I0645808

From Scratch

WELCOME TO SEA PORT
BOOK ONE

KATRINA JACKSON

Editor: A.K. Edits

Cover artist: Celia Moscote

Cover designer: Katrina Jackson

Acknowledgments

To Corey/Xan West -

You'll never know how much you're missed.

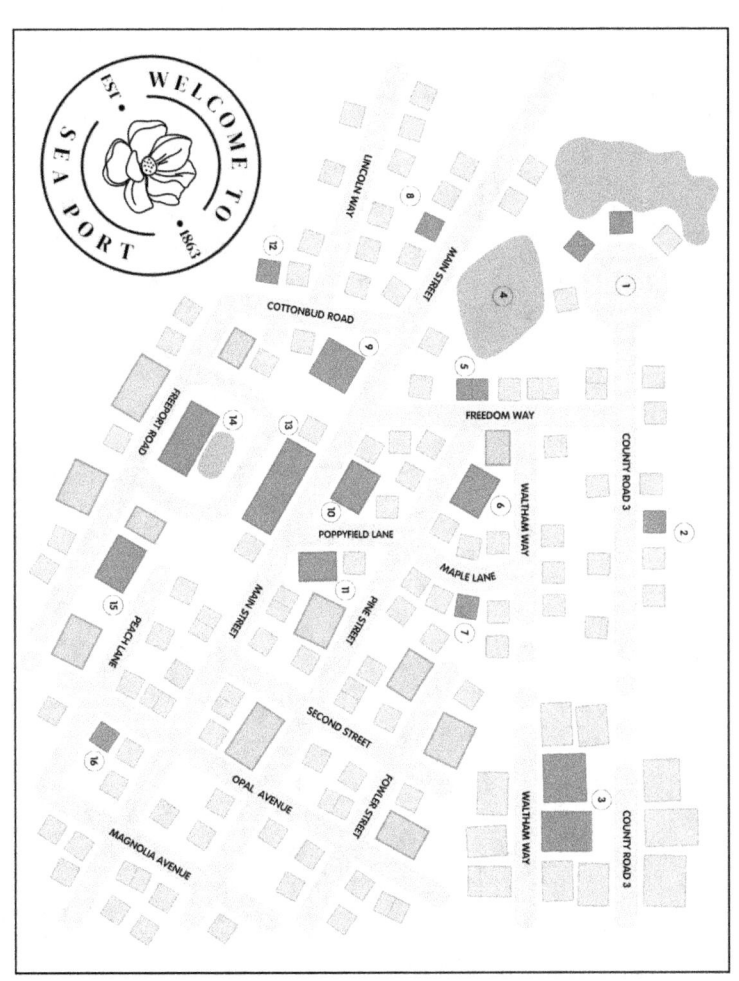

Map Legend

1. Perv Place
2. Santos's house
3. Freedom and Waltham farms
4. Douglass Park
5. Sully and Willie's duplex
6. Confections
7. Mary/Lorraine's cottage
8. The Grove
9. Knox's apartment
10. Sully's
11. Sunnyside Diner
12. Jonah's house
13. Sea Port Administrative Building*
14. Orange Grove County Library
15. La Bella Rosa
16. Bria's house

   *containing the Firehouse, Mayor's Office, Police Precinct, and Post Office

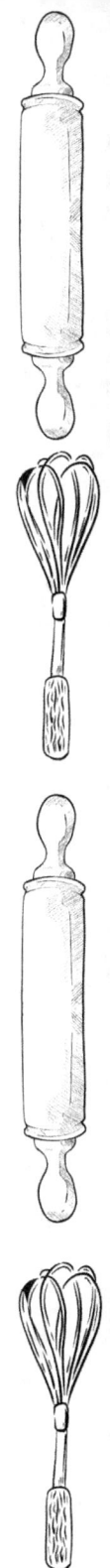

Content Warnings

Mentions of self-harm
Mentions of police corruption
Mentions of domestic violence
Mention of sexual abuse

WELCOME TO SEA PORT

ONE

Mary

"Keys, cell phone, recipe book."

Three months ago, Mary moved to Sea Port, a small Southern town in the middle of nowhere, to restart her life. She stopped in the entryway of her cute little rented cottage and went over the contents of her purse. She didn't want to forget anything, even though Sea Port wasn't but so big, as the locals liked to say, and if she happened to forget anything, she could power walk home in the blink of an eye.

Mary had lived in small towns before, but never one quite like this. Sea Port was a sleepy Southern town with great weather, and...well, not much else yet, but it was charming, and Southern charm went a long way to winning over new residents like her. She'd moved to town looking for a new lease on life and she'd found it. There were no catastrophes in Sea Port. No inbox full of stressful emails. Hell, there was hardly even any traffic, vehicular or pedestrian. So far, life in Sea Port was stress-free, and Mary was eating up every second.

She tossed the essentials into her bright red tote bag, grabbed her keys from the hook next to the front door, and turned to her cat to say goodbye.

Cat-leen Cleaver was lounging on the back of the couch as she normally did, seeing Mary off with a dispassionate but somehow also judgmental glare in her big black eyes. Mary couldn't tell if Cat-leen was sad to see her go every morning or impatient for some alone time, but it was nice to see her adjusting well to their move.

"Don't scratch up the couch. Don't throw up on the rug. Have a good day," she said, bending forward to scratch the top of Cat-leen's head - potentially dangerous contact with her lazy house cat.

Cat-leen stared at her for a few seconds before unhinging her jaw to yawn and then resting her head on her front paws dismissively.

"Great. Good talk," Mary said. She ran a hand down Cat-leen's back — at Cat-leen's discretion of course — and breezed out the front door.

Mary locked the house behind her and stopped for a second on her cute little porch to look out at her cute little street and took in a breath of fresh Sea Port air. It smelled like leaves and grass, which was nice, but Mary preferred it when there was a hint of sugar and warm bread in the air, so she skipped down her front steps and headed off to work.

Sea Port was small and a little barren. She didn't pass a single person or car on the quick walk from her cottage to work, but Mayor Waltham promised that the town would be flourishing soon enough and Mary chose to believe her.

She'd uprooted her entire life and livelihood to move to a town she'd never heard of a year ago and so far, she hadn't regretted her decision even once. Today, Mary Woods was happy — really happy — when six months ago, she'd been at rock fucking bottom.

In her former life, Mary taught English at a prestigious East Coast university. She spent nine months out of the year trying to teach students about American literature, even though they were more interested in frat parties than Toni Morrison, or Mary's lectures for that matter. Each semester seemed like a personal hell only partially of her own making. She wasted hours each week in meetings for committees with long names but short on direction. She slept too little, drank too much, pinched pennies she didn't have, and went to bed each night hating her life but hoping things would get better when she got tenure.

In Mary's experience, the average life of a junior academic was hoping and praying that tenure would make it all better. That job security would make the sacrifices worth it. Six years of working herself into an emotional frenzy was the price Mary's advisors told her they all paid to get to tenure. It was the carrot the English Department chair dangled in front of her while giving her one more committee assignment. The promise of tenure was the fable she spun for herself at the beginning of every semester, including the semester when she was denied. Receiving the email telling her that she'd failed had unraveled the fragile threads allegedly holding her life together. Technically someone, somewhere was denied tenure every academic year. It was common enough that Mary had considered the possibility. She'd just never thought it would happen to her. Maybe

3

that's what everyone who didn't get tenure said, maybe it was just her. And maybe she was the only person who let the shame at rejection make her spiral because not getting tenure cemented in her brain that she was a failure through and through.

In hindsight, there were signs; every publishing deadline she missed, every revise and resubmit, every pointless committee assignment, and every set of below-average student evaluation scores spelled her doom long before she submitted her tenure materials. The hostile teaching observations and tepid departmental support for her promotion were just icing on the shitty tenure-track cake.

The official rejection was the candles.

The worst part of it all was that she'd blamed herself and no one else. Not her unsupportive department or the lack of mentorship — just her. An hour after she'd opened that email, Mary had walked across campus to teach a class, her face hot with embarrassment and her eyes brimming with tears. If anyone noticed, they didn't care enough to comment, and that summed up her experience at that university in a nutshell.

But Mary didn't have the privilege to wallow longer than a weekend; after that, she had work to do. Literally. Mary didn't come from money and she needed a job. It was the middle of spring semester when she got the news, too late to apply for another tenure-track position —the thought alone turned her stomach sour. So she submitted her CV for every adjunct teaching position in a fifty-mile radius and started combing through online message boards for part-time tutoring gigs for any subject except math. Although she'd been willing to consider math if the money was right.

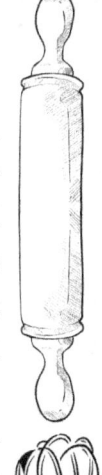

She'd been stoically spiraling the day she stumbled on the ad for a small town in the middle of nowhere looking for people, *any* people, to move there. Mary was people. She'd never heard of Sea Port when she clicked the link to the website for their Relocation Program, and truth be told, it screamed scam, but beggars can't be choosers, so she read every word.

The basic html website was ugly but full of useful information. Like a lot of small towns all over the world, Sea Port had been in population decline for decades. It was the kind of place people left at eighteen, hoping never to return; the kind of place people forgot. When the population dipped so low the town's very existence was hanging in the balance, the newly elected mayor had entered office with a plan to bring new blood to the streets of Sea Port. The Sea Port Relocation Initiative outlined various incentives for people willing to move to...well, the middle of nowhere. Remote workers got preferential rental agreements on the city's empty homes, downtown co-working spaces with the best Wi-Fi, and any other support they might need to thrive in their new town. Entrepreneurs could apply for business loans, career coaching, and free housing for a year. There were other plans for highly skilled people willing to relocate even temporarily and venture capitalists looking to invest; every scheme was more exciting than the last. The more Mary read, the more excited she got, even if the threat of a scam never quite went away.

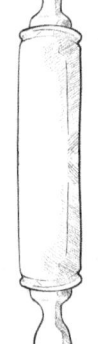

It looked too good to be true, but what if it wasn't? That question had nagged at her as she frantically pulled together an application while finishing her last semester as a professor...maybe ever.

Her life was falling apart faster than Sea Port's population statistics, what did she really have to lose?

NOTHING.

What did she have to gain? Apparently, EVERYTHING!

Six months ago, she'd been devastated at the state of her life. Three months ago, she was driving down the Eastern Seaboard with everything she owned in a van and Cat-leen in the passenger seat. And today, she was practically skipping down the street under a bright blue sky, feeling happier than ever.

Today, Mary Woods was living her best life!

It took her five minutes to walk from her cottage down Maple Lane to Pine Street where the bakery — *her* bakery — was located. Instead of teaching online and dragging her old life into the new, she'd decided to bet on herself for once. Mary had wanted to be a baker when she was a kid, so she dusted off her childhood pipe dream when applying to relocate to Sea Port, and in just under two weeks, it would be her reality. She could hardly contain herself.

Mary ducked into the alley behind her bakery and let herself into the building through the back door. She stepped into the dry storage area and walked down a short hallway into the kitchen. It was a tight space but had everything she needed — a small but mighty industrial mixer set on the metal prep table in the corner. Across the room were the double ovens she'd used most of her business loans buying — hoping they would pay themselves off in no time. There were more metal prep tables next to the ovens and a sink set right next to the swinging door that led through to the storefront. It was a bit basic for sure, but to Mary, it was heaven.

She flipped the light switch on with her left elbow and hung her bag on a hook in the small office — that was really just a closet — on the other side of the kitchen. She grabbed one of the aprons hanging on the hooks next to the office door, dropped her phone into the front pocket, and then moved to the sink to scrub her hands.

The town's rehabilitation scheme included updating older buildings for entrepreneurial use. Mary's application and small business loan were approved just in time for her to snag the town's former post office right in the middle of downtown Sea Port — although 'downtown' was a bit generous. Confections by Mary was bright, colorful, and full of joy — exactly what she wanted from her new life in Sea Port.

She'd only been in the renovated building for three months, but there was no time to waste. Mary had been caught in a whirlwind of recipe testing, planning, and more recipe testing since she arrived, putting in ten- and twelve-hour days of backbreaking work, inhaling who knew how many tablespoons of flour every day, and she'd loved every minute of it — a stark contrast to the grueling ten- and twelve-hour days she'd spent lecture planning and grading before. But now, with her soft opening just a couple days away, it was crunch time, and she was deep in her PR campaign to win over the locals.

Technically, Confections was the only bakery in all of Sea Port, but Mary didn't want to rest on her laurels. She wanted her shop to succeed because her cakes and cookies were good, not just because she was the only bread slinger in town. And she was willing to do whatever it took to get there. She had a detailed plan to target, seduce, and win over a new segment of her neighbors every day this week.

With her cookies, of course. The baked kind.

She'd just started sifting flour when her cell phone rang. Right on time.

"Morning," she trilled happily into her earbuds.

"Do you have to sound so damn chipper? I haven't even had my coffee yet."

"Leave her alone, I like New Mary."

"Same. New Mary is so much less depressing than Old Mary."

"That's because she's not depressed."

Mary rolled her eyes while her best friends' voices blended together in a familiar cacophony. They'd been thick as thieves since high school, and their group calls had been Mary's lifeline out of the darkness that was academia. Since her move, these calls had become a comforting soundtrack to her morning prep. No one had been as excited as Mary to launch Confections, but her best friends had come close. They believed Mary could take Sea Port by storm and they told her so during every early morning phone call.

"So, what's in the oven today?" Leah asked. Since she'd helped Mary drive all her earthly belongings and moody cat down to Sea Port, Leah had gotten very attached to the idea of Confections. In fact, Mary's small-town PR blitz had been her idea, scribbled on the back of a napkin at a rest stop somewhere in Virginia.

"Nothing yet," Mary said. "Just got here. I definitely need to melt some chocolate, though."

"Oooh, send me a video," Dominique sighed.

"Of chocolate?" Keisha asked. "The hell are you gonna do with that?"

"None of your business," Dominique shot back.

Mary shook her head as she pulled her double boiler from the rack above the sink.

"When are we going to schedule an intervention for Dominique?" Keisha asked. "'Cause whatever the hell she's been getting up to in Portland is weird as hell."

"Excuse me?" Dominique laughed. "Just because you have a closed mind and heart and haven't let anyone blow your back out since Obama was in that damn tan suit doesn't mean you have to yuck my yum."

"Speaking of yum," Mary cut in, trying to steer the conversation back to neutral, sugary ground, "I think I'm going to make some donuts."

"Ugh, yes!" Keisha groaned. "You can gon' head and ship some of those to me."

"And me," Leah cried.

Keisha was the group mother, Dominique was the wild child, but Leah was the group's financial advisor — she'd even offered to be Mary's bookkeeper for her first year — and now Mary was the group sugar supplier.

"Sorry, y'all!" Mary laughed. "I haven't figured out how to ship food yet and these donuts are already spoken for. I'm heading to the police department today and I don't know how big the force is." In fact, calling it a 'force' was probably giving it too much credit. Her plan was to make an assorted dozen donuts and hope for the best.

She was concentrating so hard on the flour she was sifting that it took a few moments to notice the silence on

the other end of the line. "Y'all there? Did my phone die?" she asked in confusion.

"You're bringing donuts to the police station?" Dominique asked, sighing loudly into the chat.

"Yep," Mary said, walking across the room to the refrigerator she'd paid a pretty penny to have delivered to the middle of nowhere. She grabbed eggs and milk and went back to her prep station.

A few more seconds of silence passed before Dominique started laughing hysterically. "Oh my god, I love New Mary!"

"Oh, Ems," Keisha breathed.

"Hear me out," Mary said, canister of sugar in her hands.

"Oh no, I think we get it," Leah said, chuckling lightly.

"You don't think that'll piss them off?" Keisha asked, taking up her role as the group's resident worrier. She did everything by the book and ahead of schedule; classic over-achiever. She was the youngest law professor at her alma mater, hired straight out of law school. Even though Keisha was three months younger than Mary, Mary had always looked up to her. She was smart, driven, and no-nonsense; Mary was a recovering people pleaser.

In her previous life, Mary would've started jumbling her words, rushing to explain herself and reassure her friends that she knew what she was doing — which she did, by the way. For the most part. But this new version of herself was calmer and more self-assured each day.

"I know it sounds like a mess of an idea," she said, slowly pouring the sugar into the whisked eggs with one hand while she beat them with the other. "But if I show up with a smile on my face and donuts straight off the cooling rack, who's going to say no? Even if they're massive dicks, no one can resist a good donut. And they'll for sure remember me after that."

"You sound nuts," Dom said.

"You sound high," Leah said.

Keisha gasped. "Mary, are you high? Is weed legal in Sea Port?" She whispered that question into the phone.

"A sugar high is a solid possibility," Mary laughed. "But I'm also right. I can feel it."

"You sound happy," Leah said, her voice warm and gooey as honey.

Mary sighed to herself. "I am, actually. I'm so damn happy I can't stop smiling."

"You know what would make me happy?" Dominique butted in.

"What?" Mary laughed.

"Video of that melting chocolate," she whispered in a honey tone. They burst out laughing at that.

"I got you," Mary said, setting her whisk down to pull her cellphone from her apron.

The rest of their morning chat went according to their regular routine. They caught up about everything from third dates to tv shows Mary didn't have time to watch. When the time came, Mary recorded thirty seconds of melting butter and chocolate and sent it to the entire chat, just in case other people were on Dominique's West Coast wavelength. Her friends gushed about the glossy sheen. Mary's cheeks hurt from smiling so much. And so early in the day!

She hadn't been able to have mornings like this last year. Back then, she'd been too exhausted to even feign happiness,

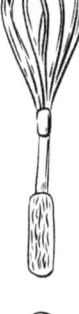
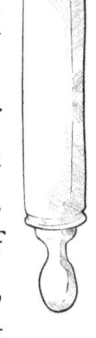

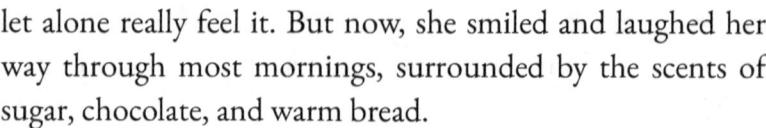

let alone really feel it. But now, she smiled and laughed her way through most mornings, surrounded by the scents of sugar, chocolate, and warm bread.

Mary's wildest dreams were coming true right before her eyes and her rock bottom was quickly becoming a distant nightmare.

"Donut holes or cake pops?" she asked the group.

"Both!" her friends said in sweet, happy unison.

The start of yet another great day in Sea Port.

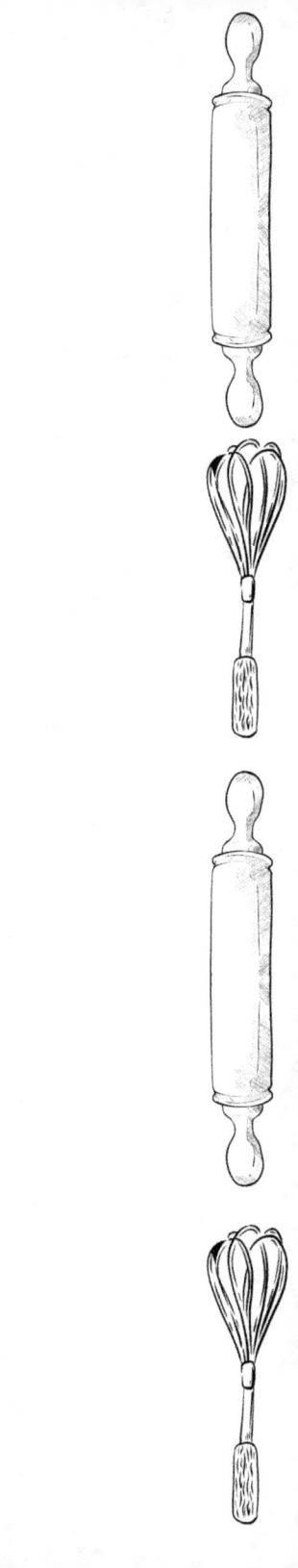

WELCOME TO SEA PORT

TWO

Santos

The first time Miguel Santos heard about a town called Sea Port, his life had been slowly unraveling. He'd been out of the Air Force for just a few months and was still adjusting to the altitude in his hometown and civilian life. No matter where he turned, Santos couldn't seem to get a firm hold on this new phase of his life and it was pissing him off.

Almost every morning, Santos left his parents' house for a slow run in a local park down a path he still knew like the back of his hand, pushing his body just a little bit harder, running a little farther, hoping to find himself in the exhaustion. He'd worn down the tread on his tennis shoes in just a few months but still hadn't arrived at any answers for where he was supposed to go next.

He'd joined the Marine Corps right out of high school with a plan. His parents had worked themselves to the bone to raise him and his little brothers. They gave their boys everything they could, but paying for college — even cosigning for loans — was beyond their means. Thankfully, Santos hated school, so the Marines and then the Air Force made more sense than college. The goal of it all was to make his parents proud, set a good example for his little brothers, and lay the foundation for a future after the service, and he'd done that.

But when the day finally came for him to leave, it was bittersweet.

The night before his discharge, he'd met up a final time with Mayra, a base psychologist who'd been his steady hookup for months. Their relationship had been perfect for Santos — no frills, no feelings, just fucking — and he was almost sad to see it end.

She rolled onto her back with a soft, satisfied smile on her face. "What are you going to do now?" she'd asked in short, panting breaths.

Their sweaty bodies pressed together on top of the sheets. "Gonna sign up for the PD," he'd said, positioning the pillow under his head.

"Why the fuck would you do that?" She asked the question in a high-pitched, sharp voice he'd never heard from her before. It piqued his attention and made the hair on his arms stand up, but Santos hadn't spent a decade in service without learning how to keep his composure. Still, his heart was racing, and not because of the sex.

Mayra ran a hand through her long, dark hair. "Sorry, shit. I didn't mean it like that. Well, I did, but...sorry."

Santos sat up and pressed his back against the cool headboard. He forced a smile onto his face. "You don't think I'd be a good cop?"

Santos had never been the kind of man who needed

other people's approval for his decisions — not even his parents — but there was something about the way she was looking at him that exposed a sore spot he'd never noticed before. He wasn't sure if he *actually* cared about her answer, but he felt the need to defend himself and only just managed to smother it. Mayra's eyes had been trained on the ceiling, and he waited silently for her to figure out how to say whatever was on her mind.

He thought about that conversation dozens of times over the next few months. He remembered trying to rein his galloping pulse in with slow, deep breaths. He'd tried not to let his own anxiety about this life transition steer the conversation off-track. And in the months since, he'd thought incessantly about how different his re-entry into civilian life would've been if she'd said nothing.

Some days he wished he could forget her words, but he couldn't. He'd eased into a light jog on the packed dirt path, her words still bouncing around in his head, trying to focus on the kindness she'd shown him with her honesty, even as she'd blown up his plans.

Mayra put a hand on Santos's chest — a much more tender gesture than they'd ever shared before — and spoke in a soft voice; a voice she probably used on her patients.

"You'd probably be a great cop," she'd said. "You're principled, fair, and kind. You'd want to be a good cop, but your local police force is corrupt as fuck. I can't imagine why you'd waste all those good qualities on that cesspool of a profession."

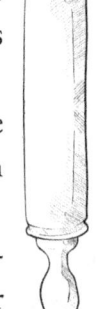

Cesspool.

That word had cut Santos to the quick. Still, he'd appreciated her candor, even if it had shocked him into silence.

Mayra had turned to him, her chest covered in sweat and nipples still hard, resting her head on her hand. "I've got a friend who used to work in Denver. Internal Affairs. He left after two years and went to law school instead. Wanna know his specialty?"

"Probably not," Santos rasped, already feeling the weight of her words on his shoulders.

"He's in civil litigation now," she'd said. "Most of his cases are against the police. Usually for battery, general misconduct, civil forfeiture, you know, corrupt shit like that."

"I... I get the gist," Santos had said, lying back on the bed and staring up at the ceiling. Mayra was quiet while Santos digested her words in silence, but not quite peace.

Her advice had brought their last night together to a close and soon enough, Mayra was dressed and ready to go. Before she was gone from Santos's life for good, she offered him some helpful advice. "You've been gone a long time. You've grown and changed, but to your family, you'll still be the little boy who said goodbye at eighteen. They love you, you love them, but they're gonna drive you up a wall and that's okay. You should be prepared for that."

After nearly two years of casual hookups, Santos had been ready for their relationship to come to a natural end. Of all the time they'd spent together, it was that last night he remembered with the most clarity. He thought about it while he packed the last of his belongings into his duffels and boarded the first of three flights home. The word 'cesspool' clung to him as he moved into his parents' basement, gorged himself on his mother's cooking, and reconnected with his brothers. Her words sat heavy on his shoulders while he

18

noted all the things that had changed since he was home last. He thought of Mayra as he filled out the application for the Denver PD, but couldn't bring himself to submit it, because of course Mayra was right.

Every article he read about Denver PD made his stomach turn, and when he thought maybe it was just Denver, he got lost in the series of ACLU lawsuits against every law enforcement agency he considered as a backup plan. Everywhere he looked, he found the exact situation Mayra warned about, and all his carefully laid plans fell apart.

He'd gone on that morning run feeling as if he was free falling when a man Santos trusted with his life threw him a lifeline.

His ringing cell phone cut through his running playlist. He grunted in frustration and pulled his phone from his running shorts. He didn't recognize the number, but he sure recognized the voice on the line when he answered.

"Mikey!" the man yelled from his end of the call. The rough, deep rumble of his Texas drawl was so thick it curled around the syllables of a nickname Santos hated like molasses. It was so lush in his ears, Santos felt like the man was jogging right beside him.

He stepped off the trail, huffing from his run and the altitude. "Sergeant," he panted, trying to catch his breath.

"I'm out. And now you're out. Call me Billy."

"No." He hadn't meant to bark that word, but he didn't regret it either. He wouldn't be calling Sergeant William Knox 'Billy' no matter what he said. Lots of people in the service had left impressions on Santos, but none so significantly as Sergeant Knox. There were lots of things Santos could call him, but 'Billy' would never be one.

Santos met Knox a few weeks into Basic. Some of the older Marines had taken a perverse pleasure in tormenting each class of younger recruits, venting their rage on them for the hell of it, but not PFC Knox — it wasn't in his nature.

"Just 'cause I ain't at the bottom of the barrel no more don't mean I gotta step on y'all who are," he used to say.

Knox was Santos's first friend in the Marines. He felt like safety and reminded him of home. Knox was the person Santos turned to when he needed guidance or reassurance or just a good laugh. Even after he moved to the Air Force, Knox was still the voice in his head reminding him not to let the service change him for the worst.

"What about Bill?" Knox asked, barely holding in his laughter.

Santos rolled his eyes. "No."

"Fine. Fine. Call me Knox, then. Anything but Sergeant."

Santos agreed with a grunt.

"Now that that's settled, are you unemployed?"

Santos only had enough breath in his lungs to let out a soft wheeze of laughter, even though it made his abs ache. Some men walked through life with the weight of the world on an already-chipped shoulder, but not Knox. For all the years they'd been friends, Knox never missed an opportunity to let that same weight of the world roll down his back like light rain. It was one of the things Santos had always loved about him. He'd never managed to emulate it, however — Santos was rigid where Knox was flexible, and neither man felt the need to change the other.

"It's only been a few months," Santos huffed.

"Sounds like you might need a job and an oxygen machine," Knox said, chuckling happily.

"Did you call me just to insult me?"

"No, but I should do that more often. It's fun."

"Sergeant," Santos ground out.

Knox laughed louder. "Alright, I'm calling to see if you're looking for a job."

"Of course, I am."

"Still wanna work in law enforcement?"

Santos's tongue had felt heavy in his mouth as he figured out how to answer that question.

Knox hummed in agreement to words Santos never spoke. "So, look, I moved to this small town — so damn small it'd probably be easier to give you coordinates than a name — and they're looking for officers. Well..." he corrected, "one officer."

"And you don't want it?"

"Already got a job. You're talking to the new fire chief."

"Congratulations," Santos growled.

"Thanks. It's a good job. I like the town. People are nice. I think there's real opportunity here."

"What's that code for? Drug running? Guns?" Santos asked without thinking — months of frustration about Mayra's words finally finding an outlet. The wrong outlet, unfortunately.

Knox was an easygoing man, the responsible life of the party...until he wasn't. "What's that you said, Marine?"

Santos stood at attention and his back tensed. While he wasn't eighteen anymore, you can take the man out of the Marines but never the Marine out of the man. Still, he didn't take back his words. In the last four months, he'd learned

more than he ever wanted to know about the hellscape that was U.S. police departments, and as much as he respected Knox, Santos couldn't just brush that aside — not even for his old friend.

"You know me better than that, Marine," Knox said in a fierce whisper. "I've never been that kind of man and I don't plan to become him now that I'm out." He bit out those words with a vehemence that made something inside Santos shrivel. But then, just as he had before, Knox's voice lightened to a gentle laugh. "Besides, if I thought you were looking for that kinda work, I wouldn't have called. You can find that kinda job right where you are. Ain't that right?"

It had been years since Santos had been on the service end of one of Knox's lectures, and it was just as terrifying as ever, but it was also familiar and comforting in a way that grounded him. If Knox didn't give a shit about you, he wouldn't waste his breath on you, simple as that.

"You aren't wrong," Santos said, finally able to breathe normally.

"I rarely am," Knox chuckled.

"So when you say opportunity, what do you mean?"

"I just mean there's a chance to start over here, Santos. You can do good, honest, *legal* work in a good town and live whatever kinda life you wanna live now that you're out. That's *all* I'm offering."

After that phone call, Knox's offer slowly edged Mayra's warning from the center of Santos's brain. In the weeks that followed, he did his research. He found Sea Port on a map — just barely — and quickly discovered that Knox had been kinder to the town than it deserved. It wasn't just small; it was on the verge of collapse. They'd resorted to paying people to move there just to survive, but instead of turning Santos off, he'd been intrigued. Knox had sent along some photos and videos of Sea Port looking like a town out of a Hallmark movie, just not as white. It looked peaceful, and peace, Santos realized, was what he was after.

Within the month, he was arriving at the closest airport — which wasn't close at all — and driving into Sea Port during the midday rush — and by midday rush, that meant the local dairy farm was dropping off their daily deliveries. The Sea Port Police Department was nothing to write home about — just two ancient men who'd been in the job for decades and received every commendation the town had to offer. Almost from the moment he'd arrived, he'd understood what Knox meant — there *was* possibility in Sea Port, and Santos wanted to grab ahold of it. With two old cops looking retirement square in the face, if he moved to Sea Port, in a few years, he could remake that police force into whatever he wanted instead of taking on the weight of Denver's years of corruption.

Every day, Miguel found himself buying into the dream Knox was selling a little bit at a time, with Knox being the biggest lure of them all.

He applied for the job, got it, threw what little he owned in the bed of his truck, and said goodbye to his parents. They'd all cried — even his little brothers — but Santos knew in his gut he was making the right decision for himself. He started the long drive south with all the hope he hadn't felt after that night with Mayra.

The slow, Southern crawl of life in Sea Port wasn't the life Santos had been planning for, but it fit him better than he expected. Santos had been settled in Sea Port for a few months and eased his way into a routine.

He woke up this morning and rolled right out of bed for a quick run around the block, followed by a long, hot shower. He put on his uniform and checked his reflection in the mirror hanging on the back of his bedroom door. He made sure every button was fixed in the correct hole, his creased pants were neat and not too tight, and his hair was combed perfectly in place. Once he approved of his appearance, he clipped the taser onto his belt, grabbed his holstered gun — which more often than not stayed locked in the trunk of his car — and walked out the front door.

Outside was a quiet, slightly humid summer morning. His shift didn't start until nine, but he had a standing appointment with Knox for coffee at Sully's, the new coffee shop conveniently located across the street from the city's main administrative building.

It was a ten-minute walk from his house on a bad day — not that he'd ever had a 'bad day' in Sea Port. Actually, he couldn't even imagine what could make this walk longer than ten minutes besides the Juneteenth parade the city was prepping for or the barbecue cook-off in July. And even then, the time it would take to pick up some ribs on the way to his office couldn't cause more than a five-minute delay.

Santos turned the corner onto Main Street. He could already see the modern sign above Sully's in the middle of the block. The Sea Port Relocation Initiative was working on two fronts — getting new residents and attracting new businesses — and Sully's was the poster child for the possibilities of what a small business could do in Sea Port. Sully's Café was West Coast relaxed, warm but professional, and as far as Santos could tell, had kickstarted the revitalization of Old Downtown Sea Port, small as it was. There weren't too many places in Sea Port where Porties and Transplants could hang out together, but Sully's had filled the gap.

Santos walked through the front door, the smell of roasting coffee beans filling his nose. The early morning crowd was thin, just Sully busy behind the counter and the silent book club in a booth at a far corner, lost in their own fictional worlds. Knox was sitting in their regular spot at the long table that ran along the floor-to-ceiling window at the front of the café. The window looked out onto Main, even though there wasn't much to see — just cool gray concrete that matched the cool gray sky. The only thing of interest was a stray cat Knox had been trying to catch longer than Santos had been in town. The cat was sitting patiently on the top of the city's only post office collection box, staring into Sully's and maybe directly into Knox's eyes.

It was still too early for most of the town's residents to be up and about, and that was exactly why Santos and Knox had made this early morning meetup part of their routine.

Santos stopped at the counter to order a pour-over from Sully before he claimed his regular seat next to Knox.

"Sergeant," Santos breathed, just to fuck with his friend.

"Mikey," Knox replied, smiling against his mug of coffee.

Santos's back tensed. Even though they'd been friends for years, they hadn't lived in the same city since Santos was in Basic, so these early morning cups of coffee were part of their slow reacquaintance. It took a couple seconds before Santos's brain could register the low, playful tone of Knox's voice, laughter hiding at the edges of his words. Santos turned to look at his friend, but Knox pointedly refused to do the same. He watched Knox's profile for a few seconds before a small smile spread across his lips.

"Knox," Santos said.

He set his mug back on the table and turned toward him. "Mornin', Santos."

"Here you go," Sully said, squeezing between them to set Santos's mug on the table.

"Thanks," Santos mumbled.

"No problem. Thanks for your business," she said, turning away.

When they were alone again, Santos turned to the view out the window. "Anything to see?" he asked, the question as much as an inside joke between Santos and Knox as a comforting routine.

"I think that little motherfucker is taunting me," Knox said, gesturing at the cat, which had curled into a ball for a nap, peacefully unaware of Knox's attention. "But besides that, not much."

Usually Knox let out a contented sigh and that was the end of the town updates portion of their morning date. Today, however, he turned his full body toward Santos. His knee bumped into Santos's thigh and a warm smile played across his lips.

"You seen the new baker yet?"

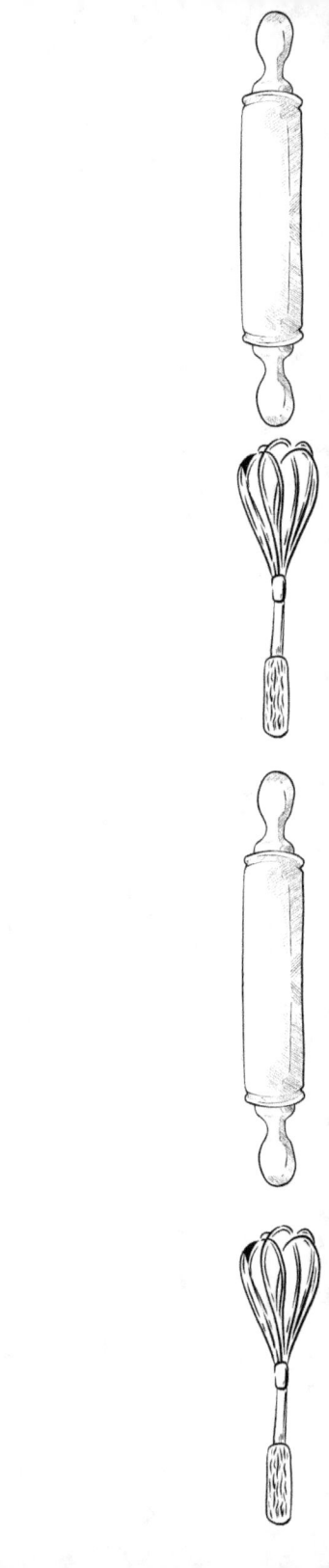

WELCOME TO SEA PORT

THREE

Knox

At some point in his childhood, Knox had looked at his parents and decided that whatever he did with his life, his only goal was to never be like either of them. This desire made him work harder in all his classes, made him train harder at sports, and forced him to plan his escape at eighteen long before it was in reach. Leaving his parents' home was such a desperate desire that he didn't even wait until graduation. He took the GED three months before his eighteenth birthday, signed up for the Marines in the same week, and left his parents' house in the middle of the night. They probably hadn't noticed he was gone for days, but he never looked back, so he didn't care. For the next decade of his life, home had been wherever the Marine Corps sent him, and he'd never been happier.

Knox had survived his childhood in the Service, but he was aimless after his discharge. For the first time in his life, he didn't have a trauma-fueled plan to stay two steps ahead of domestic abuse or the ease of his orders, and it had thrown

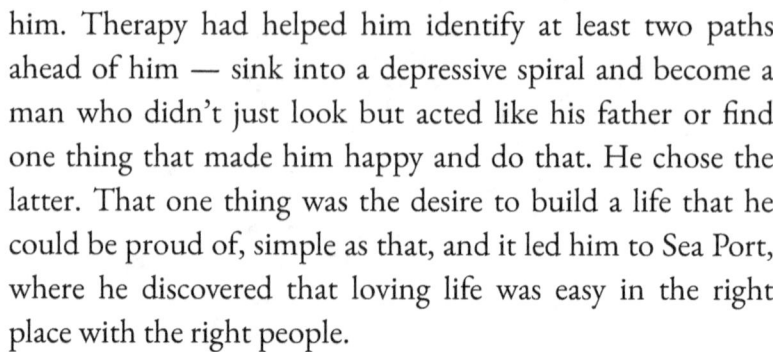

him. Therapy had helped him identify at least two paths ahead of him — sink into a depressive spiral and become a man who didn't just look but acted like his father or find one thing that made him happy and do that. He chose the latter. That one thing was the desire to build a life that he could be proud of, simple as that, and it led him to Sea Port, where he discovered that loving life was easy in the right place with the right people.

Knox believed every day could be a great day, it was all about how you used it. He'd seen a lot of terrible shit in his life but refused to let the bad eclipse the good. For Knox, happiness was a choice. Some days that choice was harder than others and some days he couldn't make it, but tomorrow was a new day. Santos used to tell him he was speaking in self-help affirmations and maybe he was right, but it worked for Knox, and sometimes it worked for Santos too. In fact, for the past few months, his time with Santos had been the silver lining that made it easier every day to choose his happiness, but the cute new baker looked like she could give Santos a run for his money.

"Shit, is that her?" Santos whispered sharply.

"That's her," Knox sighed. He took a casual sip of coffee with a smile on his face, leaning back in his stool to watch her saunter down Main Street like it was a runway.

She was wearing a pair of black jeans that hugged her full hips and thick thighs and his stomach grumbled softly with desire. She even had a little swipe of flour on her thigh that was objectively the cutest thing he'd ever seen. And sexy. She was incredibly fucking sexy. She'd tied her V-neck t-shirt into a tight knot just above her waist, exposing a delicious little strip of brown flesh that played peek-a-boo with every step.

Knox's feline nemesis lifted his head from the post office box as she passed and stepped from the curb to cross the street. Knox was about eighty percent sure there was a jaywalking ordinance in Sea Port, but the baker didn't seem to care, Knox sure as hell didn't, and when he spared a glance at Santos, the man was too busy staring a hole through the windowpane to remember the civil code off the top of his head anyway.

"When the hell did she get here?" Santos asked in a bemused voice.

"'Round about four months, I heard."

"And you're just now telling me?"

Knox sighed loudly. "I just found out about her last night."

Santos cut his eyes in his direction, but Knox was unbothered. He turned in his seat, bumping Santos's hip with his knee. Instead of moving it, though, Knox let his knee rest there, digging into Santos's side just to irritate him. He could understand his friend's irritation. If the shoe were on the other foot, he'd be just as pissed, but it was fun not to be the last to know that the town's new baker was a fucking knockout.

"When?" Santos asked. "We had dinner together last night."

Knox rolled his eyes, catching a glimpse of her as she jumped onto the curb in front of the window. He and Santos tabled their spat to watch her walk right in front of them, seemingly oblivious to the heat of their attention. They lost her for a second, but then the bell above the front door chimed in the quiet café. They turned in unison,

Knox's knee dragging along Santos's side, and tracked her progress up to the counter.

Up close, she was sexier than he thought. Curvy hips, bouncing breasts, a juicy ass, and the biggest, brightest smile Knox had ever seen. They watched her speak to Sully in a voice too low to hear over the soft music playing in the café. He leaned forward, pressing the bend of his knee harder into his friend's body, straining for the sound of her voice.

"How'd you find out about her?" Santos asked again. His voice was close, low and deep. Santos shifted in his seat so he and Knox could look one another in the eye.

"The Mayor asked me to pop by her shop to say hi and make sure she's settling in okay. I forgot about it until last night after dinner."

"Why'd she send you and not me? *I'm* technically on the Sea Port Welcome Committee."

Knox rolled his eyes. "You'd have to ask her that."

"But you went without me?"

"Do you take me on patrol with you?"

"What patrol?" Santos said.

"When you go walking around downtown."

Santos rolled his eyes. "That's not a patrol, that's my afternoon break."

"Same thing," Knox said dismissively. "Anyway, I stopped by last night on my way home. I was expecting some old lady who smelled like butter, not...that." They both glanced back in her direction just in time to catch her laugh out loud.

And Jesus, was that laugh illicit. Her soft breasts jiggled invitingly and Knox licked his lips, imagining the taste of her. "I spent a good five minutes just watching her from across the street like a creep," he said, plunging into the grips of déjà vu.

"That feels illegal," Santos murmured, a faint smile on his face.

Knox huffed out a breath of laughter and cut his eyes back at Santos. "You gonna arrest me?"

Santos's face didn't move. He didn't smile or lift his eyebrows, he just stared at Knox, thinking louder than a freight train. Normally he could guess Santos' thoughts, but not today. Without responding to the teasing question, Santos turned back to the baker, leaving Knox with a pregnant silence he didn't quite know what to do with.

Knox wasn't a jealous man by choice. What he remembered of his father, besides his low, calm, threatening voice, was the explosive jealousy. Even as a kid, he'd recognized that personality trait as something ugly and all-consuming and had nipped it in the bud long ago. Still, he filed Miguel's interest in the baker away for later so he could enjoy the view as well.

She and Sully were laughing with one another, a platter of what looked like muffins on the counter between them.

"Name?" Santos asked in a curt, gruff voice after they'd admired her a few moments longer. Most people hated when he spoke to them like that, but Knox had always appreciated it. He'd always loved a man who could get down to business.

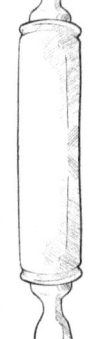

"The Mayor didn't say. Or if she did, I forgot."

"Forgot?" Santos asked.

"I didn't know she'd be fine!" he grumbled defensively.

"Fair point," Santos conceded, still with a hint of judgment in his tone.

He was just about to open his mouth to say...something

33

when the baker turned in their direction and that peek-a-boo strip of skin widened. Knox stared at it hungrily.

She trained her mega-watt smile on him. Them? In their general vicinity. And then she started moving in their direction.

"Goddamn," Knox breathed.

"Fuck," Miguel echoed.

Now that they could see her head-on, 'sexy' didn't feel like a strong enough word to describe her, but neither was 'beautiful.' Whoever the hell she was, Knox was struggling to describe how goddamn good she looked.

He'd been living in Sea Port for close to a year and he loved it, even if Mayor Waltham kept threatening to use him as a poster child for the town's relocation program and the possibilities Sea Port had to offer. Knox had been looking for a place to put down roots and he had. He'd renovated a downtown condo, gotten one of his closest friends to relocate, and had plans to rapidly modernize the fire department. In just a couple of months, he had made a home in Sea Port. Now his mornings started with a hot cup of freshly ground coffee, his best friend next to him, and a sexy baker with thick thighs and a big smile heading their way.

What could be better than that?

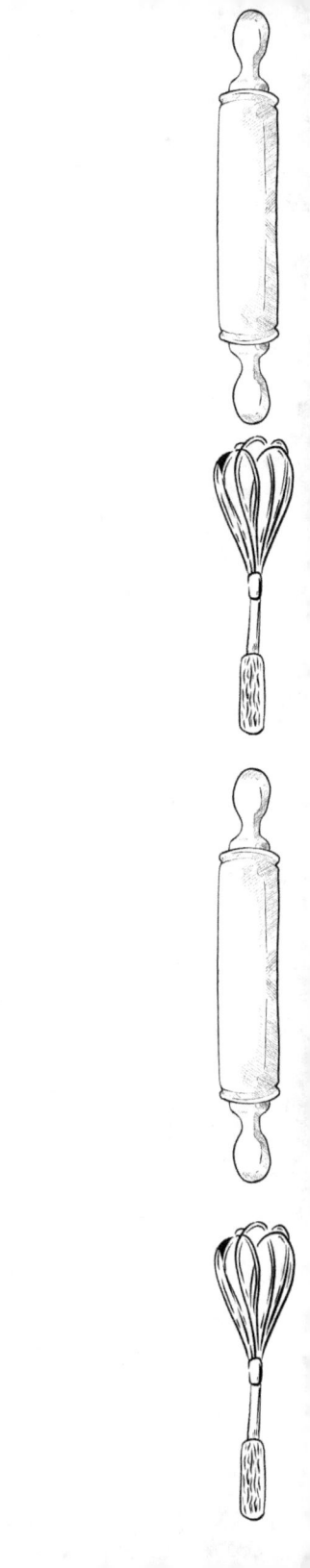

WELCOME TO SEA PORT

FOUR

Mary

ary was of the mindset that every new phase of her life should be marked with a change in wardrobe. When she started her period, all of a sudden, her closet started transitioning from the polyester floral dresses her mother bought seemingly in bulk to thrifted band tees and baggy jeans that hid her growing hips. Her mother had been very unhappy about that pubescent phase, but Mary had seen those pictures recently and she stood by that fashion glow-up.

When she'd become a professor, she'd made a similar transition, but for far different reasons and without any of the childish joy that came with pre-teenage rebellion. Mary had never wanted to *look* like a professor. She didn't want to stuff her curves into A-line dresses that didn't agree with her shape and aged her, so she settled on a uniform that worked— skinny jeans and slogan tees. Every now and again, she found the energy to dress up for a meeting with one of the dozens of deans who had endless slots in their

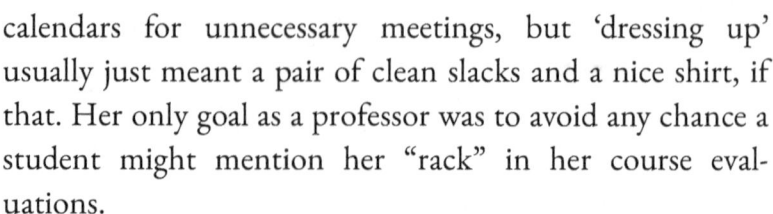

calendars for unnecessary meetings, but 'dressing up' usually just meant a pair of clean slacks and a nice shirt, if that. Her only goal as a professor was to avoid any chance a student might mention her "rack" in her course evaluations.

Not again.

It was only in hindsight that Mary realized she'd lost herself and her fashion sense in her previous job. She'd been so worried about not looking like her colleagues and avoiding unwanted attention that she'd left little time or space to find herself. But in Sea Port, Mary had nothing but time, and since her move, she'd rediscovered how much she loved her soft waist and décolletage. She liked cursing a little more now that she didn't need to censor herself for her students or her Baby Boomer colleagues obsessed with the appearance of propriety more than reality. She liked laughing loudly and with her entire voice instead of chuckling softly and murmuring "that's so funny" just to be polite. And most importantly, Mary liked to say exactly what was on her mind rather than diminish herself for someone else's comfort.

In this new phase of her life, Mary was ready to chase her own desires. Whether it was a slice of decadent chocolate cake or the delicious attention of an attractive man, she wanted it all. Besides, it had been longer than she could remember since she had really good sex.

"Where are you headed today?" Sully asked, nodding at the basket draped over Mary's arm.

"Police department." Mary pulled back the cloth covering the contents of her basket, releasing the warm scent of fried dough into the air.

Sully's eyebrows lifted with a smile. "Any chance I can get one of those?"

Mary laughed. "Not unless you're the new police officer I've heard about."

Sully rolled her eyes. "Not a chance, but if you're looking for him, he's right over there," the other woman said, pointing toward the front.

She followed the direction of Sully's hand to two men sitting at the bench along the front window staring at her. "Well, goddamn," she said, taking in two of the finest men she'd ever seen in her life. Objectively.

"Have fun!" Sully laughed, turning away to load the café's display case.

Mary hadn't dated in academia and it hadn't been a choice. Whenever Mary and Keisha used to catch up about their lives, all their conversations followed a predictable pattern — research, the job, and sex. Who was getting it? Neither of them. How much? Keisha had an extensive toy collection and she lobbied that each self-pleasure session should count. Who wasn't getting anything? Mary. Why? Because. She had no other answer besides that.

Their conversations also tended to cover whatever latest university sex scandals were hitting higher education news outlets or spreading around their gossip networks.

Dating in academia was just a microcosm of the sad state of dating in the real world, which was Mary's kind way of saying that as a fat Black woman, she'd found her dating options to be severely limited if not completely non-existent. There was always someone to tell her that their best friend's mom's neighbor said there were so many men on college campuses, so it only seemed logical that it would be easy for

Mary to find someone to date, right? Wrong. Sure, there were technically lots of men at her old university: old men, gay men, asexual men, and category unknowns, as Keisha liked to call the ones who never came to events or left the university too quick to be properly grouped by the nosy, lonely singles. But most men Mary knew in academia fit into one of two categories.

The first — and best — were the happily married men with lots of kids. They almost always had extroverted stay-at-home wives. Their favorite topics of casual conversation included private school fees, their children's extracurricular activities, the housing market, and home renovations. Mary didn't mind those men much. They were chatty, sure, but generally kind and always efficient with their time because the weekends were reserved for their families. They were also usually — hopefully — on a relatively low rung of the sleaze-ball ladder.

The other category, and Mary's least favorite, was most often depicted in Nineties prestige films — the male professor willing to "seduce" a female student who was 'just so mature for her age.' Mary had consumed so many media examples of men in academia that she was shocked to see it in real life. The male professors who seemed to delight in convincing smart, ambitious women to abandon their PhDs and trade in her own work to help him secure his intellectual legacy were real and they made Mary's scalp itch, and she'd still missed it when it was right in front of her.

He joined the university in a cluster hire the year after Mary. They were the same age; he was single, smart, and intellectually jaded, but not yet bitter. He and Mary became fast friends and Mary had developed a little crush — nothing major, just a tiny, secret hope that their friendship might develop into something more — but she got over it soon enough.

He was an academic superstar who published regularly, lectured like a full professor, and had a full page of invited talks on his curriculum vitae. Eventually, that crush had morphed into a gentle professional envy. Mary was *not* a superstar. She was perpetually two weeks behind her syllabus and every semester struggled with depression-induced insomnia. They'd been better off as friends until Mary ran into him and one of their department's first-year master's students grocery shopping early on a Sunday morning. That morning, a few puzzle pieces fell into place in Mary's brain — the line of female students at his office hours and his unexpected removal as graduate advisor, even though he was primarily hired to fill that position.

That colleague wasn't who Mary thought he was, and somehow, that realization rocked her understanding of herself. The university's subpar response hadn't made her feel more comfortable, nor did the shotgun wedding at the end of the summer. And to add icing to the cake, his young wife, adorable kids, and successful tenure application and promotion poured salt into wounds that cut deeper than she ever could've expected.

But that was her old life.

In her new life, her only coworker was Bria, the girl she'd hired to help her part-time at the bakery, and she was as single as Mary. Which, for clarification, was single as fuck. Mary had been date-less for longer than she was willing to admit aloud, and she felt every week of that drought while looking at the two men staring back at her. Watching them

watch her made parts of her body that had gone dormant come back to life.

"Goddamn," she whispered again before taking a slow, deep breath and walking in their direction. Her knees were a little weak and there were butterflies rioting in her stomach, but she kept going.

As she got closer, they stood from their stools and waited for her to come to them with hungry smiles on their faces. She stopped just out of arm's length, tilted her head back to look them each in the eye, and swallowed a hard lump in her throat. "Hi," she sighed in a small, dry voice. Beads of sweat formed at her hairline and she brushed it back into her soft, curly afro with the back of her hand.

"Good morning," they replied in unison, sending those goddamn butterflies into a frenzy.

They were each sexy in their own way. The one on her left had medium brown skin, dark eyes, and severe eyebrows offset by a plump, kissable mouth. He was grinning at her in a way that immediately made her heart flutter and Mary let out a soft breath before turning her eyes to his friend. He was about the same height but a bit more built. Her mouth was already dry, but the heat of this one's gaze had her feeling like she was baking under a full sun. Well, most of her was drying out, but not all. The second man's deeper brown skin was shining under the fluorescent lights, which was a feat because who looked good in fluorescent lighting? He did. But the kicker — the thing that made her heart throb in her clit — was his smile. He had, hands down, the best smile she'd ever seen — big, white, and gorgeous enough to sit on.

Mary felt woozy.

She cleared her throat and tried to get this meeting back on track. "Hi. I'm Mary."

"Nice to meet you, Mary," they said in unison. Hot liquid desire slid down her spine.

She had to take another beat to stop herself from saying anything she shouldn't. "Uh, Sully told me that one of you is new to the police force?" She didn't know who was who, so she let her eyes bounce back and forth between them — for professional purposes, of course.

The one on her right grunted in what sounded like frustration.

"I am," the other man said, offering her his hand with a triumphant grin. "Miguel Santos. You can call me Santos."

Mary shifted the basket out of the way and slipped her hand into his. Instead of shaking it, though, he squeezed, and her clit jumped. He seemed reluctant to let her go, but his friend was not nearly as reluctant to ease her hand from his grasp and take it into his own.

The first man frowned at the second, putting his hands on his waist — a very cop-like gesture that normally might've made Mary clutch her purse to her side. But she didn't have a purse on her anyway.

"And I'm the new fire chief, Billy Knox," the other man said. "You can call me whatever you like," he said, aiming the full force of his smile at her. He seemed inclined to hold onto her hand as well, but Santos pulled her free — all three of their hands brushing together — with a petty glare on his face. The shiver that moved through her body was seismic.

If she made it through this encounter, Mary resolved to find Mayor Waltham and tell her to consider putting these

two on the Welcome Committee immediately. The town would be packed in six months.

Mary's skin was tingling after those two handshakes. "Uh...okay, well," she said, licking her dry lips.

They crowded closer, surrounding her with their tall, big bodies, and all Mary could do was fight the urge to fan herself.

She turned to Santos. "I, uh, I'm opening a bakery in a week or so and want to make sure I meet as many Porties as I can. I made some donuts for the police department and I wondered if you were willing to introduce me to your colleagues. There's an extra donut in it for you."

Knox grunted and Mary felt that sound in her gut. Or lower.

Santos knit his severe eyebrows together while Knox took in a deep breath before he started chuckling in a low, deep rumble. It was molten, and that hot, slick heat moved from her spine to her pussy. This wasn't the way she thought her morning would go.

She turned to glance back at the counter, but Sully wasn't paying them any attention, refilling napkin dispensers and dancing to the music in her own world.

Knox pulled back the dish towel she'd thrown over her basket. "Is this all for the PD?" he drawled in a light voice. She liked his laughter — even though he'd been laughing at her — but something about the way he asked that question in a thick Southern accent felt like a lazy caress. Her nipples hardened into uncomfortably vital points.

"Y-yes," she replied in a shaking voice.

"What about the firehouse? You gonna be bringing us a basket tomorrow?"

Mary opened her mouth to tell him that according to her schedule, she'd be by the firehouse on Friday, but before she could, Santos cut in.

"Us? Who is us?" Santos asked, rolling his eyes in his friend's direction.

"Hey, don't go low," Knox laughed. "I'm training up a batch of real professional volunteers," he said, winking at Mary.

"I'm sure you are, but there's only so much you can do with an accountant, a banker, and a gardener."

"Hey, I'll have you know that banker used to be an EMT."

Mary's eyes moved from one man to the other as they sparred, imagining them naked in the darkest, horniest recesses of her brain. She was too distracted to realize she was moving closer to them, but then their colognes engulfed her and she sucked in a sharp breath, waiting — hoping — for their bare forearms to touch hers.

Santos snorted derisively and Knox didn't take that lying down.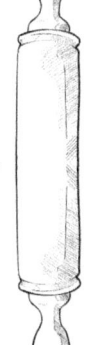

"Now, Santos, don't make me embarrass you in front of this pretty lady and her donuts." At this, he turned to Mary. "They smell amazing, by the way."

Mary loved compliments and his mouth. "Thanks. Do you want to taste?"

She didn't mean it like that.

Okay, she did mean it like that, she just didn't mean to say it out loud.

Knox's perfect smile widened at that slip of her tongue, exposing cavernous dimples in both cheeks. "I'd love to, sweetheart."

"Too bad," Santos said, pulling Mary from the abyss of Knox's eyes. "You can smell her donuts all you want, but she made them for the precinct."

Knox sighed. "'Precinct' is pushing it, Mikey."

"So is 'firehouse,' but I was perfectly willing to let you live in your delusion, Knox."

Mary's pulse was racing. Blood was rushing straight toward her pussy.

"Um, excuse me," she cut in with a voice shaky with lust. They both turned to her and she unconsciously took a step back. She cleared her throat again. "I don't mean to get in the way of this pissing contest over...whatever this is about. I've just got a business opening soon, a marketing plan my best friend will kill me if I don't execute perfectly, and some custard setting in the fridge that I want to get back to."

She licked her lips again. "I don't care who takes me over to the precinct so long as somebody does. And since you're the only regular firefighter, if I'm understanding you both correctly, you're welcome to as many donuts as you'd like."

Mary smiled at them both and was rewarded by two smiles that made her head spin.

"I'd be more than happy to carry these across the street to the police department," Knox offered.

"I work there. It should be me," Santos said in a tight voice.

"Then I guess you shoulda dusted off your manners and offered faster," Knox said, never breaking eye contact with Mary.

He pulled the basket from her hands and offered his other arm to her. She grasped his hard bicep instantly. She would try not to grope him, but she was absolutely going to have to take a detour back to her house to masturbate after this. How could she not?

"Hey, Mary, your coffee's ready," Sully called to her. She placed the carafe Mary ordered to accompany her donuts on the counter.

Mary turned to Santos. "You're welcome to carry that for me, if you'd like."

Knox chuckled under his breath and led her toward the exit. His bicep was practically pulsing in her palm as Santos followed, coffee in one hand, eyes burning a hole in Knox's back.

Yeah, she was definitely going to need that masturbation break sooner rather than later. The custard would have to wait.

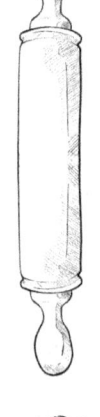

WELCOME TO SEA PORT

FIVE

Santos

S antos didn't see the point in jealousy. It felt like a lot of energy to expend on something as trivial as monogamy. If that was what you wanted and you weren't getting it, then leave, was his philosophy. And on the list of things Santos wanted in life, monogamy wasn't top of the list if it was on it at all. He liked easy, casual, and dirty, if he was getting specific. There wasn't room for jealousy in that equation, just orgasms. Many, many orgasms. So jealousy was an unfamiliar taste coating his mouth as he carried the large to-go carafe in his hands, trailing behind Knox and Mary as they walked toward the city's administrative building.

Mary and Knox strolled arm-in-arm, jaywalking across the street like they'd known each other forever. Knox leaned to his right, whispering to her in a voice too low for Santos to hear. And Mary was no better, smiling up at him, batting her eyelashes, laughing prettily at his jokes. Both of them moving as if they'd forgotten about him completely. His jealousy dug a path deep into his gut with every step, even if he couldn't quite figure out where to rest his ire, at Mary or Knox.

Or both.

Sea Port's administrative building sat at the exact center of the town. Decades ago, downtown Sea Port used to be a bustling area, relatively speaking, full of local businesses and important services, but as the population shrunk, so did everything else. At some point, the town decided it made more sense to move the most important services like the police and fire departments and post office into the main administrative building than allocate money they didn't have to maintain those departments. It was a sad state of affairs that now, most of the city's administrative offices fit in this one squat building, including the mayor's office, the jail, and a single courtroom that also doubled as the meeting room for the city council, but the town had always done what they could to survive.

Up until now, Santos had loved working so closely to Knox, usually taking his breaks in Knox's garage office — in sight of the town's ancient and singular fire truck — but right now, he hated it. Instead of him leading Mary into the building, Knox released her hand carefully as if he was loath to lose her touch and jogged a few steps ahead to open the door. She beamed at him as she walked inside.

That should've been him, not Knox.

And because Knox was Knox, he shot Santos a shit-eating grin before following Mary inside the building. He didn't even hold the door open for Santos.

"Prick," Santos mumbled under his breath.

Santos knew that look on Knox's face well. That look

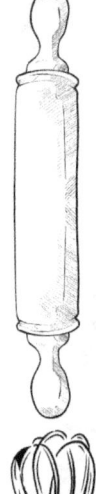

was a lesson, his grin all but yelling, "You snooze, you lose, Marine," and Santos hated that he was right.

He also hated that he had to rush forward to catch the door before it closed in his face.

"So now, what possessed you to make donuts?" Santos overheard Knox ask with a gentle laugh that made the hair on his arms stand at attention. He was planning to ask her that.

You snooze, you lose, Marine.

Santos caught up with Knox and Mary at the elevator. They could have walked up the two flights of stairs to Santos's office, but when he looked Mary up and down for not the first time, he finally took note of her tall sandals and adorable painted red toes peeking above the strap and begrudgingly approved of Knox's decision.

"I thought it would be funny," she said in the sweetest voice while shrugging casually.

Santos drank in her profile — the adorable pout on her lips, smooth deep brown skin, and cute button nose. And then Knox leaned forward, his plump lips broadening into a smile, deep dimples almost hidden by his beard.

A hungry growl moved through Santos's gut.

The elevator arrived at the ground floor loudly, the ancient doors creaking as they slid open, jostling both men into action. Knox moved his arm over the threshold to hold it open, and Santos quickened his steps just in case they tried to leave him behind. Mary stepped into the elevator and turned around, her gaze crashing into his. She blinked innocently at him, but her smile was anything but innocent. That smile spoke to Santos in a way he couldn't explain.

Most of the women Santos had dated thought men in

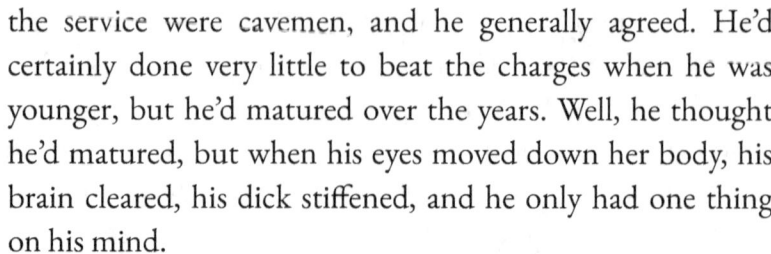

the service were cavemen, and he generally agreed. He'd certainly done very little to beat the charges when he was younger, but he'd matured over the years. Well, he thought he'd matured, but when his eyes moved down her body, his brain cleared, his dick stiffened, and he only had one thing on his mind.

So, of course, Knox ruined the mood with a deep roll of laughter. "Now or never, Marine," he said, those words a provocation if nothing else.

Santos lifted his gaze and glared at his so-called friend.

"You coming?" Knox asked with an understanding grin. God, he hated how well Knox knew him.

"You always been such an ass?" Santos shot back, stepping forward.

Knox chuckled and stepped onto the elevator, crowding close to Mary's side. They smiled at one another again. "I'm gentle as a lamb," he whispered. "Scout's honor."

She leaned into his side just as Santos stepped onto the elevator, and it shifted worryingly with the added weight. "I hope not," she replied, loud enough for both men to hear.

Santos's next step faltered and Knox reared back in shock as his face lit up in his signature smile.

Santos wedged his body on Mary's other side. She glanced from Knox to him and back. "What floor?" she said.

"Huh?" Knox asked, saving Santos from being similarly speechless.

And then Santos pushed off the wall and pressed the button to the third floor.

Mary watched him, licking her lips. "Thanks," she breathed.

"Anytime," he replied.

The door closed, trapping the three of them in the small space. Electricity filled the car, traveling up and down his spine.

Santos didn't have a type. He liked what he liked and he knew it at first sight. Mary was his type. And apparently, she was Knox's as well.

Knox offered his arm to Mary again, and she gracefully moved her hand to his bare forearm. Santos watched Mary's hand slide up to Knox's bicep. He swore he could feel that touch on his own skin as that static electricity moved from his spine to his groin with force.

After a few seconds or an hour, the elevator came to a stuttering stop, making Mary's lush cleavage bounce.

Thankfully, Mary wasn't looking at him, so she didn't see his hungry tongue taste his lips.

The elevator door creaked open again and Santos stepped out into the familiar hallway quickly. He took a breath untainted by his own lust and tried to get his bearings again.

"You doin' alright there, Marine?" Knox asked in a tight voice.

He wanted to say no, but he was too busy moving the box of coffee in front of his pants to hide his erection. He turned and found Knox looking at him with an easy smile and blown pupils.

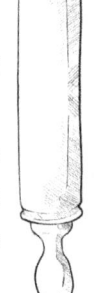

Santos pushed out a light laugh, happy to be on the same page with his friend again. "You doin' alright, Sergeant?" he asked teasingly.

"I'm doing great," Mary beamed, stepping out into the hallway hard nipples first.

WELCOME TO SEA PORT

SIX

Mary

Mary hated the college town where she used to work. It was *too* small — claustrophobic, even — and she'd withered there. Some of her colleagues had loved being able to walk to work when the weather was nice, droning on about the ease of living in a quiet, half-deserted town in the summer. But Mary had found it near to impossible to be herself in a space where any given day, she might run into one of her students at the grocery store or the chair of her department at the post office and always when she was in sweats, dirty sneakers, and a bonnet. And nothing was more embarrassing than taking a cab to the liquor store before they closed and standing in line behind one of her students when they both had class in the morning. Even in the summer, when most of them had gone home, Mary still couldn't seem to leave her house without running into someone from work.

Everywhere she looked, there was yet another reminder

that her life revolved entirely around her job, and she'd hated it.

Mary's life in Sea Port couldn't have been more different. Even though she'd been living there for a few months, she still didn't know more than a few people by name or sight, and at least half the town was still skeptical about the newcomers, so they gave them — her — a wide berth. And the few people she did know, like Bria and Sully, happily talked her ears off whenever she saw them. It was a lovely balance.

Sea Port was still on the verge of collapse and when she stopped by the town's small grocery store in the morning before work, she could peruse the store's aisles — all three of them! — in peace. But as Santos led them to glass double doors with a shield painted on them, she couldn't help but wonder how in the hell she'd missed these two men.

"So, um, what time do you normally go grocery shopping?" she asked Knox while squeezing his bicep. Again.

"Huh?" He frowned down at her in confusion.

Yeah, she definitely wanted to sit on his face.

"Come on," Santos grunted.

His face too.

Mary just barely pulled herself together and turned to find him pulling open the doors to the precinct. He was glaring adorably in Knox's direction, but then he moved his gaze to Mary and his mouth relaxed into a smile; his eyes didn't lose an ounce of the intensity he'd given Knox.

She sighed in contented lust as Knox led her forward, shocked that her panties could be so wet before noon. There was an entire workday ahead of her!

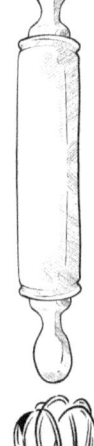

Knox disentangled Mary's arm from his and gently nudged her into the room before him.

"Welcome to Sea Port," Santos whispered as she passed.

She and her pussy floated through that door on a cloud of lust or something similarly delusional but came crashing back to earth when confronted with the reality of the Sea Port police department.

"Is this it?" she asked, too shocked to say more because her bakery was about the same size as this room and she just couldn't quite believe it. "No, this can't be it. I've been in storerooms bigger than this."

Knox appeared at her left, chuckling softly. "Not a bad comparison, actually."

"Shut up," Santos hissed, and then his hand settled at the small of Mary's back. Her mouth fell open on a gasp as he nudged her forward. "We're a small town, so we have a small department."

She started nodding because that made sense and she wanted to be reassured. Also, he had a very sharp jawline under his light beard. "So, um, how many people...uh, police officers are there?"

Knox laughed softly behind them.

Santos frowned and glanced down at her. "Three."

"Three...dozen?" she asked, looking at the half-dozen desks scattered around the small room.

Knox's laughter grew louder.

"Just three," Santos said in a tight voice. "I said we were small."

"That's not small, that's miniscule. A micro police force."

Knox snorted.

"Isn't the goal to get to know your new neighbors?" Santos asked, irritation creeping in at the edges of his voice. It was sexy as fuck, so Mary was willing to concede the point.

"It is."

"So keep an open mind," he said, urging her forward with that big strong hand at her waist.

"Fine," she exhaled loudly.

"Thank you." He didn't smile but she still wanted to sit on his mouth anyway. At that, Santos turned to the room and blinked. It was almost as if he was seeing the room through Mary's eyes and realizing that small town or not, this place was tiny, and she appreciated the empathy.

Mary turned to check on Knox behind them. He had a big, wide, pretty smile on his mouth and winked when they made eye contact, and that soothed her fraying nerves for a moment.

"There's not much crime in Sea Port," Santos said, leading her down the center of the room. "Most of it's parking-related with delivery trucks or people stopping in the road to talk to one another."

"A few years ago, it was arson," Knox offered.

"Suspected arson," Santos corrected. "But most of those cases were just ancient houses and people not paying attention to wind warnings when they burned their trash."

"Now why would they do that?" Mary asked.

"I'll take that to mean you're not from the country," Knox called.

"Nope. Where are you from?" She tried to turn in Santos's grasp but his arm tightened around her body. Maybe Santos didn't want her talking to Knox, and by the

lovely rumble of the other man's laughter, Knox didn't give a damn.

And as evidenced by her hard nipples, Mary was very interested in this dynamic.

"Most of what we do," Santos said, pulling her attention back to him, "is help people mediate their problems with neighbors. We're barely in the office, actually. In a town like this, we're part of the community. Mayor Waltham likes for us to be seen."

Mary looked Santos up and down. "I get it," she said in a soft growl.

His hand flexed on her back. "The only time we're really here is for this." Santos led her around a corner to a room with a small window set into the far wall, two benches along the short side walls.

"Uh...what's this?"

"Our jail," Santos said.

"You..." She turned to look at Knox. The other man tried to hide his smile behind his hand, her basket of donuts hanging from one arm. She turned around to gape at the room in front of her. "What the hell kind of jail is this?" she asked in a high-pitched voice.

Knox broke and let out a loud splutter of laughter before smothering it with his fist.

"The kind that rarely gets used," Santos sighed. "I've been here a few months and haven't had to arrest anyone yet."

"I...I don't know what to say," she said, and Santos's blank face indicated he didn't have a clue of what to say either.

The three of them stared at one another for a few

seconds before Knox pulled himself together. "The police and fire station work together along with some city staff that are like social workers," Knox said, his voice light with more barely contained laughter. "Or at least they will work like social workers, but the last one was Ms. Nadine and she retired the year before I got here."

Mary stepped out of Santos's hold. Now she could see both of them and they could see her.

She licked her lips as a shiver moved through her, a shiver of lust and shock. A very odd combination. "How long have you been here?" she asked Knox.

"Just under a year."

She turned to Santos. "And you?"

"Just about four months."

"Oh, me too," she said. "Um, and do you... Do you two like it here?"

They both nodded quickly, smiling as they glanced at one another.

"I don't know what kind of life you were living before you came here, but our lives were a little...chaotic," Santos said.

"This place is many things, but chaotic ain't one of 'em," Knox added.

"It's slow, predictable, and quiet," Santos said. "We like that."

Mary liked the way Santos said "we." She liked it so much that she lost herself to a beautiful and filthy little movie in her brain. "I like slow," she whispered, imagining Santos and Knox undressing in front of her.

Knox made a noise that sounded like a groan, and Mary had to cross one foot in front of the other to press her thighs

together and give her poor shuddering pussy some much needed pressure.

"Do you want to see the rest of the building?" Santos asked.

Mary nodded, licking her lips again. His eyes bored into hers, but he didn't move and neither did she. Well, her legs didn't move, but what was between them throbbed.

Knox, once again, saved them. He stepped closer on her opposite side and Mary sank into the delicious thrill of standing between them. "Come on, sweetheart," he said, offering her the arm free of her basket.

She nodded softly, lifting her hand to smooth it over his bare skin to caress his hard muscles. "So you work nearby too?"

"Mmhmm. I'll show you my office last 'cause it's the best." He leaned close and his cologne filled her nostrils. "Did you move here alone?" he asked.

She nodded eagerly. "Did you move here alone?"

His mouth tipped into a smile. "I did. And so did Santos. Ain't that right, Marine?" Knox asked without taking his eyes from Mary's.

"Yes, Sergeant," Santos ground out.

"Is he always so serious?" she whispered.

"He is, but he don't bite," Knox whispered.

"Don't speak for me," Santos spat back.

Mary's mouth fell open on a happy smile.

Knox laughed gently. "Well, excuse me."

WELCOME TO SEA PORT

SEVEN

Knox

K nox had given enough tours around town to be bored by the familiar surroundings, but this one had him so excited, he felt like electricity was running up and down his spine. He showed off the ancient building while trying to keep Mary and Santos in his line of sight. Mary's almost naïve interest and easy smiles were lovely, but when punctuated by Santos's red, frustrated face, Knox was having the time of his life. In all the years he and Santos had known each other, Knox had never seen the man jealous. Even at eighteen, Santos was practically unflappable in the few romantic relationships Knox watched him blunder through, so he was having a damn good time getting under his skin with Mary on his arm.

Unfortunately, his enjoyment started to dim about halfway through the tour right along with Mary's formerly bright smile.

Knox knew the building was nothing to write home about — the old, creaky elevator, thin, rattling windows,

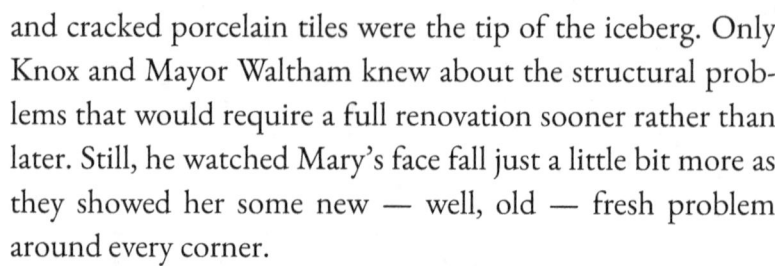

and cracked porcelain tiles were the tip of the iceberg. Only Knox and Mayor Waltham knew about the structural problems that would require a full renovation sooner rather than later. Still, he watched Mary's face fall just a little bit more as they showed her some new — well, old — fresh problem around every corner.

He tried to focus on the positives, pointing out all the stained glass he hoped they'd save in the renovation, and finally, the big, beautiful atriums on each floor right at the center of the structure — Knox's favorite feature by far. When they made it back to the third floor, the sun had burned through the early morning fog and was streaming through more of that stained glass he and Mayor Waltham loved. When it was sunny outside, the light was so pretty here, and Mary looked stunning underneath it.

Stunning, but terrified.

"And that's the end," Knox said, gesturing around them.

Mary's gaze followed the arc of his hand. Even though he loved this place, he could see the building the way she must've — the way he and Santos had when they first arrived. Most of Knox's job was identifying problems and strategizing for how to address them. His position gave him a unique appreciation for Sea Port's history and he'd hoped to transfer some of his enthusiasm for the place as it was and what it could be during his tour, but based on the look on her face, he'd failed.

"Please tell me this is a joke," she whispered. Her gaze was a little wild as her eyes moved from Knox to Santos, around the building, and back again, her voice dripping in disbelief. "That's...*it*?"

Knox winced at her tone — it was high-pitched, high-strung, and frantic.

He'd been in Sea Port for about ten months and had encountered this kind of reaction from a few new residents, especially the ones from larger cities, and it made sense. Sea Port wasn't just a small town, it was rural on top of that, set deep in a county with more cows and fallow land than people knew what to do with. It wasn't even the county seat. For some people, moving to Sea Port was like immigrating to an entirely different country.

If a town could make someone feel claustrophobic, Sea Port was it. It had one of everything — one post office, one post office box, one grocery store, one coffee shop, and, soon, one bakery.

"It's not as bad as it seems," he said gently.

"It seems really bad," she said.

"We're a small town. We don't need much here," he reminded her.

"What does that mean?" Mary shrieked, her voice bouncing around the quiet atrium.

Santos moved to Knox's side, tall and silent as usual.

"I've given lectures that lasted longer than that tour. There's more security to get in a liquor store where I come from. What if something goes wrong? A fire? A break-in? Do y'all just let people fend for themselves?" She glared at Santos. "Do you?"

Santos didn't like conflict and was a big, silent brick wall in arguments, so Knox stepped just into her line of sight to take the heat off his friend.

"We don't," he replied. "Santos and I want to make this

65

the kind of place that doesn't need a big ass police force, and not because there aren't enough people for the job."

Her eyes inched away from Santos's face, but the fierceness in her stare didn't lessen. "That's a pipe dream," she whispered.

Knox smiled down at her. "This is the kinda town that had a ribbon-cutting ceremony for the new stoplight and the coffee shop. We've got room for a pipe dream or two."

She didn't want to break, but Mary had a mouth perfect for smiling and it blossomed as he spoke. Even biting it back couldn't stop its beauty.

Knox inched close to her, slow and calm, trying to keep this moment from spiraling out of control again. "You wanna take a deep breath with me?" he asked.

Her eyes dipped immediately to his mouth and she nodded slowly, letting that smile come fully to life.

He was fighting a war in his chest to stay professional. The toughest battle was when they inhaled together, her cleavage lifting into view. He had to shift his eyes a centimeter higher to outrun the temptation of Mary's perfect, full breasts.

Even Santos joined in the slow inhalation. They exhaled loudly and in unison, the sounds of their breaths bouncing around the room.

"Feel better?" Knox asked.

"A little," she said with a slight grimace.

"Good."

"Let's go to Knox's office," Santos said, speaking for the first time in the entire tour. "You can catch your breath there."

Mary's tongue moved slowly over her lips. Knox swal-

lowed a groan as she exhaled, nodding her head slowly. Santos offered his arm to her and Knox couldn't help but smirk. He bet the man had been waiting for that since Sully's. Mary hesitated for a second, but eventually she slid her hand over his bicep, licking her lips again. But Knox could be an agent of minor chaos when he wanted and put his hand at her back as Santos led them down the east hallway toward his office.

Inside the room, they settled Mary into one of Knox's desk chairs, closing the door firmly behind them. Knox liked his office, but it was small and bare since he much preferred to spend his days in the garage or around town. It did have a pretty good view of Main Street, though, but that was about it. And Mary didn't seem interested in that anyway.

Knox had been on the Sea Port Welcome Committee from almost the moment he'd signed his contract as fire chief. He'd developed a decent grasp of the kind of things people needed to hear after their move, but he just couldn't fathom what was left to say to the new baker. So he set her basket on his desk, squatted down next to her chair, and squeezed her shoulder carefully. Not too hard, but with enough pressure to release the tension lifting her shoulders up toward her ears.

She looked at him with sad eyes and her pretty mouth turned down in a frown.

"It's okay," Knox sighed.

She opened her mouth to speak, but the desk groaned behind them and they both turned. Santos had leaned on Knox's ancient desk, one finger under the towel over her basket, looking at her donuts with the same hunger he'd

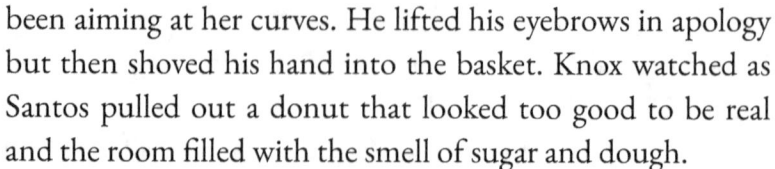

been aiming at her curves. He lifted his eyebrows in apology but then shoved his hand into the basket. Knox watched as Santos pulled out a donut that looked too good to be real and the room filled with the smell of sugar and dough.

Someone's stomach rumbled. Or maybe all their stomachs grumbled in hungry harmony. Either way, Mary's donuts smelled amazing.

"I went for a run this morning. I'm fucking starving," Santos said and ate half that damn donut in one bite. Dark purple jam oozed from the center of the donut and Santos licked it from the corner of his mouth.

"Boysenberry jam-filled," Mary whispered, and her voice shocked Knox back to attention.

"Huh?"

"I wanted to make a blueberry jam, but when I went to the store, they didn't have any. They had hella boysenberries, though, for some reason."

"The Barrett farm grows 'em," Knox told her.

"I'll remember that. They made a great jam and I stuffed some of the donuts as an experiment."

"What other kind of donuts did you make?" he asked. "I didn't eat breakfast either."

She smiled shyly. "Glazed, old-fashioned, and um, some donut holes. You should try them. They're best eaten fresh."

"Alright," Knox nodded. He squeezed around Santos with a roll of his eyes and peered into the basket.

He'd already eaten most of his donut and the man had an uncharacteristic smile on his mouth as he chewed happily. "Tastes fucking great," he mumbled with a full mouth.

Knox sighed and reached into the basket to grab a donut hole. "Holy shit," he mumbled with a full mouth himself.

"See?" Santos said, popping the last of the jelly donut into his mouth and licking a jam smear from the corner of his lips.

Knox reached back into the basket and grabbed a glazed donut this time. When he turned back to Mary, her expression had changed drastically. The abject terror had been replaced with a smile and tentative hope in her eyes.

"Good?" she asked, watching Knox take a bite of his donut like a scientist conducting an experiment.

"Great," Santos said, reaching into the basket again.

Knox was shoving his donut back into his mouth, so he nodded instead.

Mary relaxed into her chair, looking happy again for the first time in a while.

Knox hadn't planned on gorging himself on Mary's donuts, but if it made her happy, he and Santos were happy to oblige.

SANTOS

Mary came to life watching them demolish nearly half the donuts in her adorable little basket. She didn't have a pen and paper, but he could tell she was taking

notes on which donuts they ate and how much they enjoyed them.

"You should try a jelly donut too," she said to Knox, softly kicking his work boot with her sandal.

Santos and Knox turned their attention on her fully, and she looked like a completely different person from a few moments ago. She was sitting on the edge of her seat, her eyes were hooded, and the tip of her tongue was tasting the corner of her own mouth as if she could taste her own treats on their skin.

It took her a second to realize they were watching her with almost the same intensity as she was watching them, and when she did, she sat back in the chair and licked her lips fully. "For research purposes," she said. "H-he liked it. We should see if you do too," she said, glancing at Santos's mouth before looking quickly back at Knox.

Santos didn't like that. "Do you remember my name?" he asked.

Knox shifted so he could look at Santos with raised eyebrows. He managed to smile at the same time as he took another bite of his old-fashioned.

"Um...yeah. Yes," she said, stumbling adorably over her words.

Santos reached back into the basket for a donut hole. "What is it?"

"Huh?" she asked.

He popped the donut hole into his mouth.

Thankfully, Knox was always helpful. "I think he wants to hear you say his name."

Santos cut his eyes at the man he *thought* was his friend.

70

He didn't mean it like that. Okay, he might have meant it like that, but Knox didn't need to highlight it. He glared at Knox, but the other man was unfazed. In their time apart, he'd forgotten just how irritating the things he loved about the man could be.

"Santos," Mary replied in a soft voice. "And Knox."

He liked the way she said their names. A lot.

Knox licked a bit of glaze from his lips and they turned back to Mary. She was sitting at attention in the chair — back straight, thighs pressed together. Also, her nipples were hard, but that was beside the point. Mostly.

"You remember," Knox said breezily.

She rolled her eyes. "I remember this janky ass town I've moved to as well," she said, and her face fell.

He didn't like that. Santos moved past Knox and kneeled at her feet. He grabbed the chair's armrests, bracketing her thick thighs with his arms.

She didn't look at him the way he'd watched her look at Knox. She softened under Knox's gaze, but not with him. With Santos, Mary bunched her hands together in her lap and looked at him with a challenge in her eyes.

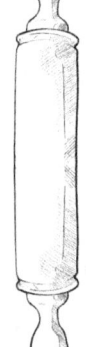

He loved that.

Santos moved one hand to the side of her leg, not to cop a feel, just to reassure her.

"I could tell you you're safe here until I'm blue in the face, but you probably wouldn't believe me."

She shook her head. "Because I'm not safe here," she sighed. "My mother was right. I made a completely unhinged decision. I'm *not* as smart as I think I am." She started wringing her hands as she spoke, so Santos moved his other hand to her left knee as Knox moved closer.

71

"I should've just gotten a shitty adjunct job, but I moved to the middle of nowhere Southern Hicksville instead. And now I'm giving away donuts to cops who are sexy but probably corrupt. What the fuck is wrong with me?"

"Now, wait a minute," Knox said at the same time as Santos said, "Hold on."

But Mary didn't pay either of them any attention. She was on a roll of self-recrimination. "Keisha was right! I let the shock of not getting tenure send me on a spiral. What was I thinking?" she shrieked.

Santos glanced up at Knox. There was a little sugar in his beard, but he looked just as confused as Santos felt.

"No, seriously," Mary said, looking between them. "What the hell was I thinking?"

"I thought that was a rhetorical question," Knox mumbled.

Santos focused his attention back on Mary's face, but she was looking up at Knox with an eager gleam in her eyes as if he could really answer her question. Santos had probably looked at him in just the same way dozens of times over the years.

He wanted to be empathetic to her, but she had the sexiest mouth and smelled like sugar, so most of his attention was focused on breathing through the hard-on growing down his left pant leg.

"Look at me," Santos said in a low, deep tone.

Mary jumped at the sound of his voice. Even Knox shifted behind him.

Knox's office was small, but somehow the three of them had squished themselves together more than was probably necessary. And when Knox leaned forward, his arm brushed Santos's shoulder and settled there.

"We don't know you—" Santos started.

"You don't know anything about me," Mary said, cutting him off.

"But we'd like to get to know you," Knox added.

"Oh," Mary breathed, her eyes shifting back to him.

Even Santos's eyes shifted up. "I wasn't going to say that."

"So you don't want to get to know me?" Mary asked in a gentle, curious voice.

He turned quickly back to her. "That's not what I meant. I was going to say that even though we don't know you, we can already tell that you seem very smart *and beautiful*." He put the stress on those last two words, eyes shifting to Knox briefly again.

"And we get it," Santos said. Mary scoffed. "You're in the middle of nowhere, the Wi-Fi's shitty like it's buffering into this century, and everybody seems like they're too damn nice."

"Yes. Oh my god, yes!" Mary cried.

"My Wi-Fi's okay, and what's wrong with being nice?" Knox asked.

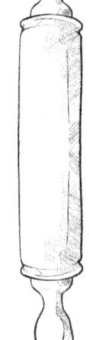

"Anyway, other than all that, Sea Port isn't too good to be true. I researched the fuck out of this police department. No lawsuits, no police brutality, no corruption as far as I could find. And if I find any now that I'm here, I will rain hell down on this force, this damn town, to bring it to light." He waited a minute and then cocked his head toward Knox. "And so will he."

"Damn straight, but I did all that same research, so I

don't see us needing to do all that," Knox replied in his characteristic breezy tone.

Mary's gaze jumped back and forth between them. She blinked a few times and took a deep breath. "That all sounds good" — her voice was small and hesitant — "but how do I know I can trust you two?"

Knox kneeled down in the space between his desk and her chair, on the same level as Santos. "Because it sounds like we moved here for the same reason as you — we just wanna build a good life. We wanna talk to our neighbors and leave this town better than we found it. We don't wanna get stressed out about bills or work."

"At all," Santos sighed.

"And these donuts are fucking amazing, so now that good life includes your baked goods."

She was beautiful from the moment they spotted her, but when she smiled, Santos felt something low and hot in his gut.

She leaned toward Knox. "Anyone ever told you your smile is a panty-wetter?"

Santos's eyes nearly bugged out of his head, but Knox just laughed softly and leaned in even closer. "A time or two."

"Mmhmm, I bet." She smiled and turned to Santos.

"My soft opening is in a few days," she said.

Knox choked on his laughter.

"Any chance I can convince you to show up in uniform?" she asked shrewdly.

"Depends," Santos said.

"On?" Mary asked.

"What you'll give us in exchange," he shot back. He

wasn't sure why he'd said *us*, but he said it, and now there was no taking it back.

Her mouth slanted into a grin. Santos watched as the wheels started turning in her head. He added 'cunning' to the list of things about this woman that made his dick pulse.

"You want a reward?" she asked, her voice dripping in something warm, sweet, and sticky.

"We do," they replied at the same time.

"Okay. I'll be prepping and baking like a bat out of hell until the shop opens. But if the soft opening is a success, I'll think of something."

"That's not an answer," Santos said.

Mary moved as if she wanted to stand and Santos and Knox stood, bumping into one another to give her space. She seemed amused by that as she eased to her feet.

"After the soft opening," she said in a playful voice, reaffirming her stance but hinting at so much more.

Santos was sure he was reading too much into her tone and hoped she wouldn't notice what it had done to his dick.

And just as soon as he thought that, her eyes dipped, first down Santos's body and then Knox's. She licked her lips and lifted her gaze.

"I made too many donuts. You two can keep them and fight over who's going to bring my basket back to me," she said with a suggestive wink.

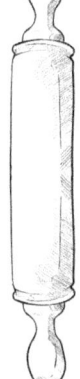

They watched her turn and breeze through the door, letting out deep, shuddering breaths that sounded to his ear like moans. They stood there for a few tense moments before Santos broke the silence.

"I won't fight you for her," he said, turning to his friend.

"Wouldn't dream of it," Knox said breezily, licking his

lips. "So we just let her pick and the other man's gotta be good with it. No matter what."

Santos considered Knox's proposition and then nodded, but an intrusive question formed in his brain and fell from his lips before he could stop it.

"What if she wants us both?"

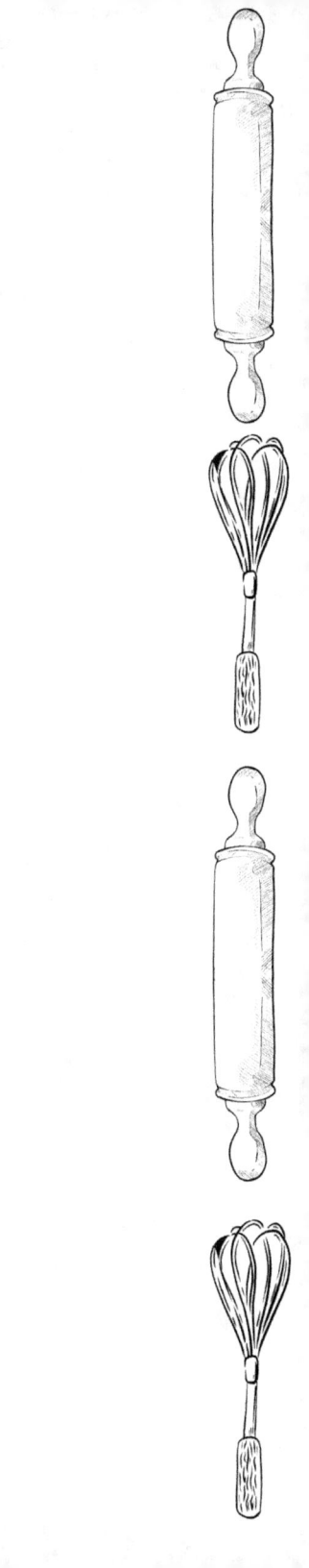

WELCOME TO SEA PORT

EIGHT

Mary

M ary left Knox's office in a daze. She'd planned to jump right into bundt cake experiments for Sea Port's over-sixty crowd, but that was before she met Knox and Santos. Now, her cake plans would have to wait for another day.

She bypassed her shop and headed straight home to masturbate. She'd learned a lot during the tour and most of it she wanted to forget, so she focused on the parts that made her happy, like how fucking sexy Knox and Santos were. So sexy, she locked herself in her bedroom with a couple of fully charged clitoral stimulators and went over every second she'd spent with them until she passed out, stress-free, with the biggest smile on her face. Workday over.

Sometimes, the life of an entrepreneur was wonderful.

Unfortunately, she woke up the next day still feeling yesterday's unease.

If Mary's life were a romcom, she was right about at the

point in the movie where she was being forced to reconsider the state of her entire existence by anxiously second-guessing every decision she'd made in the last few months. In most of the movies she'd seen while just barely hanging on mentally in grad school, the romcom heroine usually processed her feelings with a long run. Mary preferred therapy, but there weren't any therapists in Sea Port and she couldn't afford health insurance anyway, so she crawled out of bed before the sun was up, grabbed her favorite waterproof clitoral sucker, and walked to the bathroom for a long, hot shower to start her day.

Nothing better than starting the day with a few orgasms.

Fresh out of the shower, Mary opened the bathroom door and was immediately accosted by her howling cat.

Adopting Cat-leen Cleaver was objectively Mary's worst *and* best decision of the last decade or so. She'd adopted her from the local Humane Society, just one of the dozens of kittens students abandoned at the end of fall semester when their parents refused to let them bring their new pets home. Cat-leen was the only black cat in the bunch and looked scared as all get out. So, of course, Mary had to take her home. It took a few weeks for Cat-leen to acclimate to, and approve of, Mary's apartment, but when she did, Cat-leen ruled Mary's house and life from then on. Even in Sea Port, her cat demanded that Mary stick to a strict schedule of feeding her first thing in the morning. If Cat-leen had to wait, Mary was going to hear about it. And she did.

"Calm down," Mary sighed.

Cat-leen howled louder. In fact, Cat-leen trotted behind Mary from the bathroom, through the living room, and into the dining room where her food bowl and waterer were nestled against a wall, yowling at ever greater volumes.

Mary opened the airtight container of dry food in the pantry and dumped a scoop of food into her bowl. Cat-leen nudged Mary's hand out of the way and dove face-first into her breakfast as if she hadn't been fed in days rather than hours.

"Dramatic as hell," Mary mumbled under her breath, picking up Cat-leen's waterer to wash and refill it.

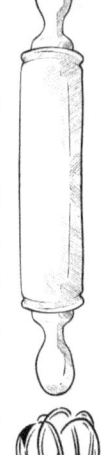

Now that she'd orgasmed enough to dehydrate herself and Cat-leen was momentarily appeased, Mary finally let herself think about yesterday with a clear head. And she was still stressed. She didn't even like the police, but she'd taken for granted her safety in a small town. It was one thing to assume Sea Port was safe, it was another to live thousands of miles away from everyone she knew and loved and realize the only thing standing between her and harm was a police department smaller than her Rhetorics class. She wouldn't have thought she wanted to live in a town with lots of cops, but when confronted with the reality, it shook her. It was still shaking her, to be honest, but she would have to deal. All she needed was rest, a dozen or so orgasms, and a good night's sleep, and all the obstacles that seemed insurmountable yesterday seemed slightly more manageable today.

Did she want to live in a town with a police force the size of an Intro to Composition course? No.

But was she ready to live in a town with a police force the size of her senior seminar on Love and Grief in African American Literature? Also no, but she didn't have a choice.

With the ambient sounds of Cat-leen's happy chomping and her drip coffee machine, Mary decided to just deal with

it. She had a brand-new life to build for herself, small town and all.

"Speaking of," she whispered to herself while moving to the dining room. She sat in the chair closest to Cat-leen's food bowl. "So I met some men yesterday, Cat-leen. Wanna hear about 'em?"

Mary stared at the back of Cat-leen's head ducked low into her bowl. She didn't even bother to throw Mary a pity glare, but this was their dynamic; had been since the day Mary brought Cat-leen home from the shelter. In exchange for a cushy life with plenty of food, catnip, toys, and pets whenever she wanted, Cat-leen agreed to stand in as Mary's therapist. So she kept talking anyway.

"A cop and a firefighter. I'm not sure if we're holding that against them yet, but they were fine as hell, so excuse me for my loose morals. Potentially," she added at the last minute, just for clarity's sake.

Cat-leen's response to her info dump was more greedy crunching, but Mary was too wrapped up in replaying yesterday's events to bother about being ignored.

"One of them had a smile that made my panties wet. Didn't even think that was possible," Mary mused as a shiver ran up her spine. "The cop was a little *too* serious, but you should have seen his arms, girl."

Cat-leen took a break from eating to clean her front paws for a second and then dove back in.

Mary had moved to Sea Port with hastily drawn up but still meticulous plans for her new life, but in all that work, she'd never considered dating. Not even once. But this morning, she was considering it — considering it so hard she left her coffee on the table and went back to bed for a little more quality time with her vibrators.

"Okay, good chat," Mary called to an uninterested Catleen.

Mary was in the zone today.

After Knox, Santos, and her libido had derailed her plans yesterday, she was back in the kitchen, working on her next baking project.

Cake.

Mary learned to bake in her grandfather's kitchen. He hadn't gone to culinary school, he'd just always loved baking, and he was fearless with it because he couldn't read well enough to follow a simple recipe, which was where Mary had come in handy. Everything he couldn't learn from books, he figured out through trial, error, and the strength of his taste buds. They'd cemented their bond on browned butter and sugar. Mary's time as her grandfather's kitchen assistant were some of the best memories of her childhood. He'd passed on all his hard-won knowledge to her with a deep Georgia accent, a keen eye on the texture of her bread dough, and a big, rough hand on her shoulder as she whisked, making sure her form was up to his standards.

Mary's grandfather was a man of few words and showed his love through food — a plate of cookies for all his grandkids after the first day of school, an elaborate and delicious

birthday cake, and a dozen or so sweet potato pies on Thanksgiving. He'd taught her the joy in understanding her ingredients well enough to try new things, make mistakes, and then try again. The kitchen in Confections looked nothing like his, but she could imagine him here all the same.

When she was a child, Mary had harbored the small, secret hope to become a baker but had gone to college instead of culinary school, thinking she'd set that childlike dream aside. But her grandfather always said you can't run from your destiny, and he was right. She'd rounded up all his knowledge and all her determination and in just a couple of weeks, Confections would open. She could only hope he would be proud.

She needed that kind of support today while she tried to perfect the vegan version of her gooey dark chocolate cake. Unfortunately, her grandfather hadn't known what a vegan was, let alone how to make a gooey vegan cake, so she'd been working on this recipe like her life depended on it — researching, testing, and researching some more. Most of her other vegan desserts had come together easily with simple swaps, but this one had been giving her hell for months. It was either too dry or it simply refused to set. She knew her proportions were off, so she'd been tweaking her recipe one ingredient at a time, and today, she thought she'd finally figured it out. She moved her spoon through the batter and it looked good — creamy, dark, and glossy. She grabbed a clean tasting spoon and skimmed it over the top of the batter, coating the back lightly. She brought it to her mouth, closed her eyes, and licked the chocolate from the cool metal.

Immediately, her taste buds started dancing happily. It wasn't just good, it was great. She'd made it, but her brain

still couldn't believe there were no eggs, milk, or butter, which made Mary even happier. But the batter was the easy part. The real test came in the oven.

She tossed the spoon into the sink and poured the batter into a small, greased loaf pan, pushing it into the oven with heartfelt prayers.

Vegan treats hadn't been part of her business plan until Leah had implored Mary not to abandon the vegan dollar. They'd laughed at that for a bit before Mary agreed to give it a try. She hadn't expected that decision would lead to her fiddling with a cake recipe for the hundredth time, but here she was.

She set the manual timer and glanced at the clock before turning to the sink full of dishes.

It was still early; barely even eight in the morning. Mary had been working by herself for the last couple of hours, but there weren't any windows in the kitchen so it felt like longer. She'd just filled the sink with hot, soapy water when the little bell over the shop's front door clanged.

Mary's eyes bunched together and she cursed under her breath. That door was supposed to be locked. She wiped her hands on the towel cinched in her apron strings and pushed through the swinging door that led from the kitchen into the display and dining room.

She expected Bria, but standing just inside her shop in running shorts and a damp tank top was Santos.

The vegan cake batter had distracted her from playing and replaying their time together, but seeing him again in all his sweaty, fine ass glory instantly made yesterday's attraction return with a vengeance. It took a few seconds for her to process what she was seeing — the sweat drying on Santos's face, his jet-black hair sticking to his forehead, his heaving chest and hard nipples.

Mary licked her lips and stepped fully into the storefront. "Um...we're not open," she said in a voice as weak as her knees.

"Obviously. We need to talk." He ran a hand through his soaked hair. His damp skin caught the dim light in the shop and his biceps flexed with the movement.

Mary shivered from head to fucking toe. "Uh...about what?" she whispered in a daze. "I mean, I don't have to talk to you without a warrant." It was a weak addition.

Santos rolled his eyes. "A warrant for what?"

"You tell me, officer," Mary shot back.

He sighed loudly and shifted gears. "We need to talk about us. You, me, and Knox."

Mary squinted in deep confusion at his words because none of them made sense together. Although she was imagining a world where they did fit together, and snugly at that.

She had to swallow a surprising lump in her throat while her skin flushed. "Do you mean you and me, *us*, plus Knox? Or you and Knox plus me? Or is it you, me, *and* Knox us?" She inched closer to him while she spoke.

Santos had clearly been out for a run and was still out of breath, panting loudly in her quiet shop. He looked caught out, like he'd said something he meant to keep private, and his eyes darted nervously around the room.

His nerves somehow eased her own and she walked with a little more confidence. She licked her lips again before she spoke. Maybe it was the exhaustion from her early morning in the bakery, maybe it was her perpetual sugar high spiking a little earlier in the day than normal. Or maybe she just liked how cute Santos looked after exposing himself unwittingly. Either way, Mary decided to expose herself as well since he was here anyway.

"Because if you mean all or any of the above, you should know that I dreamed about that last night. All. Night. Long."

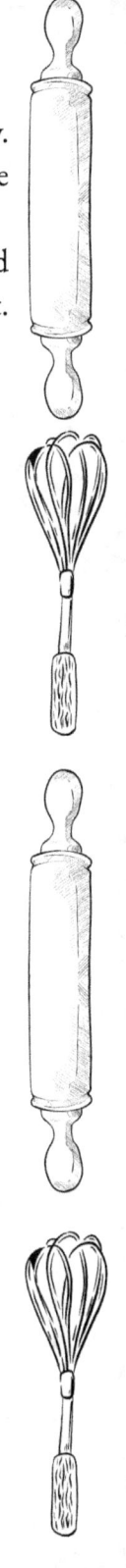

WELCOME TO SEA PORT

NINE
Santos

W hen Santos was stressed, angry, anxious, or sad, he went for a run. Physical exercise was his therapy and it worked. Going for a run was his most dependable form of stress relief besides sex, so when he woke up this morning with a stitch in his lower back and a hard dick, he knew he'd need a long run today.

He couldn't remember his dreams clearly, but after yesterday, they were surely about Mary and Knox — and himself — and he didn't want to think about it too hard. He washed his face, brushed his teeth, put on his running shorts, and left his house just as the sun was peeking over the horizon. The air was still chilly first thing in the morning, but he turned away from Main Street, heading toward the farms and woods ringing around the heart of town.

Downtown Sea Port was no more than six square blocks, but every time Santos said that, he was sure that couldn't be right; it had to be smaller. In only a few minutes, he was leaving the town's few paved roads for packed dirt trails.

Santos had run this trail before and was coming to know it like the back of his hand. He'd tried to convince Knox to run with him, but the other man had refused each time. Santos wondered if Knox would reconsider if Santos could convince Mary to join them, and that conundrum pushed him the next couple of miles.

Santos knew from a map he'd seen in Mayor Waltham's office that this path would stretch through the town's nature preserve — a dense forest of untouched land that was the southernmost point of a large stretch of woods that spread across three states. Sometimes, he considered running along this path just to see where he ended up, but today all he could think about was Mary and Knox, and that thought made him turn around, heading back toward Main Street far earlier than normal. He wasn't on shift until later this afternoon and still had his regular coffee date with Knox at Sully's in a few, but not now.

Right now, he had time.

The closer he got to downtown, the stronger the smell of baking bread and warm sugar in the air, filling his nostrils, throat, and lungs with every breath. How had he never noticed that before? By the time he made it back to Main, there were a couple of trucks on the road, so he moved his run to the sidewalk. It was garbage day, and Santos waved at Mrs. Johnson behind the driver's wheel, her daughter Celia hanging off the side of the truck. They waved back as he jogged past.

On Poppyfield, he eased into a walk, slowing by degrees. He didn't know exactly where Confections by Mary was, but Sea Port was too small to hide, and he came to a stop, dripping in sweat and exhausted in front of her shop. He walked up to the front door and peeked inside the dark windows. There was a sign taped to the door announcing the soft opening in a couple weeks.

He tried the door handle. "If it's locked, that's a sign," he mumbled under his breath. The handle turned and Santos pushed it open with his heart pounding a fast beat against his chest. An old-school bell above the door chimed as he walked inside and his brain flooded with images of Mary, naked, covered in a thin sheen of flour. His blood was pounding in his ears as it rushed from his brain down to his groin.

He didn't have time to second-guess himself and get the hell out of there because one second, he was stepping into Mary's bakery and the next, she was peeking into the storefront with a cute little bun on top of her head. It hadn't even been twenty-four hours but she'd somehow gotten sexier.

She took him in with wide eyes, her teeth digging into her plump bottom lip, and best of all, there was a light smear of flour over her right cheek.

He swallowed the lump in his throat as adrenaline and lust flooded his veins like pure diesel.

"We need to talk," he ground out.

"About what?" Mary's voice was saccharine-sweet, maybe even a little bit mocking, and it made his dick hard. But then her voice shifted into a slightly harder tone. "I don't have to talk to you without a warrant." His dick was hard as steel.

He knew what he wanted to say and that he shouldn't, so of course, he said it anyway. "About you, me, and Knox." He didn't have any expectations of this moment because he hadn't been expecting to tell her or Knox any of the things

91

he'd been thinking since they met her, so he was unprepared for the slow, eager smile that spread across her mouth.

He felt like he blacked out for a minute, but he came to at her next words.

"I dreamed about that last night, *all night long*," Mary murmured in an intimate whisper. Goosebumps emerged on his arms as Mary shut her eyes for a few seconds, not even trying to hide that she was, in fact, thinking about the three of them together right now.

Santos watched with lumps in his throat and his running shorts. "What does that mean?" he asked with a tremor in his voice.

He tried to speak casually, but the brain in his head wasn't in full control so the words came out like a rough demand. Knox was the smooth talker and Santos wished he was here. For many reasons.

"I'm... I'm honestly not sure," Mary said, licking her lips nervously as she stepped from behind the register.

"But you're dreaming about Knox? You want him?" he asked, squinting at that smear of flour.

"He has a beautiful smile," she whispered dreamily.

Santos stole a glance at her eyes but then couldn't look away. They moved slowly and deliberately toward one another in accidental unison until they were standing in front of her display cases, close enough he could smell the scent of sugar on her skin.

Santos's eyes moved down her body following the curve of her wide hips, licking his lips hungrily.

Mary cleared her throat, pulling his gaze back to her face. There was a look of amusement in her dark eyes that matched the playful smile on his own mouth. "I said I was thinking about you too," she reminded him.

"So you...want me?" Santos asked, his brain sluggish from lust.

"Also," she added.

He nodded once and took a sharp breath in through his nose.

"And what about you?" she asked.

His eyes went wide. "What about me?"

She stepped closer. "Do you want him too?" She was close enough that he could wrap her up in his arms if he wanted. And he did want that, but her question was bouncing around his brain, heating his blood by degrees.

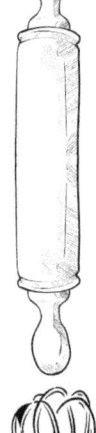

Santos could feel every vein and blood vessel throbbing in his dick, but he couldn't find the words to respond. He couldn't find the words to encapsulate a thing he knew was true.

She tilted her head back and batted her eyes at him. "Because if you did, I'd definitely be into that," she admitted.

That was all it took. Santos bent forward until their noses touched. "How much into that would you be?" he growled.

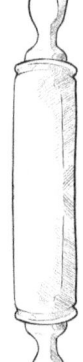

She pressed her mouth against his, swiping her tongue hungrily across his lips. "So into it, my pussy is dripping right now."

Mary was straight, no chaser, and Santos loved that about her.

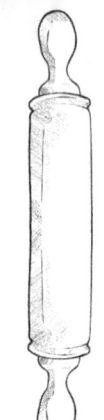

MARY

Before her failed bid for tenure, before grad school, before adulthood got its hooks in her, Mary had been a free spirit. Well, a freer spirit. Her overbearing and over-protective mother made sure she could never be too loose, but Mary had grabbed onto whatever bit of free self-expression she could hold onto until grad school and the tenure track stripped it from her. But the best thing about the move to Sea Port was that she was finding that freer version of herself again — maybe even building a new version entirely.

Whoever she'd become in the last not even twenty-four hours was horny as fuck, though, and Mary thought that was a great new development.

So was Santos's kiss.

Mary couldn't remember the last time she'd been kissed. She hadn't dated for years and had missed sex. Her sex toy stash had grown with her isolation, but she didn't own a single toy that could simulate...*this*. For all Santos's silence yesterday, he was saying a lot with his lips and tongue this morning. And his hands. She couldn't ignore his hands.

Mary sucked Santos's tongue between her lips while his hands moved from her waist to her backside, squeezing her soft flesh. Santos kissed Mary like he'd been waiting for years rather than a day. It was almost too good to be true.

Mary reluctantly pulled away from Santos's mouth and licked the taste of him from her smile.

"You taste like sugar," Santos whispered, dipping his head and licking across her mouth.

"You have no idea," Mary sighed.

Santos's pupils were blown wide open and his eyes were full of hunger. Mary felt sexy and powerful under his heated gaze. When she finally found the breath to speak, she felt bolder than normal; bolder than she'd felt in years.

"Would you two really make me choose?" Mary purred, smoothing her hands over Santos's bare, warm skin. "That seems so sad."

Mary could hardly believe the words coming out of her mouth or the audacity she had to say them. On the one hand, she wasn't looking to come between Santos and Knox — that sounded messy — but on the other hand, they were all adults, and adults could compromise.

Adults could share.

Santos took an unfortunate step out of Mary's grasp, his hands moving over her hips as if he was reluctant to let her go. He cleared his throat and glanced nervously through the window. Mary's eyes roamed over his profile. His jaw was chiseled with a cute little five o'clock shadow. Mary had been primarily focused on Knox's smile yesterday, but now that she had the chance to take in Santos's features, she concluded that he definitely had a great mouth for sitting.

"We'll be fine. No matter who you choose, we'll be fine," Santos said in a grave, gravelly voice.

"That wasn't what I asked," she said.

"We've been friends for years," he said, ducking around the question some more.

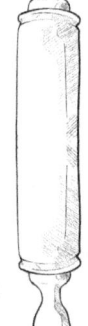

Mary stepped into the space he'd created between them. "I asked," she said in a slow, deliberate tease, "if you two will really make me choose."

He watched her approach with bated breath. When she pressed her hands against his chest again, he sighed softly and shook his head slowly.

Mary's insides were shaking as the audacity grew inside her chest. "What if..." she whispered, brushing herself against him again.

His hands settled back on her ass quickly, as if those few moments apart had been more than enough.

Mary wrapped her arms around his shoulders with a smile. "What if I want you both?" she mused. She asked the question in a voice full of wonder. In all the hours she'd spent masturbating about them yesterday, Santos and Knox's images had rolled one into the other, exciting her more than she realized until just this moment. "Yeah," she whispered. "I think I definitely want you both."

"Why would you—" he started.

Mary cut him off with a hearty laugh. "Why would I not? Have you seen yourself? Have you seen Knox? Oh."

Santos's eyes widened at the mention of Knox's name and his hands flexed on her ass. He averted his gaze quickly, but she'd already seen the look on his face and was watching his cheeks flush into a lovely bright red.

"Oh," she sighed.

"You want to date us both," he said.

Mary pressed herself firmly against him, against the hard bulge in his running shorts; the bulge that hadn't been there in the same force when his tongue was halfway down her throat.

Mary thought she was being very clear, but she spent years as a professor and had no problem clarifying her point. "If you're okay with it, I'm open to dating you both," she whispered. "But I'm also open to more. What about you, Santos?" She liked the way his name tasted on her tongue. She liked how his eyes widened while she spoke. And how his fingers dug into her ass at the same time. "How open are you?"

"Very," he growled in a low, deep whisper.

"Really? You're not just saying that 'cause you think it's what I want to hear?"

Santos shook his head and frowned beautifully. "I'm open," he whispered. "Knox probably isn't, though."

"But you don't know for sure?" She laughed.

He rolled his eyes. "There's nothing funny about this."

Mary smoothed her hands over his chest. She could feel his heart beating against her palm. "I disagree. This is very amusing. But you know what's really not funny is how long you've been blocking your blessings."

Santos's thick, dark eyebrows bunched together. "What do you mean?"

Mary moved her right hand down Santos' chest, smiling as she hooked her fingers into the waist of his running shorts. "Like I said, have you seen Knox?" She stopped here to lick her lips. Santos watched and mirrored her movement with his own tongue. But it was the gentle press of his hips toward her when she mentioned Knox that told her all she needed to know. She pulled Santos's face down toward her.

"If my best friend had a smile like that, I'd have married him years ago just so I could lick it every day," Mary whispered against his lips.

Instead of answering, Santos closed the distance between their mouths and practically shoved his tongue between her lips again. Mary welcomed this kiss with a smile and a gentle peal of laughter muffled by his hungry mouth.

This kiss was different than the last. Instead of kissing her with nervous excitement, this time Santos tasted her like he was starving and thirsty at the same time. He kissed her as if he wanted Knox to feel it, and Mary welcomed every press of his delicious mouth. She wrapped her arms around his neck and offered her lips up for exploration and experimentation, moaning against his tongue.

Once again, Santos broke their kiss, but at least he didn't pull away this time. He pressed his warm forehead against hers. Their breaths were equally ragged and Mary's lips were still tingling.

The day was just starting, but she was feeling very optimistic about what was to come.

"I don't know what I'm doing," Santos admitted softly.

Mary gave Santos a sympathetic smile. "Neither do I. Maybe we should ask Knox if he has some suggestions."

His next breath left his lips on a shudder and Mary felt it in her nipples.

"Come with me," she purred, taking a step back.

But Santos had already taken a step forward, his tongue moving over his lips again.

Mary had mapped the layout of her tiny bakery in a day. Without taking her eyes from Santos's face, she led him from the front door past the small eat-in section. There was only enough room for three circular white tables clustered in front of the window, set in a small alcove to the side of the storefront. There were only two doors back here, one to a small storage closet for cleaning supplies and then the small bathroom for customers next to that.

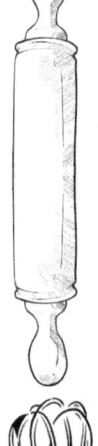

The bakery had a perfect view of Pine Street, a quaint little avenue just behind Main. Anyone standing on the curb would have been able to see her pulling Santos away, but the street was empty at this hour. Actually, the street was empty at most hours because Sea Port was in a population crisis.

Thank god for that.

Mary turned to open the door and Santos wrapped himself around her from the back with his larger body. That bulge in his shorts pressed against her ass, nudging her forward impatiently. They crowded inside the small powder room, unable to move without their bodies brushing together.

Santos turned her around and grabbed her behind her thighs, lifting her onto the counter. Mary was too shocked to do anything but moan happily as he manhandled her in the best way.

"God, I want you," he groaned against her mouth while shoving his body between her knees.

She snuck a hand down the front of his shorts and caressed the length of his shaft. Santos groaned loudly and she licked at his pleasure. "Are you gonna tell Knox about this?" she moaned.

This time, she felt his reaction at hearing Knox's name firsthand when his dick jumped in her palm while she stroked him. He tried to stifle his next groan with another kiss, but Mary heard it, felt it, and eagerly swallowed it down. She refused to let any second of this moment go to waste. Mary squeezed the head of Santos's dick until his back bowed and he broke their kiss to groan louder than ever.

She kissed a path across his cheek to his ear. "Will you?" she whispered, unrelenting, because she thought Santos could handle this level of scrutiny. If anything, with every stroke of his throbbing dick, Mary thought he was craving it, and she was happy to oblige. "Are you gonna tell Knox I made you this hard?" she moaned against his ear.

"Yeah," he grunted, hips jutting toward the apex of her thighs. "Fuck. Yes."

She smiled and kissed her way back to his mouth, accepting that she was just going to have to let the vegan cake in the oven burn — a sweet casualty to her changing circumstance.

Santos sucked her soft flesh into his mouth, licking her pulse while his hand moved between her legs, his fingers searching for her clit, stroking her sex through her leggings. She pushed that cake completely from her mind. She could make another — she could make a dozen other cakes if she wanted — *after* she and Santos got one another off.

"Fuck," he grunted into her mouth while slipping his hand into her pants.

She swiped at the precome leaking from the tip of his dick while his fingers slid through her lips and down to her opening.

"Yes," she moaned eagerly as Santos pushed two thick fingers deep inside her pussy.

Absolutely fucking yes.

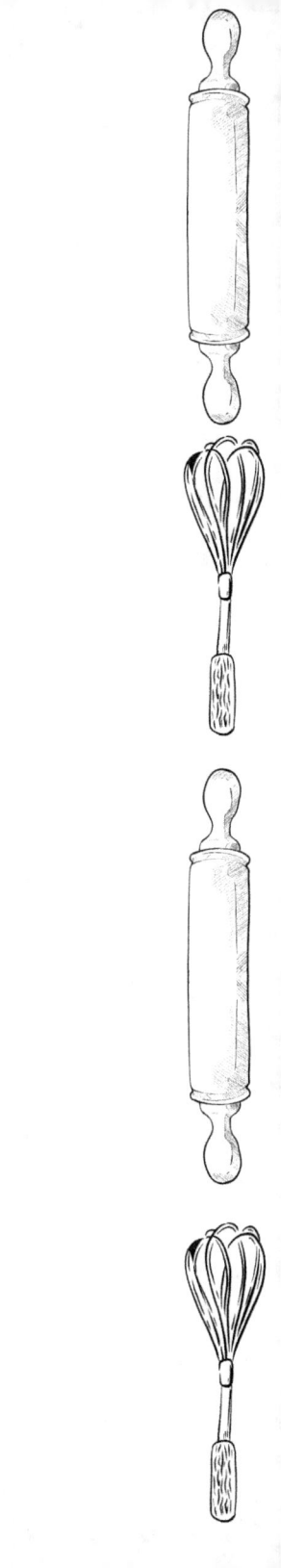

WELCOME TO SEA PORT

TEN

Mary

Her little encounter with Santos in the bathroom gave Mary a lovely little burst of energy. By the time he left, she was energized and ready to bake. She threw the crispy block of cake away and put on a disco playlist to whip up another small batch. Easy-peasy. Thankfully, she kept meticulous notes while she worked through a recipe, and after her first couple of assisted orgasms in years, she worked with a smile on her face and a little pep in her step.

She shoved the cake pan into the oven just as the back door opened. Mary's assistant Bria breezed into the kitchen.

"Hey, boss. What'd I miss?"

"Huh? Nothing. Why would you miss anything?"

Bria stopped in her tracks halfway through the kitchen, one hand on the long strap of her crossbody bag. She stared at Mary with furrowed brows and a small smile on her face. A bead of sweat trickled down Mary's back and not just because the oven was right behind her.

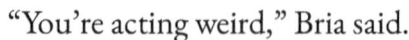

"You're acting weird," Bria said.

"I always act weird," Mary deflected.

Bria stared at her for a few more seconds before shrugging. "That's true. I took those cookies to the community center on my way in. Everyone loooved them," she said dramatically.

Mary hadn't originally planned to have an assistant, but the moment she met Bria, the two had just clicked. She saw a glimmer of herself in the younger woman and wanted to take her under her wing, but Bria was no pushover. As soon as she expressed regret that she didn't have the budget to hire her, Bria had gone to the mayor and gotten Mary an application for a grant to employ a local. It was a win-win situation, but it also taught Mary something important about how Sea Port worked. It was a small town, a place where some people still did business with a handshake rather than a contract, and having a homegrown Portie by her side would open doors normally closed to someone like her.

Bria was her best ambassador to the town, but Mary did sometimes regret her smartass mouth. "You weren't supposed to agree," she deadpanned. "About me being weird."

Bria pulled the strap of her bag over her head. "I can't lie to you, boss. I respect you too much?"

Mary rolled her eyes. "Anyway, thanks for making the cookie delivery."

"No problem. What else are you getting up to today?"

"Isn't today your day off?"

"Definitely, but there's literally nothing to do in this town."

Mary stared at her assistant as she hung her bag in the office and grabbed an apron from the hooks on the wall.

"Besides, our soft opening is right around the corner." Bria sang that last sentence at Mary while she started washing her hands. As if she knew Mary would change her mind.

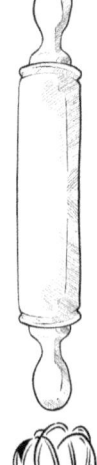

Mary thought about kicking Bria out, but Bria was stubborn, especially when she was right. Also, Mary was still riding her post-orgasmic high, so she sighed and pulled her notebook from the pocket of her apron and flipped to the marketing plan she'd scribbled down all those months ago — very official. "Okay, small business association, city council, police department and fire department, now the community center, all done and dusted. Next is local restaurants."

Bria nodded. "Have you met Sal?"

"Who?"

Bria rolled her eyes and turned to the handwashing station. "He owns the Italian restaurant. He's a close family friend. He already loves you because you gave me a job."

"Oh. Cool. Guess I can check him off my list, then."

Bria smirked but shook her head. "I think we should make a play for his dessert menu. It's old and not the best."

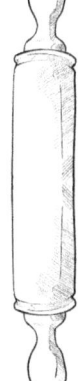

"Oh?" Mary said, her interest piqued. "What kinda dessert menu are we talking about here?"

"All over the place, honestly. Tiramisu, dry chocolate cake, banana pudding, peach cobbler."

"Peach cobbler?"

"The mayor's family owns a peach orchard, they're cheap."

"Is the cobbler good?" Mary asked.

"No, ma'am. Sal doesn't even like dessert, but he feels

like he has to have a menu for the people who love a little something sweet to end a meal."

"He's right," Mary said seriously.

Bria nodded. "That's why I've been priming Sal to outsource it to us so he can focus on making pasta."

"Is *that* good?"

"Oh, the best. You have to try it. I suggest going for dinner. It's not too crowded."

"Is anything in Sea Port ever crowded?"

Bria laughed. "Relatively speaking. Anyway, the dinner specials are good and the atmosphere is great for a date."

"Oh, yeah?"

"Yeah. I mean, I guess. I don't really date, but it looks nice."

Mary shrugged. "I don't date either, but I'll remember that if anything changes."

Bria smiled and lifted her eyebrows. "I heard you met Santos and Knox."

"How'd you hear that? Also, you knew who they were and didn't tell me?"

She shrugged. "They're not my type. Are they yours?"

Mary dodged that question. "How'd you hear I met them?"

"This town is this big," Bria said, snapping her fingers. "Remember that. But in this situation, my best friend, Keith, said he saw you three leaving Sully's yesterday morning when he was heading to work."

"Oh. Okay," Mary breathed, trying not to let her nerves show in her voice.

"I was just dropping some donuts off at the precinct and Knox gave me a tour of the Admin building. That's all," Mary said in a rush of words, tripping over her own tongue.

"Chill," Bria laughed. "You don't have to worry about the gossip mill. Keith hates gossip. I still love him, but damn." She shook her head sadly.

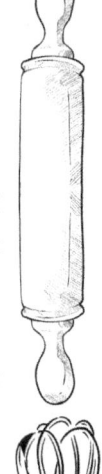

Mary giggled, having a hard time imagining anyone in Sea Port *not* liking gossip since it seemed to be the only part of the town still thriving despite the population loss.

"But I'm not nearly as respectful. He said they were looking at you like you were one of our sweet treats," Bria beamed.

"I don't know what you mean," Mary lied, trying not to let the things she'd whispered to Santos about Knox show on her face. Mary had become accustomed to denying herself — closing a door before she ever had a chance to see if it was unlocked — but she didn't want to do that anymore. The fantasies she'd been whispering into Santos's ear had been as much about riling herself up as exciting him, but even she thought they were just fantasies.

But what if they weren't?

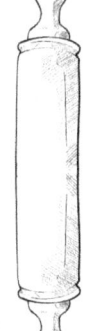

Thankfully, Bria had busied herself sifting flour for... something, leaving Mary to replay her time in the bathroom with Santos in relative peace.

"So...is the feeling mutual?" Bria asked. Mary blinked out of her filthy imagination to find her refilling the bread flour container.

"Um..."

Bria snorted. "Perfect. Then what I need you to do is to use this little love triangle to get us contracts for the city."

"Wait, what?"

Bria snapped the lid on the airtight container and rolled

her eyes. "Sully's sends coffee *and* tea to the mayor's office for her open office hours, press conferences, whatever."

"She does?"

Bria sighed loudly and stared at Mary as if she couldn't believe she didn't know that. Maybe that was fair, but damn.

"Alright, chill," Mary mumbled under her breath.

"Yes, they do," Bria said in a voice full of exasperation. "And Confections needs the same kind of contract. We can bring donuts, assorted pastry platters, cookies, whatever they want."

"That's a good idea," Mary said, nodding. She reached into her pocket and started scribbling in her notebook.

"I know! And so what I need you to do is to get Knox and Santos on your side so when we bring the proposal to the Mayor, we can say they support it."

"Umm, are you telling me to date them so we can get more work?" Mary asked incredulously, mostly to hide that it sounded like a great idea.

"Date, sex, flirt, whatever it takes," Bria said with a shrug, turning back to the dry goods.

"You can't be serious," Mary mumbled in return even as she was internally putting that in the column for why she should definitely date them both.

Bria glared at her over her shoulder. "I can and I am. Before you got here, I was waitressing for Sal during the lunch rush for pocket change. I need this job, and I'm going to make sure you're successful enough that I can keep it."

"Aw," Mary trilled, "that's so sweet. A little unhinged, but I love your loyalty."

"Exactly. So the next time you see one of them, show a little cleavage and—"

"Alright, get out. You're done for the day. Thanks for your help."

"I just got here!" Bria cried.

"And now you're leaving," Mary said, shooing Bria toward the office.

Bria started laughing, untying her apron. She tossed it back on the hooks and ducked into the kitchen office. She came back with her bag. "You don't want to hear me, but I think we both know I'm right."

"Out," Mary said again.

Instead of complying, Bria walked to the fridge and grabbed a box of cookies she'd baked yesterday. "The elementary teachers are having a professional day. I'm gonna drop these off on the way home."

"Damn, that's a good idea."

"I'm full of them." Bria smirked, heading toward the back door. "I'm doing what I can to get us that win. Don't let the team down."

"Leave!" Mary yelled around a laugh.

When she was alone again, Mary started tidying the kitchen while her sample loaf baked and cooled, keeping her hands and mind busy so she didn't daydream about Santos and Knox.

When the chocolate cake was ready, she sliced it carefully, checking it thoroughly with her eyes first — the crumb, the texture, the ooey gooey center. She cut a small sliver from the center and set it on her tongue. Mary closed her eyes and tried to find a fault in the recipe but couldn't. It was sweet but not too sweet, and the center melted on her tongue like butter. It was so good, she worried there were

eggs and butter in the batter, even though she'd made it herself.

For weeks she'd been trying to get it to the same gooeyness as the regular chocolate cake and she'd done it, but now she was terrified it was too gooey.

She cut off another sliver and ate it with a frown.

She stood in silence, tasting the cake, worrying about how perfect it was while already thinking of ways to make it better. What if she added a little icing? Maybe even some espresso for a cute kick? The cake was so good, Mary had nothing but ideas, and she pulled her notebook out again to jot them down alongside Bria's suggestions, including the risqué one.

Mary scribbled Santos and Knox's names at the bottom of the page with a smile on her face while licking a smudge of chocolate off her knuckle just as the bell from the front door chimed again. She immediately wondered if Santos was back and her pussy shivered.

But then sense returned and she turned toward the storefront. "Didn't I lock that door?" she muttered to herself, pushing through the swinging door eagerly.

Knox was standing just inside her door, her basket clutched in his hand, looking nervous, confused, and sexy as hell.

She'd never been more excited to have her day disrupted for a second time.

KNOX

K nox was a secret romantic.

Not a show up at your door with flowers or a boom box kind of romantic, but a tortured poet kind, which really just meant he could romanticize anything and anyone.

It had been twenty years and Knox could — and did — feel a little stitch in his chest when he talked about his first real situationship. He was fourteen and her name was Cristina Wilde. She was a high school junior, cheerleader, class president, and way the fuck out of his league, but she'd laughed at all Knox's jokes and didn't ignore him when they ran into one another at school.

The summer before his sophomore year, they met up at a youth protest about a fire that had destroyed a Black housing project in their neighborhood. They talked about everything and nothing while marching with the crowd, paper signs clutched in their hands. Sometime after sunset, they'd ended up in her bedroom, smoking a half-joint she stole from her dad's ashtray, listening to grunge music, and nervously playing with each other's bodies in that young, experimental way that felt risqué at the time but was so innocent in hindsight. Sure, she made out with another boy a couple of nights later, but the night he spent with Cristina was the most tender of his young, tumultuous life up to that point. He'd felt something so close to love, and that feeling stuck with him long after.

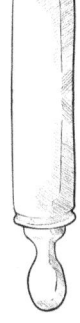

That same feeling welled up in Knox's chest as he stood just inside Mary's bakery while the bell above the door was still ringing in his ears. His heart was galloping in his chest as

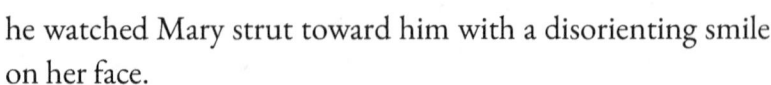

he watched Mary strut toward him with a disorienting smile on her face.

Knox knew he'd be romanticizing the hell out of her tomorrow at the very least, no matter how this conversation went.

"Well, hello," she purred, sweeping through the small swing gate.

"Hello," Knox said around the lump in his throat.

"How can I help you?" she said, running her tongue over her lips.

He took in a shaky breath now that he could see her without her display cases in the way. Her apron was tied snug to her body, accentuating the curve of her soft waist and her breasts. He looked her up and down as she closed the space between them.

"Knox? You in there?"

"What?" he asked, tearing his eyes from her thigh. "Sorry. Yeah. What?"

Her smile was almost painfully sunny. "What are you doing here?"

The question sobered him quickly and made him want to shrink in on himself because for whatever reason, he was always waiting for someone to break his heart. Thankfully, Knox knew all too well how to hide his pain behind a smile.

"I just came to bring back your basket and see how you were settling in. You seemed stressed out yesterday."

"I was," she admitted, stopping just out of arm's reach.

"You feeling better now?"

She bit her bottom lip and nodded, pulling her own mouth into a broader smile that he mirrored with his own.

"I'm settling in just fine, Knox," she said, caressing his name with her lips. She took another step forward.

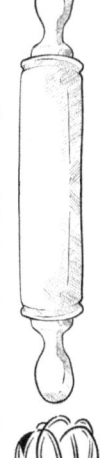

He swallowed a sound that couldn't have been anything but a groan, biting back the first filthy thing that came to mind. He waited a second before he trusted himself enough to speak, and when he did, all he could say was, "Good. That's good."

Mary moved her hands to her back pockets and his eyes went immediately to her breasts. He knew he shouldn't be staring at her like this — and so shamelessly — but there was just so much of her to see and he liked it all.

"How 'bout you?" she said in that soft, warm honey voice. "What's life like for a fire chief in a town this small?" she asked in a voice full of playful curiosity. He liked it so much, he had to casually cross his hands in front of his groin.

"Uhhhhm." He cleared his throat. "Um, it's slow mostly. Thankfully."

Mary licked her lips and watched Knox for a few silent moments. She stared for so long, Knox started to worry he'd said something wrong. Or maybe he'd spoken in another language?

"That must be boring for you."

He shrugged. "It can be," he said, gaze darting back and forth a few times between her nipples and her eyes before he managed to pull himself together and focus on her face — her lush mouth especially. "But not always. I'm the kinda person who needs people. I moved here after I left the Marines so I could live in a community. I like that I can get to know damn near all my neighbors, maybe even everyone in town with enough time." He stopped here to lick his lips

briefly but kept going. Now that he was speaking and Mary was listening, Knox wanted to hold her attention.

"I like that I can get home in a few minutes or I can stay out all night and no one's gonna hassle me or anybody, really. I like that I can walk a couple blocks from my office and check in on somebody like you." He hadn't known what he was about to say until the words were already out of his mouth.

Mary inched forward while he spoke, flustering the hell out of Knox the closer she got. "It ain't so bad," he finally said before pressing his lips shut.

She took one more step forward and pressed her soft belly against the back of his arms.

"It ain't so bad, huh?" she breathed, imitating his accent.

Knox was chatty. If given the opportunity, he'd run his mouth about any and everything, whatever it took to fill the silence, mostly as a coping method. But Mary had him speechless even though his brain was full of things he wanted to say. He wanted to ask if she'd seen Santos recently 'cause the man had been ducking his phone calls all morning. He wanted to let her know her nipples looked sexy today. He wanted to tell her to stop toying with him. Or beg her to let him suck her pussy while she kneaded some dough. He had a lot of things on his mind but none seemed appropriate, whatever appropriate meant in this context.

Mary tipped her head back and smiled up at him, her eyes searching his face. "Is this how you thought your visit would go?" she whispered.

Knox shook his head quickly.

"What'd you imagine would happen?"

His eyes went wide at the way she practically purred the

word 'imagine,' as if she knew exactly what he was thinking. "I-I don't wanna say," he replied in a hoarse voice.

Her mouth curved into the perfect O and Knox couldn't have stopped the groan that rumbled in his chest any more than he could stop a runaway freight train with his bare hands. "Oooh, that means it's probably good." He felt that whisper run down his spine like the ghost of a caress.

"Bad," he whispered.

She lifted onto her feet, moving her body against his bare arms. "Then I definitely wanna hear."

"Why?" he said, bending forward.

Her gaze dipped to his mouth as she strained her neck to get closer to his lips. She blinked the longest, silkiest eyelashes he'd ever seen. "'Cause it just might come true." Her whisper tasted like chocolate.

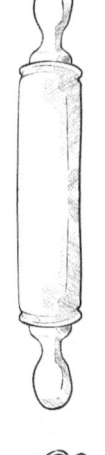

WELCOME TO SEA PORT

ELEVEN

Mary

Mary was a people pleaser, but not a people person. Like at all.

Most days, she preferred to be alone, usually in her house, with her cat, a good true crime documentary series on TV, and a bread recipe she wanted to try out. She also didn't enjoy making small talk with strangers in line at the coffee shop or other inconvenient and unwanted public encounters. Before she moved to Sea Port, Mary's best days were spent holed up in her apartment talking to Cat-leen. She wasn't, generally speaking, a chatty person, and her last job had somehow made her introversion worse.

But Knox made her want to talk his ears off. Or his clothes. "Come on, Knox," she purred. "I promise not to bite."

Knox huffed out a soft laugh, shaking his head. "You seemed nicer yesterday."

She laughed and took a step back. "No, I didn't. I was

scatterbrained and rude yesterday. Equal parts flirty and confused."

"Were you trying for that?"

"Trying to be confused?" she asked, reveling in the ability to toy with him.

He rolled his eyes and clarified. "Were you trying to flirt with me? Us?"

She shrugged. "I wasn't trying *not* to flirt. I guess you two inspired me."

"Us...two?"

"You *two*," she echoed, feeling giddy.

Moving to Sea Port had inspired in Mary a kind of hopefulness she couldn't explain; a hopefulness that stood in stark relief to how she felt about the life she'd just left. She certainly hadn't meant a situation like this, but Mary had hoped to feel abundant in her new life, and today she did. Vegan cake, Santos's dick pulsing in her hand, and now Knox's big, warm body — this was the stuff of her horniest dreams.

Knox, however, seemed conflicted, but so had Santos. Mary doubted it was intentional, but Santos had primed her perfectly for Knox, had shown her there was hope for her to get under his skin and behind that smile. So when a ripple of frustration moved over his face, she didn't respond. Instead, Mary waited to see what emotion was next and was not disappointed. For all his bluster yesterday, today Knox looked nervous, almost sheepish standing in front of her.

Mary was already aroused, but Knox had her ascending to a new level. "I think we should stop beating around the bush, don't you, Sergeant?"

Knox's nostrils flared. He pursed his lips and stared

down at her for a tense moment that felt like electricity on her skin.

And then he rolled his eyes. "Santos teach you that? How to annoy me?"

She wondered if he even noticed the change in his tone — how it had gotten deeper, lower when he said Santos's name — because she certainly took notice, and it made her bolder.

Mary licked her lips before she managed a shaky smile. "He might've mentioned something about you hating when he called you by your rank..." She stopped here to take in and release a shuddering breath. "In private," she finally finished on a soft moan.

Mary said those last two words deliberately slow, mirroring Knox's tone as best she could. She also leaned forward, pressing her breasts against his chest.

Knox's jaw tightened in response. "Traitor," he whispered, his gaze glued to her lips.

"If it makes you feel any better, I was rubbing my breasts up against him when he told me."

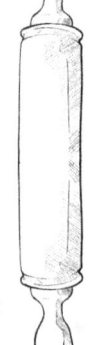

He grunted and lifted his eyes to hers. "I don't need to know that," he ground out.

"Does it make you angry?" she asked, stepping into him now, shamelessly rubbing her nipples against him like a cat in heat.

"Jesus," he hissed, shaking his head.

"You sure? You seem angry to me, Sergeant."

He watched her with hungry eyes and it seemed like his mouth moved of its own accord, closer and closer to hers. "I'm fucking furious," he admitted, and she smiled.

"You two are close?"

"Very." His breath started coming in short, minty pants that caressed her lips.

"Do you wanna get back at him?"

It took a few seconds for her question to sink in and his gaze to lift from her mouth. "What?"

"He told me how to get on your nerves. Why don't you tell me how to get on his?"

She almost had him on the hook, but then he shook his head and backed away. Mary frowned so hard it hurt.

"I'm not a vindictive man. Santos has been my friend for too many years to be petty."

Mary cocked her head to the side, reconsidering Knox one more time. "Seriously?" she breathed.

"Seriously. If you and Santos got something going on, that's none of my business. He's a good man. A good friend. I don't wanna get in the way of that. I just..." He shrugged sadly. "I guess I just wanted to hear it for sure."

Mary sighed, realizing that she'd definitely read him all wrong. Knox was clearly more complicated than she was giving him credit for. He and Santos were much less alike than she'd realized and she liked it — as if each man was an individual puzzle she got to unravel. Hopefully slowly.

Mary rocked back onto her heels. "You're giving up so easily," she sighed, resting a hand on her hip. She sucked her teeth before gesturing down her body with her other hand. "You're telling me all this ain't worth getting in a little scuffle for?"

Knox's eyes followed her hand down her body. The man had the nerve to lick his lips while taking her in. When he spoke, his voice had changed yet again and it made Mary shiver; something he certainly noticed.

He stared at her for a few more seconds before his face fell and he shook his head sadly. "If it was anybody else but him," he said in a deep, contemplative whisper. "I been thinking about you so hard I can damn near taste you on my tongue."

Mary preened at that, but the warmth in her chest only lasted for a few short seconds.

"But that don't mean I'm gonna fight over you like a piece of meat I can win. And with my best friend at that." He shook his head again. "If you want him, you've got damn good taste. Like I said, he's a good man, and he'll treat you right."

Mary dropped the hand from her waist and let her gaze wander over his face, liking everything she saw and had learned about him in these last few minutes. She hadn't met a man worth a damn in over a decade, but now she'd met two. Knox was honest, fair, sexy, and Mary really wanted to sit on his face.

Unfortunately, the man was throwing obstacles in their path, and for no good reason.

"This was so much easier with Santos," she muttered.

"Huh?"

Mary knew what she wanted. Her old life had been full of indecision, confusion, and fear. She'd been so bogged down by a life she wasn't really living that she never got the chance to be happy, but she wanted to be *really* happy in Sea Port. She felt surer of the person she was becoming and the life she wanted to live. This morning, that had meant making out with Santos, and now it hopefully meant doing the same with Knox. Who knew what tomorrow would bring?

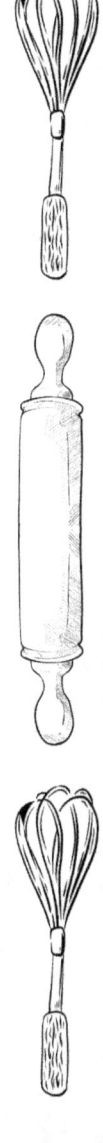

She sighed and walked to the bakery's front door. She glanced at Knox over her shoulder and turned the lock. The sound of metal grinding was unnaturally loud in her warm, quiet bakery. It was still early in the day and the streets were mostly empty, but even if there had been pedestrians walking by her shop, that wouldn't have changed her plans.

She turned back to Knox, smiling bigger than ever, and stepped to the side. Knox watched her like a hawk as she walked toward the same small hallway she'd led Santos down.

She turned to him, hard nipples forward. "You want a tour of my shop, Sergeant?"

He swallowed hard.

Now that there was space between them, Mary could see the nice bulge in his pants and she licked her lips.

"Yes," Knox said quickly.

"Good, 'cause there's lots to see," she said, turning on the balls of her feet. She looked over her left shoulder at him. "So much I can't wait to show you."

Mary hardly recognized herself. She'd been so quiet and reserved for most of her life, but that had gotten her nowhere. Well, technically it got her a PhD and a bakery, but that was neither here nor there, and in the end, nothing mattered more than when Knox took his first step forward.

They had to squeeze inside the powder room, just like she had with Santos, but Knox was reserved in his desire, so Mary took over, pushing him back against the sink.

She ran her hands over his chest, feeling his muscles through his thin t-shirt. She could feel his heart pounding as she pressed herself against the hard, rhythmic thump. Knox

opened his legs just enough to bracket her thighs in his, and she rewarded him by rubbing her stomach against his bulge.

"I'm not gonna fight him for you," Knox whispered.

"Okay. Do you wanna touch me?" she asked, a greedy whine in her voice.

She was expecting to have to tease him just a little bit harder but was happy when he proved her wrong again.

One second, his hands were hanging straight at his sides, his fingers twitching toward her body but no more. But when she asked — okay, begged — she heard his breath hitch before his fingers brushed the back of her thighs, and all that reserve he'd had before fell away in front of Mary's eyes.

His touch was so similar and different to Santos's all at the same time — they were like different pages of the same book. Two pages she wanted to get in between.

Knox's hands moved roughly up to her hips and waist. His fingers sank into her flesh and they groaned together.

"Goddamn, you feel good," he moaned.

Mary's clit jumped and she moved her hands over his shoulders, enjoying every inch of his hard muscles. After Santos, Mary thought she'd be riding the wave of those orgasms for days, maybe even weeks, but now that she was pressed up against Knox, a whole new reserve of lust opened up and she wanted him more than she could say.

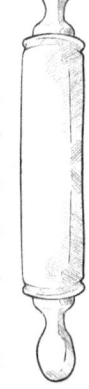

Mary leaned forward and pressed her lips against the corner of his mouth, but then he turned his head, opening his mouth to taste her. She tried to tease his bottom lip with her tongue, but Knox greedily sucked it into his mouth.

Mary let out another giggle-moan just like she had with Santos, which couldn't be a coincidence, right? A week ago, she hadn't even known that sound was possible, but the

more these men pulled it from her throat, the sexier it sounded to her own ears. And based on the way Knox was kissing her with hungry sips, Mary thought he liked it as well.

With Santos, their hands had greedily pushed clothing aside, desperate to get to warm skin. Knox's hands were a hurricane, setting down in one spot just long enough to do some damage — i.e., make Mary moan — before moving on for more. Now that she could compare, all Mary really wanted was to feel Knox *and* Santos's hands on her at the same time.

The thought was so good, Mary had to break their kiss.

"What...what's wrong?" Knox asked with hooded eyes.

She laughed softly and his eyes dropped immediately to her mouth. "Nothing's wrong. I just had a thought."

His eyebrows bunched together. "O...kay?"

She licked his minty taste from her lips. "I was just thinking about you and Santos touching me at the same time."

Knox's mouth fell open in shock, but it was the way he unknit his eyebrows and they lifted in serious interest that steadied Mary's resolve. Her right hand started moving down his chest. His muscles jumped as her fingers skimmed over them.

"How does that sound?" she asked. Instead of answering, he clamped his lips shut. Mary rubbed herself against his bulge again, kissing the groan from Knox's lips. "'Cause I think it sounds perfect. Both of your hands on me. My hands on you. Your hands on each other."

Knox's hips jumped forward into her waiting palm but touching him through his pants wasn't enough. Mary pried open the button of his jeans. Their lips brushed together, but they held their breath as she pulled the zipper down casually.

"Wouldn't that be good?" she whispered against his mouth.

"Which part?" Knox groaned, his eyes on the place where her hand disappeared inside his pants.

"All of it," she sighed wistfully. "All of you on all of me. And Santos."

He moaned beautifully.

Mary moved her free hand up to cradle the crown of his head. He leaned close and dug his fingers into her thick thighs. Their mouths brushed. She couldn't wait to taste his tongue again. But first, she wanted to be clear.

"Like I told Santos this morning, I want him and I want you. The only question is—"

"We want you," he said quickly.

Mary rolled her eyes, smiled, and smoothed the palm of her hand down his length. "Obviously."

He took in a slow, shuddering breath as she covered the soft head of his hard shaft. "The only question is if you start to leak precome when I mention Santos's name like he did when I mentioned yours."

"Jesus Christ," Knox groaned as he finally — *finally* — kissed her with everything he had.

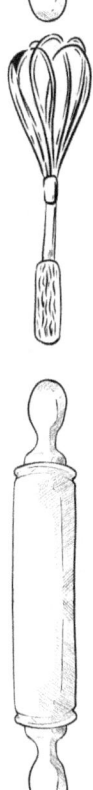

WELCOME TO SEA PORT

TWELVE
Santos

When Santos decided to leave the Air Force, everyone had an opinion about what he should do with himself; the kind of life they thought he should live. He'd listened to every stitch of advice knowing he had no plans to follow any of it. No one knew what kind of life Santos wanted to live as a civilian, not even him. The only opinion he might've entertained was Knox's, but Knox didn't give advice — that wasn't his style. Still, when Santos got back to Denver, there was a gift from Knox in the pile of presents welcoming him home — a world map and a framed photograph of the two of them from nearly a decade before. Santos would have preferred Knox's presence, but the map was a nice, sentimental nod in the right direction.

That map was hanging in his bedroom now on the wall above his dresser, surrounded by pictures of his family and that picture of him and Knox. He'd pushed pins into all the places he'd visited over the years, including one as close to tiny Sea Port as he could get. And when he woke up this morning with a riot of knots knitting themselves together in his gut?

All he could think about was Mary and Knox as guilt built in his chest.

As soon as he opened his eyes, Santos knew he couldn't go about his morning routine as normal. He didn't even try — because of the guilt, but also the lust he didn't know what to do with. He opened his eyes to his dark gray bedroom. He looked around the room and most of the details were fuzzy in the dark, but not that map. Santos's eyes drifted there as he slipped his left hand under the blankets.

If he'd hoped stopping by Confections would settle things between him and Mary, he was wrong. He probably could've guessed things wouldn't work out the way he planned, but he hadn't been thinking yesterday. Well, he'd been thinking, but his brain wasn't running the show yesterday or this morning. He closed his eyes to slits and started stroking his soft shaft, thinking about Mary's sweet tongue sliding between his lips. He covered the head of his dick with his palm and squeezed. A light ripple moved up his spine and he arched his back away from the mattress. How was he supposed to taste vanilla and sugar again and not get hard?

He normally rushed around in the morning, always in a hurry to get out the door for a run and work, but not today. Today, he stroked himself to a slow arousal and even slower release. He'd gotten off yesterday with Mary, but it wasn't enough.

The thought pulled a desperate grunt from his chest and

he pressed his shoulders back into the bed as a shudder moved through his body. Santos tightened his grip on his shaft and started stroking himself harder and faster, but then his brain betrayed him.

"What would you do if Knox was here?"

Mary had whispered those words against his lips while stroking him yesterday and he came almost instantly, hard, wet, and sticky. Today, in the privacy of his home, that question made his toes curl. He was normally a one-hander, but he was overwhelmed this morning and shoved his right hand under the covers, caressing his balls until he was panting loudly and shoving the back of his head into his pillow. A needy warmth spread through his chest at the thought of two sets of hands on his shaft.

"Fuck. Fuck," he groaned, low and deep, at the thought that one set of those hands could be Knox's.

Touching himself like this and thinking what he was felt wrong in the way so many new things often did, and only because this feeling and these thoughts were new and unfamiliar, but not bad. Not bad at all based on the electric feeling of an orgasm building around the base of his dick.

Cool hope grew in Santos's chest, but he smothered it with a firm grip on the head of his shaft. Precome leaked from the tip and he used that moisture to ease the path down his length, but it wasn't enough. He pulled his left hand free, spit into his palm, and started stroking again. The thought of staving off his orgasm flew out the window with lubrication, so he kicked the blankets from his body and really focused on getting himself off.

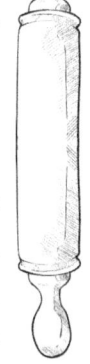

Santos was the kind of person who needed a physical relief to clear his cluttered thoughts. It didn't matter if that

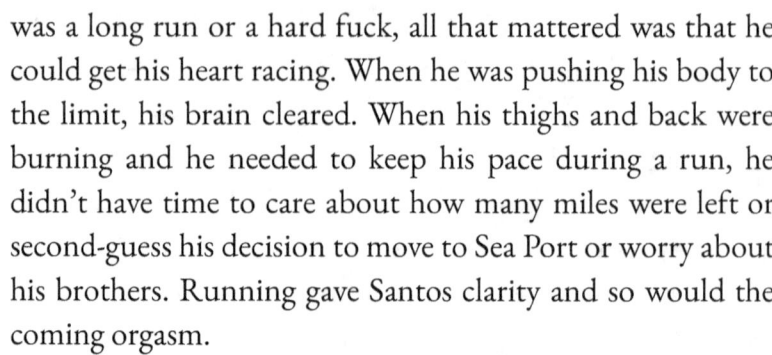

was a long run or a hard fuck, all that mattered was that he could get his heart racing. When he was pushing his body to the limit, his brain cleared. When his thighs and back were burning and he needed to keep his pace during a run, he didn't have time to care about how many miles were left or second-guess his decision to move to Sea Port or worry about his brothers. Running gave Santos clarity and so would the coming orgasm.

He could taste Mary on his tongue, but he wanted to taste Knox as well. He'd wanted that for years, but the man had always seemed so far out of his grasp that he pushed that desire away. After yesterday, he couldn't anymore.

The silent bedroom filled with his own muffled grunts and the sound of skin moving over skin. He bit his lips shut for a second before a loud moan burst from his chest. "Knox," Santos grunted at the end of that long, desperate moan, and then he came in a wet, sticky puddle. It splattered over his boxers and thighs and left him out of breath but satiated.

The honesty in that orgasm was purifying.

After his orgasm, Santos fell back asleep and fucked up his morning schedule. He left his house late and had to rush to Sully's for coffee with Knox. Sea Port just wasn't big enough to have to rush anywhere.

He drove the few blocks to work and parked along Second Street. It might have been faster to just walk, but he had to head out to the farms — what Knox called Santos's rural route — and he wouldn't be walking that. He slammed the driver's door, hopped onto the curb, and walked quickly around the corner onto Main just as Knox stepped out of Sully's with a paper coffee cup in each hand. He spotted Santos and stopped. The two men stared at one another and Santos noticed that Knox wasn't smiling — a rare sight.

Santos resisted the urge to fidget, but a few hours ago, he'd been jacking off, fantasizing about Knox and Mary, and he was terrified Knox would somehow see that on his face, so he stayed as close to still as possible.

After what felt like ages, Knox pursed his lips together and extended his arm, offering one cup to Santos.

It took a few seconds for Santos's feet to start moving again, but each step closer to Knox made the nervous flutter in his stomach all the more pronounced. He walked down the block, trying to get his stubborn brain to forget what he'd done this morning, but it refused. In fact, the closer he got to Knox, the stronger the memory burned itself into his brain.

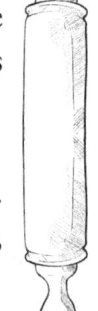

"I got your regular," Knox said in a hard grunt.

His back muscles spasmed at something in Knox's tone. It sounded deeper than he remembered from just yesterday, which didn't make an ounce of sense, but it was how it felt.

Santos plucked the cup from Knox's hand and his fingers brushed Knox's briefly. It took all the energy Santos had in that moment to swallow the moan in his throat, chasing it with a hot sip of coffee.

He just knew he was going to have to run home at his lunch time to masturbate.

"Let's walk," Knox said, shrugging his right shoulder

and turning away. Santos followed silently, wishing the ground would open and swallow him whole.

Or maybe... He shook his head, refusing to entertain that thought any further.

They headed east, away from Sully's, Confections, and the little nugget of downtown Sea Port where they spent most of their time. They walked in the direction of Sea Port's library where the methodical emptying of the building had been the most interesting thing in town until a couple days ago. He and Knox had walked this path together before, but this time felt different. After yesterday and this morning, Santos didn't think he could ever feel the same about Knox again, which had him terrified of what that could mean for their relationship in the long run.

After about a block, the silence started to get to Santos. He cleared his throat. "What's up, Sergeant?"

"Don't call me that," Knox snapped.

Santos swallowed the sharp retort that formed on his tongue and washed it down with another sip of coffee, but he didn't correct himself.

"How was your day yesterday?" Knox asked.

Santos choked on the hot liquid running down his throat. "Fine," he croaked out, wiping his chin with the back of his hand.

"Mmhmm," Knox hummed and then waited for Santos to catch his breath. "Didn't see you yesterday."

"I was busy," Santos lied.

"Oh, yeah? Anything interesting happen?"

Santos wiped the tears from his coughing fit from his eyes. "No. Nothing happens around here," he said, forgetting his lie immediately.

"Then what were you busy doing?" Knox asked.

Santos's eyes went wide and he knew he'd fucked up as soon as they locked eyes.

"I went to see the baker yesterday afternoon," Knox said, looking at him with a lazy precision. Santos remembered this look from Basic. "You sure nothing interesting happened?"

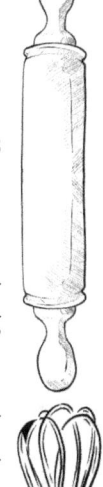

If Santos were a different kind of man or he respected Knox less, he might've leaned into the lie. If he respected himself less, he might have tried to convince himself and Knox that he didn't owe his friend an explanation about yesterday. That would have been the easy way out of this awkward conversation. If he just ignored the anxiety he was feeling, he could remind Knox that they met Mary at the same time and she was fair game, but Santos didn't think Mary would like him talking about her like a prize to be won.

Especially not to Knox.

If anything, Santos thought he and Mary had bonded over the realization that actually, Knox was the prize they both wanted to win. So he took another sip, cleared his throat, and tried to remember how to speak again.

Before he could say anything, though, Knox cut him off. "Just so we're clear, Marine, I already know about the bathroom."

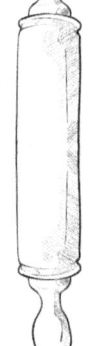

Santos felt like his heart was trying to beat its way up through his throat. "And how do you feel about that?" he croaked, biting the inside of his cheek to stop from calling Knox by his rank.

"A lot," Knox replied carefully, stopping and turning toward Santos. "But mostly I've been wondering why she

was the one telling me and not you. Not my best friend? What's up with that?"

Santos's ears warmed in shame, but he took the knock because he deserved it. "I didn't know how to—"

"You didn't know how to gloat? I don't believe that." Knox laughed drily.

Santos shook his head. "Nothing to gloat about." Knox raised his eyebrows and Santos rolled his eyes. "You know what I mean."

"Do I?"

Santos squinted at him. "What exactly did she tell you?"

Knox took another sip. They stared at one another, and Santos could tell Knox was enjoying torturing him over his morning caffeine fix. This was such a typical response that all he could do was roll his eyes again.

"What you think she told me?"

"Have you always been such a dick?"

"Yes," Knox said, smiling.

Santos licked his lips. He and Mary had shared a lot with one another in that small bathroom, things he didn't think Knox would've received with this kind of easy, playful response.

Right?

Santos couldn't be sure and he felt like it was eating him alive. "I asked her if she was interested in either of us. She said both."

It was a small tic, but Santos saw Knox's jaw tighten, and he grunted in response.

He took a beat to breathe slowly, steeling his nerves for the next sentence. Knox waited patiently. "She kept asking if I was going to make her choose between us."

"And what'd you say?" Knox's voice was rough.

It was a pretty mild morning, neither cold nor hot — a beautiful spring day in Sea Port, but Santos felt like he was baking under a full summer sun. "I told her I wouldn't make her choose," he admitted.

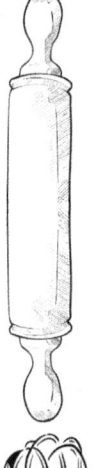

Knox grunted again. Santos pressed his lips shut and waited for the next question, whatever the hell it would be.

"She told me," Knox said carefully, "that you told her to call me Sergeant 'cause it annoys me."

"That wasn't exactly what I said," he replied, grinning in relief, "but that was about the gist."

Knox rolled his eyes, grunting again. The sound went straight to Santos's heads.

"What'd you say when she told you that?" he asked in a soft whisper.

Knox sucked his teeth before he turned back to Santos. "Not much, but she said I shouldn't blame you since she was rubbing up on you when you started spilling secrets."

Santos couldn't help but laugh at that. It was true, and he remembered every rub fondly. "She was," he replied. "I guess I could gloat about that."

"You missed your chance," Knox said flatly.

"Don't y'all have jobs?" someone called.

They turned toward the voice to find Bria, riding in the middle of the street on her bike, weaving left and ride to slow down and judge them for as long as possible.

Some Porties seemed hellbent on rejecting the new townspeople no matter what. But then there were Porties like Bria, who'd taken it upon herself to become friendly with everyone who moved to Sea Port, thanking them for breathing new life into the small town. The only person

more excited than Bria for the new arrivals in town was the Mayor. Still, Bria was a pain in Santos's ass.

"Shouldn't you be wearing a helmet?" Santos yelled to her.

Bria opened her mouth, but Knox cut her off. "Definitely should," he answered for her.

"Whatever," she said and turned at the corner — without signaling — to make her escape.

Once she disappeared, Knox and Santos stopped on the corner and stared down Freedom Way after her for a while.

"So we both like her," Knox said. It wasn't a question, and Santos could have let it go and pushed the conversation hanging above them off for another day. But he'd done that for far too long.

"We both like her," Santos said. "And she likes us both."

Knox nodded his head.

"This gonna come between us?" Santos asked carefully.

"Hopefully not," Knox laughed. Santos swallowed the lump in his throat. "Definitely not," Knox added quickly.

"Good," Santos sighed and then smirked. "She's a lot."

Knox chuckled and turned back toward Sully's. "Sure as hell is. She taste like vanilla when she kissed you too?"

It was Santos's turn to grunt.

Knox's laughter was lighter now. "I'll take that as a yes. And her laugh..."

"Sexy," Santos cut in.

They arrived back at Sully's and turned toward one another. Their walk had only lasted about ten minutes, but it seemed like everything in Santos's world had shifted back into place somehow. The walk didn't erase this morning or yesterday, but it gave Santos hope that it didn't have to be one or the other for Mary or for him.

"So what's this mean?" Santos asked.

"You and me and her, this?" Knox asked.

"Yeah."

"It's a bit...unconventional, but people date around every day. At least she's being upfront with us."

"Maybe we should sit down and talk to her," Santos offered.

Knox breathed for a few beats before nodding. "That's a good idea."

Santos smiled big and broad, a rare occasion. "I have 'em every once in a while."

Knox rolled his eyes. "Once in a blue damn moon," he said, and the two men laughed together.

WELCOME TO SEA PORT

THIRTEEN

Mary

The Confections soft opening would last a week. Mary's plan was to test the market and introduce herself to as many Porties as possible and give them a little taste of what was to come before the real launch in a few weeks.

It was *just* a soft opening, she reminded herself, even as her inner perfectionist was freaking out.

Mary had been running around like a chicken with its head cut off all morning, but she held onto the last bits of her sanity by reminding herself that this was just a practice run and she'd planned it meticulously.

Mary needed to know what her customers liked, loved, and on the off chance someone in town had absolutely zero taste, hated. But Mary refused to believe that anyone could hate anything she and Bria slid into the display cases.

Refused.

She was also trying to remember that she could fail, people did it every day, but she was a bruised perfectionist,

139

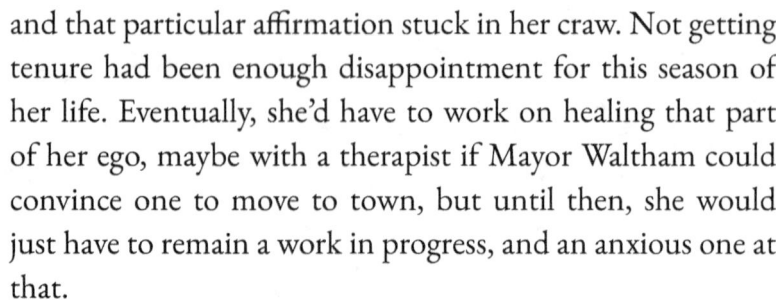

and that particular affirmation stuck in her craw. Not getting tenure had been enough disappointment for this season of her life. Eventually, she'd have to work on healing that part of her ego, maybe with a therapist if Mayor Waltham could convince one to move to town, but until then, she would just have to remain a work in progress, and an anxious one at that.

Confections opened just after dawn and had been slammed for the last few hours. There was a momentary lull in the crowd and Mary used the downtime to quietly disassociate at just how many people had come through her door. She hadn't been able to keep count, but it was more people than she'd thought lived in all of Sea Port.

"Where the hell have they been hiding?" Mary whispered to herself in a daze.

"Stop freaking out," Bria huffed, stepping back into the storefront with a rack of fresh chocolate muffins clutched in her arms.

Mary jumped at the sound of her assistant's voice. "I'm not freaking out," she cried. "And be careful."

"You are and I am," Bria said in a clipped tone, entirely unconvinced. "Open the case, please."

Mary jumped into action, moving along the back of the display cases and sliding the second open. Bria shifted the rack in her hands before carefully pushing the tray into place. They held their breath until the muffins were safe and sound and ready to be sold.

"Thanks," Bria sighed.

"No, thank you for staying on track while I'm freaking out."

"So glad you've come around to seeing things my way."

"Chill," Mary said.

Bria shrugged. "Nope."

"Can you go move the chocolate chip cookies from the oven?"

"The timer hasn't gone off yet," Bria said right as it started buzzing in the kitchen.

"Now it has." Mary beamed.

"That's a very spooky trick," Bria said seriously before turning back toward the kitchen with an adorable flourish. Mary had considered firing Bria half a dozen times this morning alone, but she liked her too much to let her go.

When she was alone again, Mary turned her attention back to the sidewalk. Across the street, a man stepped from the flower shop. Mary squinted and leaned over the cash register, certain it was Knox for a full second before reality let her down. The man who wasn't Knox walked away without even looking in Confections's direction, so she sighed and got back to work.

According to Mary and Leah's business plan, the soft opening was supposed to whet the town's appetite for more Confections to come. She'd spent weeks targeting select constituencies around town to try a very limited sampling of treats, hoping they'd spread the good word about Confections, and they had!

The Sea Port morning rush was relative, but Mary and Bria had lured them in with the smell of freshly baked bread and warm sugar. She'd spent weeks guesstimating the right amount of each treat to prep based on her informal introductions to Portie society, but it still wasn't enough. It wasn't even noon and the display cases were nearly barren.

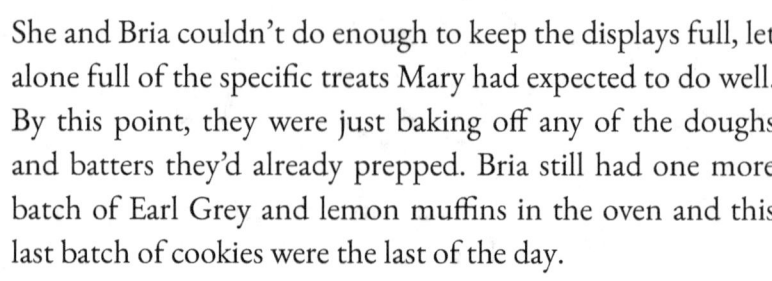

She and Bria couldn't do enough to keep the displays full, let alone full of the specific treats Mary had expected to do well. By this point, they were just baking off any of the doughs and batters they'd already prepped. Bria still had one more batch of Earl Grey and lemon muffins in the oven and this last batch of cookies were the last of the day.

As soft openings went, this one was a success but stressful as all hell. And no matter what happened in the next few hours, today would go down as a win in Mary's book.

The display case had become littered with napkins and the small wooden forks for samples. Mary started tidying the area, mostly to keep her nervous fidgeting at bay. It was good mindless work to keep her hands busy while the fact that she *hadn't* failed started to sink in.

This was also a soft opening of Mary's new life and that, too, was a success. Mary could hardly believe it. As soon as she finished, the bell above the door chimed.

"Welcome to Confections," she chirped automatically, plastering a big smile on her face at the two women stepping into her shop. Mary was a people watcher and nosy, and an unexpected benefit of finally opening the bakery was that she got to do both without even stepping outside.

"Thank you," the older woman replied with a strained smile. She turned pointedly in the other woman's direction.

Mary blinked in confusion until the young woman mumbled a greeting without even looking up from her phone. She recognized mother-teenage daughter tension immediately. With that out of the way, she shifted into sales-woman mode.

"Thank *you* for stopping in today. What do you have a taste for?"

The woman's eyes lit up at the display cases, which made Mary feel like she was on top of the world.

"I've been hearing about your sweets all week from my mother's knitting group. They said your snickerdoodles reminded them of *her* mother's."

"Oh, wow! That's too sweet. Literally," Mary said, giggling at her own joke.

The woman didn't laugh with her, but she did smile — unlike her daughter, who ignored them both.

"You just moved here, right?" the woman asked.

Mary nodded. "A few months ago."

"Welcome to Sea Port," she said.

"Thanks. I'm Mary." She shrugged. "Obviously."

"I'm Sandra," she replied with a warm smile.

"So we're fresh out of snickerdoodles," Mary said. "But I do have a batch of chocolate chip cookies that just came out of the oven."

Sandra's eyes widened. "Really?" she breathed.

Mary nodded quickly. "So fresh, they're cooling in the back, but I can grab one for you."

"Can you grab two?" Sandra asked excitedly.

"Definitely." Mary walked back to the swinging door, pushed through, and called out to Bria to box up two cookies for Sandra. "Anything else strike your fancy?"

Sandra bent forward to look closely at the brightly lit display case. Mary had put her blood, sweat, and the most expensive butter she could find into her treats and knew they could stand up to scrutiny, so she turned to the woman's

daughter. She could practically hear Leah's voice in her head saying not to let a single sale slip through her fingers. No bear claw left behind.

"What about you?" Mary asked.

"Lisa," Sandra said.

"Is there anything you'd like to try, Lisa?"

The young girl's fingers stopped typing the novel on her cell phone. She lifted her head with a look of disgusted disinterest on her face — the kind of look only teenagers could wield with such devastating accuracy; Mary knew it well. When her students had sprung it on her in her former life, she'd wilted, but Mary wasn't the same person anymore, so she widened her smile and kept eye contact with the girl until *she* sighed dramatically and answered the question.

"I'm vegan," Lisa replied in a brittle tone. Sandra let out a dismissive snort and Lisa rolled her eyes. This quick exchange gave Mary a glimpse into their relationship and she used her assumptions to go in for the kill — figuratively.

"Everything in the last display case is vegan, actually."

Mary moved to the right and stood behind her vegan display. Lisa followed, but the skepticism was written all over her face.

It was small, but Mary counted Lisa's begrudging interest as a win.

"Seriously?' Lisa whispered.

"Vegan?" Sandra asked, moving to stand next to her daughter.

"Yep," Mary beamed. She rocked onto the balls of her feet as pride swelled in her chest.

"But...how good can they really be without milk, eggs,

or butter?" Sandra asked. At first glance, she thought she saw disdain on Sandra's face, but Mary decided to give her the benefit of the doubt and treat that look as curiosity.

And Mary could always work with curiosity.

Mary saw Lisa give her mother a side-eye and guessed this had been a point of contention between the two. She didn't want to step in the middle of that, but she had dairy-free treats to sell, so she got to it.

"I've put in a lot of hard work and I think they taste great," Mary said. "But, hey, I'm biased. You shouldn't take my word for it." As she gave her customers the setup, she slid the case open and pulled a plastic glove over her right hand for the alley-oop. "Do you two like almonds and chocolate?"

"Yeah," Lisa and Sandra replied at the same time.

Mary plucked an almond thumbprint cookie from the top tray and grabbed a napkin with her other hand, placing it atop the display case. She reached back inside for a vegan chocolate dollop, her version of a brownie bite. "Give those a try," she said, setting the brownie onto the display. "On the house, of course."

Sandra and Lisa looked at one another before grabbing the treats. Mary's eyes flitted from one face to another as they each took a bite. She didn't want to creep on them, but this was her business after all.

Sandra's eyebrows lifted into her hairline and Lisa smiled around her brownie bite. And then, to make matters even better, the mother and daughter exchanged their treats to share. Mary's heart felt like it was pumping rainbows and brown butter directly into her veins.

The vegan treats had been a gamble. Mary wasn't vegan, and if she'd ever had a vegan dessert before moving to Sea

Port, it was probably an accident and she couldn't remember it anyway. But Leah had been insistent. Even if there were only two vegans in Sea Port, Leah told Mary to give them something to hold onto. Leah was going to love learning she'd been correct — her favorite state of being.

Mary was busy beaming at Sandra and Lisa when the bell over the door chimed again.

"Welcome to..." she started, but then her voice gave out at the sight of Santos *and* Knox crowding inside her shop. "Oh," she breathed.

"Did you miss us?" Knox asked with a devastating smile on his face.

"Fresh hot cookies!" Bria called as she moved from the kitchen into the storefront.

Santos lifted an eyebrow, grinning while Knox chuckled low and deep in his chest. Mary's pussy went from dormant to *awake* in an instant.

"Open the case, please, Mary," Bria said.

"Mary," Santos echoed, shocking her into movement.

"Yes. I mean, huh? What?"

Knox's laughter was louder now.

Mary turned away from the men with a hot face, only to find Bria staring at her with a smug smile. "Open the cookie case, please."

"Yes. Yep. Sorry." Mary slid the case closest to the till open. For the first time all morning, Mary was too out of sorts to freak out about Bria dropping the cookies. She was too busy feeling self-conscious because she could practically feel Knox and Santos's eyes on her and it felt almost as good as their hands.

Once the cookies were in place, Bria dusted her hands off

triumphantly. "We getting shut down?" she asked, looking at Santos and Knox.

"No," Mary said, laughing nervously. She turned to Sandra and Lisa. "We're not getting shut down. Bria's just... being Bria."

"Hey, Mrs. Porter," Bria called.

Sandra smirked. "Hello, Ms. Stone," she said in a voice that screamed long-suffering teacher. She turned to Mary. "I'm well aware of Bria's sense of humor."

Mary stifled a laugh before turning back to her assistant. "Don't forget Sandra's two chocolate chip cookies," she said. "And then help them with anything else they want?"

"Sure. I mean, it's my job!" Bria beamed.

"The daughter's vegan," Mary whispered.

"They try the dollops?" Mary nodded. "Cool. I've got this. Do whatever it takes to keep us from getting shut down. And I do mean whatever it takes."

Mary rolled her eyes. "We're not getting shut down."

"That's the spirit," Bria replied.

Mary sighed and shook her head, rethinking the decision not to fire her.

"Hey, Lisa, is the cheerleading squad doing their spring fundraiser?"

"Yeah," Lisa replied.

Mary shook her head, amazed at Bria's ability to keep everyone on their toes. She pushed through the gate into the seating area, Knox and Santos shifting in her direction like plants seeking sunlight. Mary bit back a smile as a shudder moved up her spine, the warmth of their gazes pulling her into their orbit.

She'd spent most of last night touching herself, thinking

about them in excruciatingly erotic detail — comparing, contrasting, and reliving their time in the bakery's powder room.

She straightened her back and pressed her chest forward. "Boys," she chirped, trying to sound surer of herself than she felt.

Knox's eyes dipped momentarily to her breasts, and for whatever reason, that made Mary's confidence lift. She didn't know what it was about them, but things that would've normally turned her off with other men turned her all the way on with them.

Both of them.

Mary cleared her throat to catch Knox's attention.

He lifted his eyes with a sheepish smile on his face. "Boys?" he asked playfully. "Been a long time since someone called me 'boy' without repercussions."

Mary got lost for a quick second in his smile, wondering how anyone could be this damn beautiful on a regular ass weekday.

"We're very grown," Santos replied in a whisper that made Mary's scalp tingle and her nipples harden all at the same time. Her body's physical reaction only worsened when she made the mistake of making eye contact with him.

"I remember," she replied in a sultry whisper before licking her lips.

Santos had the nerve to lick his lips right along with her before letting his gaze move down her body brazenly. She moved her hand to the small of her back, mostly to stop herself from reaching out to touch them, probably inappropriately.

Knox cleared his throat while smirking at her. He

opened his mouth to say something, but Sandra's voice cut him off.

"What the hell is gluten-free? You're just making that up."

The other woman's voice reminded her that she was not, unfortunately, alone with Knox and Santos. "Maybe we should go outside," she said. Santos nodded quickly and moved behind Knox to pull the door open. Knox gestured for her to lead the way with the promise that they would follow because they were gentleman. And also because they probably wanted to stare at her ass, which made perfect sense to her.

And she was happy to oblige.

"I'll be outside," Mary called to Bria.

"Sure thing," Bria called back.

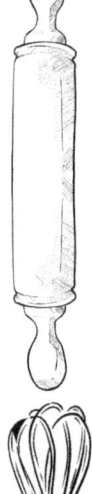

Mary stepped out onto the quiet sidewalk and blinked at the sunlight. She'd been cooped up in the shop all day and took in a deep breath of fresh air, enjoying the warmth on her face. After a quick shot of vitamin D, she turned to find Santos and Knox standing side by side, all their attention focused on her.

The sidewalk didn't give them any more privacy than inside the bakery, but Mary didn't care. She took a step forward and huddled close to these two men, pretending like this small little block in small little Sea Port was all theirs.

"What brings you boys to my shop?" she asked, hoping they couldn't hear the nerves or need in her voice.

Knox crossed his arms over his chest and grinned at her in a way that was intimate, playful, and a little bit dirty — an elite combination. "You know why we're here," he said in a deep, sensual whisper.

"I assure you I don't, but believe me, I'm listening."

"We came here for you," Knox said.

Mary raised her eyebrows in serious interest. "Music to my ears. Does that mean you talked to each other?"

"Yeah," Santos said.

"And now we need to talk to you," Knox said, shifting closer.

A trickle of sweat dripped down her back. Maybe she could've convinced herself it was because of the midday Southern sun, but a warm wetness also developed at the apex of her thighs and she couldn't blame that on the heat. She licked her lips and shoved her hands into her back pockets, once again unable to trust herself not to reach for them.

"I definitely think we should talk, Sergeant," Mary said.

Knox grunted, dragging his eyes up to her face from her chest again. "Don't call me that."

"You didn't have a problem when I called you that yesterday."

He took a deep breath and pushed it out of his nose in frustration. An adorably angry nerve in his neck pulsed as he breathed. Mary imagined licking that little patch of skin.

Knox shifted close. "It sounds dirty when you say it."

"Good," she breathed in a sultry challenge.

He blinked at her as if he couldn't remember how to speak.

Thankfully, Mary was having no such problems. She moved forward and they bent in her direction, enclosing one another in a bubble just for the three of them. "I just want to know, though, does it sound dirty when he says it too? Or is it just me?"

She'd been dreaming about asking this question since

Knox pushed her t-shirt up to suck on her nipples. She hadn't trusted herself with that kind of bravery then, but today was a brand-new day. She wanted Santos *and* Knox. She didn't want to choose, so she steeled her nerves because this was the moment not to deny herself.

On this plain Southern sidewalk on a bright summer day, Mary couldn't see anything besides Knox and Santos, so she decided to put her cards on the table.

Knox's eyes widened in shock. "What?"

She worried he might be about to have a stroke or sprint across town just to get the hell away from her, but then she remembered Santos's hot length pulsing in her hand when she mentioned Knox. And she'd never let herself forget the way Knox had groaned onto her tongue when she mentioned Santos. There was, of course, a chance she might've miscalculated, but it was slimmer than the space between their bodies.

She glanced in Santos's direction and was fortified by his smile.

She'd read both men correctly, but apparently Knox needed a little more encouragement.

Mary focused her attention on Knox again. She barely knew him, but she imagined they might be kindred spirits — the kind of people who talked themselves out of good things and used practicality and insecurity as brick walls between the things they wanted more than anything. It was, of course, just a guess, but Mary thought Knox was someone who seemed to think he didn't deserve to be desired, and she was ready to take it upon herself to convince him otherwise. Although that wasn't a mission she had to complete on her own.

Santos shifted closer, his chest brushing Knox and Mary's arms. "She's asking, Sergeant," he started, tipping his mouth toward Knox's left ear, "if your dick gets hard when I call you Sergeant as well, Sergeant."

This was, objectively, the most perfect moment of Mary's life. She tried to take it all in — the scent of fried dough and lightly roasting coffee hanging in the thick air, the sunshine — but there was too much to keep, so she focused on the most important things, like Santos's lips brushing Knox's ear and Knox's soft pants.

As far as Mary was concerned, the rest of the town fell away and there was only the three of them. She had to bite her lips closed at that thought, mostly to keep from moaning.

"Sergeant?" Santos nudged, whispering into Knox's ear.

"Yes," Knox whispered. Or maybe he groaned. Either way, he sounded delicious.

Just then, the bakery door swung open. Santos and Mary jumped away from Knox's body. He closed his eyes and let out a breath as Mary turned to find the Porters exiting the shop with a medium-sized bag in Lisa's hands.

She felt triumphant. "Enjoy your treats," Mary said.

"We will," Lisa said.

"You'll see us again," Sandra said.

"Excellent," Mary replied, waving them away.

She watched them walk down the block, waiting until they were out of earshot. When she turned back to Knox and Santos, they were staring at one another, clearly having a silent conversation without her. It made her a bit jealous, but lust overrode any sore feelings.

"So, what comes next?" Mary asked, knowing they only had so long before Bria came out to interrupt them.

"I don't know," Knox said, still watching Santos.

Santos smiled. "We'll figure it out."

Knox licked his lips, but he didn't disagree.

Another win in a great day.

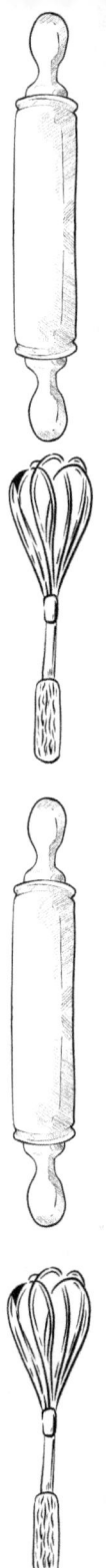

FOURTEEN

Knox

It wasn't what Santos said but how he said it — the way he moved close and crowded into Knox's space, lowering his voice and whispering to him as if he was a lover rather than a friend. And Mary's excitement as it all went down had Knox's head spinning.

He and Santos had found themselves in more compromising positions before, but it had been years since he'd thought about him in ways he shouldn't. He'd chosen his friendship with Santos over selfish urges long ago, but apparently Mary and Santos himself were hellbent on cracking open a door Knox had already closed.

Okay, he'd cracked it open a couple inches in that bathroom with Mary, but that was fantasy. They'd just been toying with one another — with their hands and words — none of it was real. He'd thought Mary understood he and Santos were too close friends for anything they'd said in that bathroom to be serious. But when Santos's lips brushed his

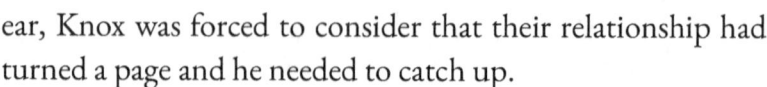

ear, Knox was forced to consider that their relationship had turned a page and he needed to catch up.

Now here he was, standing on the sidewalk in the middle of the workday, with his semi-hard dick making his left pant leg uncomfortably tight. He was getting hot under the collar and his skin was still tingling where they'd touched him. He smoothed a hand across his chest, trying to hide the riot of his emotions and probably failing.

"Sooo, we're good here?" Mary asked cheerily.

Knox nodded in a daze, but Santos's voice cut off their agreement.

"You sure about this, Sergeant?" Santos asked. Knox's dick pulsed while Mary bounced excitedly at Santos's question and Knox's discomfort.

Knox swallowed the lump in his throat before turning to his friend — the man he'd known for most of his adult life. The Santos staring back at him wasn't a Santos Knox recognized. His eyes were hooded, his gaze was hot, and he had the nerve to inch closer, brushing his thigh along the length of Knox's dick.

"You've gotta say yes or no, Knox," Santos breathed. "I want this to be clear."

"You want *what* to be clear? What am I saying yes to, *exactly*?"

Santos's eyes lowered to slits and he opened his mouth to speak, but Mary spoke first.

"I used to teach at a university," she admitted quietly. Santos's eyes opened and they both turned toward her.

Mary's bright smile disappeared as she spoke and she refused to return their gazes. "Before I moved to Sea Port, I hated my life. I spent years doing the things people expected of me — things that were supposed to get me tenure but didn't — and I hated it. I spent years making sacrifices, trying to make other people happy, and somewhere along the way, I lost track of how to make myself happy. I'm still trying to figure that out, actually."

She finally lifted her eyes to meet theirs, nervously licking her lips. "I think I can be happy here," she said. "But if that's possible, I need to make it a priority. I can't put anything above my own happiness. I can't choose. I don't *want* to choose between you two." She looked from Knox to Santos, her smile widening again. "What do you two want?"

Santos shifted against Knox's body. "I moved here to start a new life after I left the Air Force. I'm still trying to figure out what comes next, but I think I've figured something out." He turned to Knox and the two men stared at one another for a long, heated moment while Mary drank them in.

Knox's gut was tied in knots.

"Tell us," Mary hissed.

"I want you both as well," Santos said in an intimate whisper. Knox tried not to shudder, but then Santos deepened his voice. "And I'm possessive."

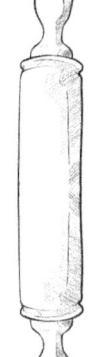

Mary hummed contentedly. "Now it's your turn, Sergeant."

"We've been friends a long time," Knox said.

Santos smirked. "Nothing's gonna change that. I don't see you missing an opportunity to get on my nerves anytime in this lifetime."

"You say that—"

"I mean that," Santos said quickly.

"You're getting caught up in the negative," Mary offered

gently. "Been there. Done that. The three of us together sounds so much more fun."

"I agree," Santos said.

"I agree," Knox replied. "But—"

"But?" Santos and Mary nudged at the same time.

"But this town is so damn small. If we fuck this up or this goes bad, we'll see each other every day. We'd have to give up all we wanted out of this place if it goes bad."

He hadn't expected this conversation to go quite like this, but one of them had to say the obvious.

Mary was undeterred. "Or maybe we should stop worrying about what could go wrong and focus on all the things that have gone right."

"Like what?" Knox asked, forcing himself to laugh softly.

"Like whatever the hell magic had to happen to bring the three of us to this small ass town in the middle of nowhere, ready to fuck."

Santos's laughter burst the tension of the last few moments, his chest bouncing against Knox's arm he was so close.

Knox chuckled softly. "Keep your voice down. We're outside."

Mary shrugged. "No, thanks."

"You always been this way?" Knox asked, squinting at her.

She rolled her eyes. "I just told you I haven't. I've been overworking myself for years and now I finally feel free. But my sex drive isn't the issue."

"Clearly," Santos mumbled.

"The question on the table is if you want to help Santos twist me up like a pretzel."

"Goddamn," Knox whispered.

"Or do you want us to twist you up first? I'm flexible," Mary offered good-naturedly.

"I bet you are," Santos said. Mary winked at him before they both turned their attention back to Knox. "It's a yes or no type of question, Sergeant," Santos said, getting them back on track.

Mary lifted her eyebrows and bounced onto the balls of her feet. Knox knew what he wanted to say — he knew what he wanted — but the words stuck on his tongue, waiting for him to be brave. Mary and Santos watched him with hope radiating off them like pheromones.

Knox took a deep breath. "Yes," he said on a long, terrified exhalation.

She clapped her hands. "Perfect! I'm so excited."

Knox let out a dry, surprised huff of laughter at her enthusiasm, every move rocking him against Santos's body.

"Alright, I really need to go back into work now before —" Mary started, but then the bakery door opened, cutting her off.

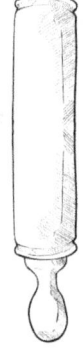

"Hey, Mary, you want me to make some more brownies? These display cases are looking raggedy," Bria called.

"No, I think we're good. Gimme a second."

"Okay," Bria said, but then she leaned against the door-jamb and smirked at them. "What y'all doing?"

"Nothing. Go back inside," Mary said, shooing her away even as she started moving in that direction.

"Wait," Knox said, his heart pounding in his chest. "What do we do next?"

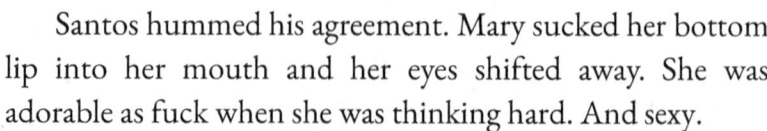

Santos hummed his agreement. Mary sucked her bottom lip into her mouth and her eyes shifted away. She was adorable as fuck when she was thinking hard. And sexy.

"I've got a bunch of stuff to do this week. I need to get ready for the grand opening, but once our soft open is over..." her voice trailed off. "Opening day. After we close?"

"When's that?" Santos asked.

"A week from today."

"A week is a long time," Knox said, and they both turned to him. Knox could feel Santos's smile, which was why he kept his eyes on Mary.

"Someone's eager," she purred. "I like that. And I agree! What about Friday after we close. Just two days. How about that?"

"Works for me," Santos said, finally stepping back from Knox's body. "That work for you, Sergeant?"

"Yeah, that works," he replied in a hoarse voice.

"Perfect," Mary chirped. "Come by when we close. Now if you'll excuse me, I have fresh hot cookies to sell."

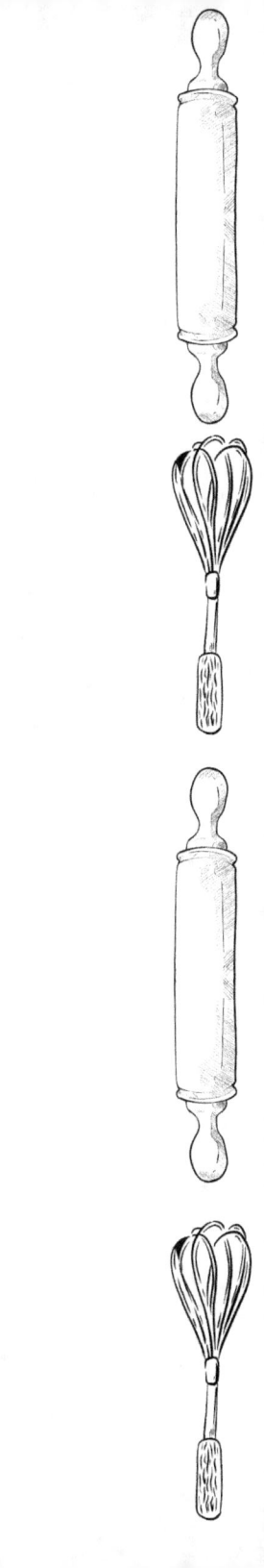

WELCOME TO SEA PORT

FIFTEEN

Knox

Knox woke up with a pit in his stomach after one of the worst night's sleep of his adult life.

Instead of conking out for an easy eight hours of dreamless rest, all night, his brain had been conjuring images of Mary and Santos doing the filthiest things he could imagine. He tossed, turned, and kicked the sheets and blankets off the bed. At some point, he woke up covered in sweat, his dick so hard it was throbbing, and all he could do was push his boxers down his legs and jack off. It was the middle of the night and he was half-awake. It should've been the easiest nut of his life, but every time he got close, his brain would shift away to another scenario so he had to start all over again. What finally tipped him over the edge was an image of Mary moaning onto Knox's tongue, his fingers sinking into her soft flesh, while Santos's hand wrapped around Knox's dick, his warm breath tickling the shell of his ear.

The mess he made brought him fully awake and the

feeling of shame dragged him out of bed and into the shower to rinse off. He stripped his sheets, remade his bed, and fell immediately back asleep, only to wake up hard and horny all over again.

The sun wasn't even out when he opened his eyes, and as soon as he did, Knox wanted to go right on back to sleep. He was awake but nowhere near rested. He wished for one more hour of unconsciousness, but he was also desperate to come again and that won out.

Knox yawned while reaching into his bedside table for the bottle of lube he kept at hand.

After a night of running from his dreams, he finally gave in to his imagination, letting his desires run free. He hadn't bothered with underwear after his shower last night, so he squirted a dollop of lube on the head of his dick and smeared it down his length with his other hand. He was close — he'd been close for hours. He pictured Santos and Mary naked in his bed like a fly on the wall. He knew Santos would be gentle with her, but his back arched when he thought about Santos digging his fingers into Mary's hips the way Knox had. Imagining his friend pushing her thick thighs open and kissing a path over her soft, round stomach got him close, but it was too fast, too soon. He wanted to enjoy this fantasy, so he forced himself to stop. Besides, Knox only had two sets of sheets and one was in the washing machine.

In the cold half-light of morning, he walked from his bedroom to the bathroom naked, hard dick still dripping with lube. He stepped into the shower and turned on the water, picking his fantasy back up while he waited for the water to heat. Except this time, he was in the mix.

Knox started stroking his shaft again while he imagined

kissing his way down Santos's back, caressing the ass he knew would be hard from long runs and squats. He grabbed his balls with his free hand and slowed his strokes, massaging himself in deep presses, refusing to let this end too soon. In Knox's mind, his fingers played along the crease of Santos's cheeks, charting a path along the underside of the man's ball sack and down the length of his shaft and back again.

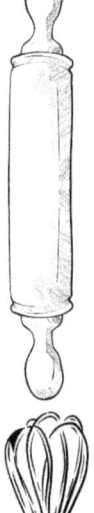

Knox pressed his back against the cool shower tile while teasing himself and the fictional Santos in his mind at the same time.

They'd been friends for almost two decades but Knox would be lying if he said he'd never thought about Santos like this before. He'd masturbated to thoughts of Santos so many goddamn times over the years, it had consumed him at times. But then the post-nut clarity would hit, triggering a deep shame he'd buried alongside years of inconvenient pining. And he'd never told Santos a word about it.

Crushes came and went, but Knox refused to risk their friendship for a one-night stand at most. But now that he knew there was no danger of that, he let the picture fully unfold in his mind while stroking his dick at the same pace he stroked Santos's in his mind. He recycled the memory of Mary moaning in that little bathroom for his own desires as he joined Santos while eating her out. His hands sped up as the desperation grew. He just wanted to come, even though he didn't want the fantasy to end.

It had been so many years of wanting Santos but knowing he shouldn't that opening that door was too much for him. He couldn't control himself and his knees went weak when he came. His toes curled. He was out of breath. His muscles were relaxed for the first time in probably hours.

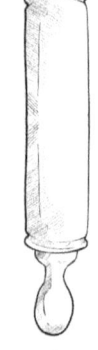

When that old familiar shame started creeping in at the edges of his brain, he stepped into the shower directly under the hot spray, feeling sated and refreshed.

Ready to start the day.

Knox was procrastinating with chores around the apartment — moving his sheets to the dryer, straightening his bedroom, even pulling out the iron and ironing board, something he hadn't done since his discharge. But every time he looked at the clock, he felt a tightness in his chest and went in search of some new task to take his mind off his regular coffee date with Santos.

When his bed was made and he was fully dressed, Knox moved to the kitchen and started seriously contemplating deep cleaning his coffee pot when a knock on the door interrupted him. He knew who it was immediately.

Knox took a deep breath — two, actually — before shuffling across the living room to his front door. He pulled it open with a sigh. "What are you doing here?"

Santos wasn't that much taller than Knox, but his presence seemed to fill Knox's hallway. He had the same blank, bored look on his face as always. He held a paper coffee cup in each hand and lifted an eyebrow at Knox's greeting. "Is that how we're saying good morning these days?"

"No," Knox said, rolling his eyes. "It's how I ask why you're here and not at Sully's."

Santos smirked. "Were you going to show up?"

"I have every other morning."

"That wasn't the question."

"I'm dressed, aren't I?"

Santos smirked. "That ain't the question either, but I think I got the answer I was expecting. You gonna invite me in?"

"No," Knox said, finding it easy enough to answer that question.

"I brought you coffee," Santos teased, lifting his left hand.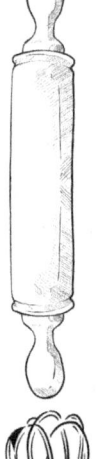

Knox reached for it, but Santos stepped back, his smirk turning into a full-blown smile. "You want the coffee I paid for, you let me in." He said it like a playful threat, which pissed Knox off 'cause that was his normal tone.

"And if I don't?" Knox ground out.

"I guess I can give this to my boss. Or maybe I can drop by Confections. Maybe Mary needs a pick-me-up."

The best thing about the version of Santos Knox had been dreaming about all night was that he never spoke; he didn't have the chance to get under Knox's skin. The real Santos was far less considerate. He stepped forward, the toes of his boots crossing the threshold into the apartment. His voice dropped when he said Mary's name and his eyes zeroed in on Knox's mouth.

Santos crowded into his space, the slightly bitter scent of coffee mixed with his cologne suffocating Knox in the best way. Knox felt a tugging in his chest and his groin. Every filthy thing he'd dreamed last night and this morning flooded his brain. He worried Santos might see what he had done written all over his face.

He turned abruptly away from the door before his dick

could inflate. While Knox walked back to the kitchen, breathing deeply to settle his libido, Santos breezed into Knox's apartment like he owned the place. He kicked the door closed, followed Knox into the kitchen, and set their coffees on the island. He leaned casually on one of the stools and then they stared at one another across the counter.

"Don't look at me like that," Knox ground out.

"Like what?"

"Like you know what I'm thinking."

Santos laughed drily. "Okay. Wanna know what I'm thinking?"

That question tugged at Knox's chest. The answer was yes and desperately, but he didn't trust himself to speak, so he nodded instead.

And because Santos was fucking insufferable, he reached for his coffee cup and took a sip while he stared at Knox.

Knox needed something to do with his hands, so he reached for his own coffee and took a sip. Black pour-over, no sugar, no creamer, just one shot of brown sugar syrup. Of course, Santos knew his coffee order, but tasting his regular drink made his heart race.

Santos set his cup down and licked his lips. Knox was thankful the lower half of his body was hidden from Santos's view.

"I slept really fucking well last night," Santos breathed.

Knox rolled his eyes. "Good for you."

"But I did wake up in the middle of the night."

"Okay," Knox said, feigning annoyance.

"Remember that trip we took to Atlantic City?" Santos asked.

Knox squinted in confusion but nodded. "Barely."

Santos's lips split into a smile. "Yeah, but remember when we met those two girls at that club?"

"Yeah," Knox rasped, lifting the cup to his mouth again as panic and desire coursed through his veins.

As it happened, Knox didn't remember much about that trip besides that night and those girls, but they weren't the details that stuck in his brain. No, the things Knox remembered with crystal clarity were the four of them shoving themselves into the back of a cab, his side pressed into Santos's while their dates sat on their laps. He remembered making out with the girl who'd become faceless in his memory because every time he moved, some part of him rubbed against some part of Santos. He remembered being back in the hotel room, fucking her, even as all of his attention was on the sliver of Santos he could see in his peripheral vision while Santos fucked her friend.

Yeah, he remembered just enough of that trip to make his pants feel uncomfortable.

"I was dreaming about that night. I've been dreaming about that night every now and then since it happened."

There was a dismissive joke on the tip of Knox's tongue, probably something he'd said before in a moment like this, but he couldn't bring himself to say it now. And not because he'd grown but because his dick was so hard he was starting to sweat.

Santos tipped his head back and smiled down the bridge of his nose. Devastatingly beautiful. "When I woke up last night, it's 'cause I wasn't dreaming about those two women we were with."

Knox licked his lips. "It was Mary," he whispers.

169

"Yeah." Santos gave him a lopsided, hungry grin. "She was begging you to fuck her."

Knox couldn't have stopped the groan that rumbled through his chest if he tried.

"And so was I. Begging for you," Santos added, so there was no confusion.

Knox shook his head. Santos nodded.

"If it's too much for you—" Santos started.

"It's not that," Knox said.

"Then what is it?"

"How are we supposed to look each other in the eye after?"

Santos chuckled deep and low. "The same way we looked each other in the eye the morning after we watched those girls give us head."

"It's not the same," Knox said, frustrated.

"How so?" Knox licked his lips, and Santos picked up the tell. "Oh." He smiled, standing from the stool.

Knox felt a frisson of fear run down his spine at the same time as his dick throbbed. If Santos really did know what Knox was thinking, it didn't deter him. If anything, it seemed to spur him on. He moved around the island until he was standing next to Knox, crowding his space again.

Santos put one hand on the island and the other on the small of his back. His touch was tentative at first, as if he was worried Knox might bolt and run — a strong possibility. Knox managed to keep still, even as his heart was jackhammering against his chest as Santos's hand moved up his spine.

Santos's lips brushed Knox's pulse. His breaths were even and warm. His tongue tasted the shell of Knox's ear in

one long swipe. "If you want to know if we can look each other in the eye after I suck your dick, let's figure it out now. Before we waste any more time."

Maybe there was another way to test this theory without potentially jeopardizing their friendship, but they both knew it wouldn't be nearly as good as the option on offer. Would one blowjob be worth a friendship he cherished? No.

But would it be good?

Santos sucked Knox's earlobe into his mouth. His fingers scraped Knox's back through his shirt.

"Is that really what you want?" Knox moaned.

He felt Santos's smile against his neck while his hand moved down Knox's back. "You have no fucking idea how long I've wanted you in my mouth," Santos whispered.

Knox was a strong man, but sometimes it was good to be weak, to give in to his own desires. And apparently, Santos's as well.

He turned in the cage of Santos's arms. "Prove it," Knox rasped. "On your knees, Marine."

It was the look on Santos's face that made those next few moments too easy — the desperation and also the relief as he followed Knox's orders.

SANTOS

He didn't need to be told twice.

When Santos was twenty-one, he'd promised himself that if he ever got the chance to be with Knox, he wouldn't miss it and he sure as fuck wouldn't hesitate. Lowering to the floor in front of this man was easy, welcome even. Santos didn't feel the tile under his knees and if he was still in pain later, he knew he'd consider every ache worth it.

Santos tugged Knox forward by his belt buckle before he started opening it. He pulled the zipper and tugged his pants down his legs until they pooled at Knox's ankles. Santos caressed Knox's bulge possessively.

"Shit," Knox hissed, and his eyes fluttered closed.

Santos had been waiting years for this.

He hated tearing his eyes from his face, but he'd been waiting years to give Knox's dick the attention it deserved. Santos squeezed it again before moving his hands to the waist of Knox's briefs and tugging them over his hips. He smelled like oatmeal soap and the same spicy cologne he'd been using for years. Just the scent made Santos's dick throb and his mouth water.

Knox's shaft was the same smooth dark brown as the rest of his body, long and thick with a fat head. Knox moaned again as Santos smoothed a hand over his neatly trimmed pubic hair and down his length.

He lifted his eyes to Knox's face and their gazes locked. They watched one another while Santos held the head of Knox's dick. "We don't have to wait until after," he whispered against the fat head of Knox's shaft, his lips brushing the sensitive skin and the faint, salty taste of precome.

"Fuck," Knox ground out through a clenched jaw.

Santos smiled against Knox's dick. "Don't look away,"

he breathed. Knox nodded quickly and then moaned when Santos's tongue dipped into his slit.

"Fuck," he cried out.

That was all the encouragement Santos needed. He opened his mouth and slipped his tongue down the underside of Knox's length, using his fist to guide his path. He tasted exactly like Santos had dreamed and he closed his eyes, savoring the blend of his coffee and Knox's skin.

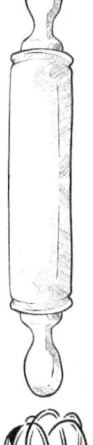

Knox grunted and then his hand brushed the back of Santos's head. "Don't look away," he groaned.

Santos smiled as he moved back, but then he tightened his lips around the head of Knox's dick before inhaling him again. They watched one another as Santos sucked Knox slowly. They both had to be at work eventually, but Santos didn't give a shit about being late. Hell, he'd skip the entire day and spend it on his knees if that's what it took.

If Knox would let him.

Knox hit the opening of Santos's throat and they both groaned. Knox's head fell back as he panted up at the ceiling, his stomach muscles spasming as he breathed through it.

Santos was endlessly patient with Knox and waited, breathing through his nose, caressing whatever of Knox's shaft he could reach with his tongue.

"Fuck. Fuck," Knox gasped before finally lowering his head to watch Santos again, laughing softly. "I shoulda knew you'd be petty, even now."

Santos couldn't smile because his mouth was moving again and faster. He'd kept himself together at first, but not anymore. He'd wanted this for so goddamn long. He wanted them both to enjoy this experience fully. He wanted to wring

every ounce of pleasure from this moment, figuratively and literally.

"Ah, shit," Knox said as Santos inhaled him almost to the base.

When Santos pulled back, Knox's hips jutted forward, and that was when they really hit a rhythm. The formerly quiet kitchen filled with Santos's mouth and throat working, opening wide for Knox, and Knox's increasingly loud moans.

"Ah fuck, I'm gonna come. Shit, I—"

Santos shoved Knox's dick as deep into his throat as he could manage this first time. He'd take it all next time, but for now, he tightened his grip on Knox's hips, leading him as they jerked forward and he came down Santos's throat with a loud, desperate moan.

Knox was holding onto Santos's shoulders for dear life as Santos swallowed every last drop of Knox's release.

It wasn't just good, it was everything Santos knew it would be.

Santos held Knox between his lips until his balls were empty and his body stopped spasming. He pulled back from his groin, stroking his saliva into Knox's shaft, making it hard for Knox to catch his breath. Santos sat back on his heels, breathing heavy as well, licking the taste of Knox's come from his lips, waiting until he could catch his own breath before he climbed to his feet.

Knox was bent over the island, his spent dick shrinking. He looked wrecked, and that made Santos feel triumphant as he wiped his mouth and chin with his hand. Santos moved to the sink and washed his hands, using wet paper towels to clean his face.

When he turned around, Knox was just pulling himself together, stuffing his still-wet dick into his underwear. Santos waited until Knox pulled his zipper closed before he spoke.

"So," Santos rasped, leaning his hip against the island. "Can you look me in the eye?"

He forced himself to breathe even though he wasn't sure how he'd survive if he'd gambled wrong. If his friendship with Knox came crashing down because of one blowjob, Santos would be devastated.

Knox buttoned his pants and reached for the ends of his belt, then slowly lifted his head and they locked eyes again. It wasn't the same as a few moments ago, but Santos didn't want it to be the same. He hadn't waited all these years for Knox to look at him in the same way he had in Basic. He hadn't tried to deepthroat him to stay friends.

"Yeah," Knox whispered after a while with a soft smile on his face. Santos smiled back, relief flooding his veins. "We're not done yet," he said.

Santos lifted an eyebrow in confusion.

Knox licked his lips. "The only way to know for sure is to give and receive."

Again, Santos didn't need to be told twice. He leaned back against the counter and started unbuckling his own belt. "Makes perfect sense to me," he said in a voice desperate and shaky with need. "On your knees, Sergeant."

He knew when Knox smiled, big and white, and his tongue moved over his thick lips that he and Knox would be okay.

That all of this would absolutely be worth it in the end.

WELCOME TO SEA PORT

SIXTEEN

Mary

Mary was high on adrenaline, sugar, and money. Her skin was tingling, and even though she'd been running around her shop all damn day and her feet and back were killing her, her cheeks also hurt from smiling for the same amount of time. After months of planning and prepping and baking, the Confections by Mary soft opening was officially a success! And it wasn't even over yet.

"You should try the peanut butter protein balls," Bria was telling her customer. Mary didn't recognize the man, but Bria knew almost everyone in town and had a knack for selling them the exact thing they would want, ensuring her job security for another day.

"I don't know," the man said in a voice dripping with skepticism. He scratched his beard and shook his head gently.

Mary was sweeping up the service area, silent so she didn't get in the way of Bria's upsell.

"I do," Bria said confidently. "We've got one left. I'll give it to you half-off, and tomorrow, eat it before you go play basketball with the old people rec league."

The man sucked his teeth. "We're not old."

"Sure. Anyway, the protein ball'll give you all the energy you need to dunk on my great uncle."

The man sighed loudly, but when he grunted, Mary looked up from her sweeping to see him nodding in clear resignation.

"Excellent. Trust me, you won't regret it," Bria said, dropping their last protein ball into a paper bag before packing his treats into a small white box stamped with the Confections logo. She walked him over to the cash register to ring him up while Mary moved to the small seating area, smiling when her gaze landed on their almost empty display cases.

They started baking before dawn only to be sold out by noon, happily scrambling through their lunch hour to make fresh donuts and cookies, anything to keep the cases — even the vegan case — full. They didn't complain because this was a good problem to have. A great problem, actually.

"If it's not good," the man warned Bria, "I'll be back."

Bria beamed at him, completely unfazed. "We'll be here. Bring your friends."

The man rolled his eyes and turned toward the door, nodding politely in Mary's direction on his way out.

"You need to stop antagonizing our customers," Mary sighed, leaning on the broom handle.

"Ribbing," Bria sang. "It's just a little banter."

Mary shook her head as she moved to the front door. She

turned the lock and flipped the light switch to turn off the 'Open' sign, sighing in exhausted relief.

"Well, maybe you should tone down the banter," she said, turning back to Bria.

"That sounds so much less fun than not doing that. Anyway, what's left to close?" Bria chirped brightly.

Mary smiled tiredly. "I'm exhausted. Aren't you?"

Bria shrugged. "I feel like Sal says he feels after a long night at the restaurant, but I'm here to do whatever you need, boss. We're a team."

Mary hadn't hated teaching entirely. There had been moments of connection with her students that she cherished, but they'd been few and far between. In some ways, the relationship she was building with Bria was reminiscent of those moments without any papers to grade. "We're good. The kitchen is clear. Go home. We can reset everything else tomorrow."

"You sure?" Bria asked.

"Definitely. You did amazing today. Thank you."

Bria's face lit up. "No problem. It was ridiculous, but so much fun."

Mary stored the broom and dustpan in a corner as she and Bria moved back to the kitchen. Bria ducked into their small office. She returned with her backpack hanging off one shoulder and a smile on her face. "Mayor Waltham probably lied to you about how boring this place normally is, but *today* was not boring."

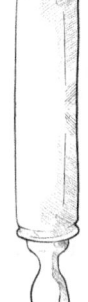

"My life was boring where I came from. Maybe Sea Port isn't as boring as you think."

Bria screwed her face up. "Let's agree to disagree," she

offered, and Mary laughed softly. "See you tomorrow, boss." She waved and turned toward the exit.

"See ya," Mary said, following behind to lock the door after her. Once she was alone, Mary closed her eyes and listened to the sound of *her* empty bakery. Hers. She could hardly believe it.

She'd had a few okay days in her last couple of years as an academic, but this single day in Sea Port blew every good day of her former life out of the water. She'd never been this happy or felt so accomplished, even though she was sore to the bone.

Sore and happy.

Mary was exhausted but also energized. She was full of nervous energy that needed an outlet and she wanted to put it to good use. In fact, she was seriously considering pulling out some butter and sugar and riding out this wave of adrenaline until she literally passed out when she heard a soft knocking from somewhere. Mary opened her eyes and turned in a circle, looking for the sound in confusion. All she heard was the hum of appliances. Unless the building was falling down, Mary concluded she must be having an auditory hallucination, which made sense since she'd been too busy to eat a proper meal. If she was about to crash from her day-long sugar high, she'd prefer to do that at home in her own bed.

Mary grabbed her bag from the office and flipped off all the light switches on her way out the front door. She pushed through the swinging door into the storefront and stopped dead in her tracks. The best part about the bakery was the two picture windows on either side of the door and the glass panes that ran the length of the front door, giving her a clear view of the quaint little street she'd come to love. But that quaint evening view was currently obscured by Knox and Santos huddled in her entryway, which was the best view she'd seen so far.

In the rush of cookies and cakes, Mary had forgotten their deal, but it all came rushing back to her as she practically floated across the shop to let them inside.

The tension crackled between them and more adrenaline flooded her veins.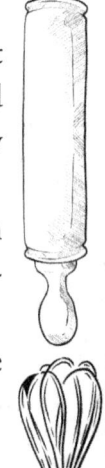

"Boys," she whispered and licked her dry lips.

The left side of Santos's mouth curved into a wry grin.

Knox shook his head but managed a small smile before he spoke. "How was your day?"

Mary lit up. "Amazing," she cried out before launching into a disjointed but excited description of her day. "We sold out of damn near everything."

"We heard," Santos said.

"From who?"

"Sully," they said in unison.

She rolled her eyes. "Then why'd you ask?"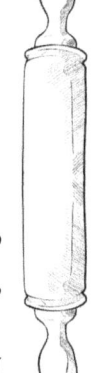

"Because we wanted to hear it from you," Santos said.

"And because we tried to send someone down here to pick up some donuts, but you were sold out," Knox added, sounding lightly disgruntled.

"Why didn't you stop by and pick them up yourself? I would've made 'em hot just for you." Mary smiled.

"Good to know," Santos grumbled.

"You know why," Knox said in a deep voice while he took a step toward her.

Mary started nodding. She sure as hell did.

"And you know why we're here now," Santos added.

She'd been so excited for today that she'd hardly been able to fall asleep last night. Her head had been full of butter-sugar ratios and the only way to clear her mind had been to shove her hand into her panties and think about their date. She'd twisted her body into knots, thinking about all she wanted to do with them while she fucked herself to sleep.

But they hadn't hashed out specifics and Mary frowned. "I thought I'd have time to run home, but we just closed and I've been running around all day." Her stomach grumbled right on time. "And I didn't have time to eat."

"That's why we're here," Santos said. "Let's go."

"Where are we going?" she asked, and her stomach growled again. She grabbed her middle and sighed, looking away. "Damn."

"We're taking you to dinner," Knox said.

Mary brightened. "Like a date?"

Santos shook his head in one sharp slash of his chin. "Not *like* a date. It is a date. The three of us are going out on a date. Wasn't that the plan?"

"I wasn't sure if we had a plan. Or if we were all... comfortable," Mary said, glancing in Knox's direction.

Knox looked between her and Santos before nodding slowly. "It's gonna take a minute to adjust, but I'm here. I'm comfortable."

Mary bounced onto the balls of her feet and beamed at them. She reached into her pocket for the keys to her shop. "Okay, I'm ready. Let's go."

Knox offered her his left arm while Santos pulled the front door open.

Mary used to wish for someone to greet her with dinner

and a hot bath after a long day on campus. She used to masturbate to the thought of a man who'd rub her feet after a long day after years without nearly enough physical affection. It was such a small gesture to Knox, probably, but Mary rested her hand on his hard bicep and leaned into his side, thinking about all those nights she'd gone home to a dark, cold apartment alone.

It felt like a lifetime ago.

Santos took the keys from her hand and locked the door behind them while she and Knox gave one another giddy, goofy smiles.

"What are you hungry for?" Santos asked, handing over her keys and pressing his palm against the small of her back.

"Don't say it like that," Knox sighed.

"Like what?" he asked.

"Like it's dirty," Mary whispered excitedly. "Besides, there are only two options anyway."

Santos chuckled. "I mean, if you're only thinking about food, then yeah."

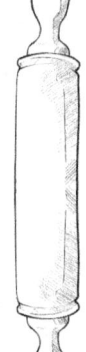

"See?" Knox said, shaking his head. But Mary saw the smile on his face and it matched hers.

"I don't really care what we eat," she whispered. "For dinner, I mean."

Knox sighed loudly and Mary winked at a smiling Santos.

"My thoughts exactly," Santos said.

WELCOME TO SEA PORT

SEVENTEEN

Knox

K nox wouldn't call Sea Port a ghost town at night, but if someone else did, they wouldn't be too far off the mark.

When Santos arrived in town for good, Knox had helped him move his meager belongings into his small cottage and then they'd walked back to downtown to Knox's place for dinner — the only two people out past dark. Santos had been unnerved at how quiet the town was, but the quiet was Knox's favorite thing about the place, and over time, Santos had come around to his point of view. There were a few more people strolling around tonight, but Sea Port was still on the verge of collapse, so Santos led Mary and Knox to the one and only diner in town.

Mayor Waltham's five-year plan to grow the town was ambitious, and no one besides her thought she'd actually do all the things she'd promised, but if they got a couple more restaurants, Knox wouldn't be mad at that. Not at all. Still,

185

even with all Mayor Waltham's hard work, it would still be a few more years before Sea Port became anything more than a small Southern town time forgot, and in a town that small, if someone wanted a good burger or the best chicken-fried steak, the only option was the Sunnyside diner, owned by Mr. and Mrs. Wright. If they wanted something a little fancier — and were willing to stretch the definition of fancy — they could walk a few blocks over to Mr. Genova's Italian restaurant, La Bella Rosa. Knox was happy when Santos led them to the former since the Sunnyside customers were the perfect mix of nosy and unbothered. They might notice all your business, but they left you alone while noticing, and Knox appreciated that, especially tonight.

They strolled in the middle of the street like three peas in a pod, Mary holding onto their biceps with both hands. The sun set behind the city administrative building in a final blaze of glory, casting half the town in an elegant shadow. Maybe it was the comforting bump of Mary's hip bouncing into his. Maybe it was the warmth of her hand on his skin or Santos's steely presence on her other side. Or maybe it was the euphoria he'd been riding all day after his morning blowjobs with Santos and anticipation of this exact moment. Either way, by the time Santos rushed ahead of them to pull the diner door open, all the anxiety that had been eating away at Knox seemed to settle in his gut.

He was hungry, horny, and excited. A perfect combination.

Knox eased Mary's hand from around his bicep, smiling as she whined softly, before ushering her ahead of them into the restaurant. Santos squeezed her soft waist as she passed, which made Knox chuckle softly. Santos inclined his head for Knox to follow her and then squeezed his side in the same possessive manner. Knox was too choked up to laugh at that.

Stepping into the Sunnyside was like walking through a time machine. Knox didn't know exactly when this diner was built, but based on the décor, it couldn't have been too long after the Civil Rights Act passed. Mr. Wright had said something about renovations in the Eighties, but Knox was dubious about those claims. A lunch counter ran the length of the building, with two rows of booths — four to the right of the door and three to the left. As fire chief, Knox had inspected the diner's kitchen with trepidation that whatever he found would force him to eat elsewhere, but the Wrights took such pride in their business that he stopped by at least once a week. More if he could help it.

The diner was practically empty. There was someone sitting with their back to the door in a corner booth to the left and a couple perched on stools at the counter. Santos crowded in behind him, his front pushing into Knox's back, nudging him into Mary's back in turn.

Mr. Wright was at the pass-through window, laughing with their part-time cook. "Seat yourself," he called over his shoulder, barely looking in their direction.

The food was good, but the customer service was optional.

Mary tugged at Knox's hand and pulled him toward the farthest booth on the righthand side, in a corner as far away from the front door and the pass-through as they could get. It wasn't exactly privacy, but it was close enough.

She slid into the booth and Knox sat across from her. Mary furrowed her brows and frowned at him until Santos eased onto the bench beside her and her face lifted into a smile. She crossed her legs and her foot bumped the side of Knox's shin. He started to move, but then Santos's knee bumped into his other leg. No matter who moved or how, their limbs kept tangling together under the table.

"Is it hot in here?" Knox asked, pulling the neck of his t-shirt away from his throat to get a little cool air onto his overheated skin.

Mary's foot slid along the side of his leg. "Nope. Just you," she teased, and Santos smirked.

"You two are gonna be a problem," Knox muttered.

Santos started to say something — probably something filthy — but a waitress arrived at their table just then, breaking the tension crackling between them.

"Here you go," she said, sliding three frosted red plastic cups of water into the middle of the table, followed by three straws from her apron, and then the menus before she turned and walked away without another word.

Mary grabbed her glass and drank nearly all of it in two gulps. "You want that?" she asked Knox, already reaching for his cup. Knox shook his head and pushed his glass toward her. While she was drinking, Santos pushed his in her direction as well, just to make things easier. By the time she made it to the third glass, she was able to sip rather than gulp.

"Feeling better?" Knox asked.

Mary smiled around the rim of the glass before swallowing another sip. She sighed and sat back in her seat. "As soon as I saw the water, I realized I haven't had much to drink today either. We were so busy." She said that last sentence with a smile.

"You need to take better care of yourself," Santos said in short, even clips.

"It was a wild day," she said with a shrug. "It won't be like that all the time." She smiled sweetly at Santos, disarming the man Knox had, until recently, thought was unshakable.

After a few beats, her smile shifted from something sweet to heated as they stared at one another, his face closed and still, hers bright and open. Knox watched them as a pit of something hot and fiercely protective unfurled in his gut. For all the years he'd known Santos, Knox had been protective of him; still seeing him as a fresh recruit, that buzz cut so new and sharp it made the young man's features look severe and a little otherworldly. Most people never made it past Santos's stern exterior to all the warmth underneath, and for some reason he'd never understood until right now, Knox had always taken that personally.

Knox worried for a second, terrified that for all their flirting, Mary might not see Santos the way he did, but then Mary burst into an adorable, melodic giggle and drank the last of their water.

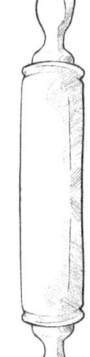

"I think I get it now," she laughed.

"Get what?" Santos grunted in a voice that made Knox shift uncomfortably in his seat.

"You two," Mary said. "You're the lover." She pointed at Knox. "And you're the caretaker." She aimed at Santos. "And you two are a package deal."

Knox blinked at her, shaking his head. "We've never done this before," he said.

Mary shrugged and her smile never wavered. "Maybe that's why you're both single now. Maybe you're better together." She licked her lips and shuddered, a wistful smile on her face.

Santos pressed his knee against Knox's. "Does that mean you're single because you haven't found the right package deal for you?"

Knox held his breath.

Mary's smile widened and she sat up, shifting from side to side in her excitement. "That definitely feels like a possibility. Does that mean I'm right about you two?"

Santos glanced in Knox's direction. "*I* think so," he whispered.

"Have you tried this before?" Mary asked.

"Not quite," Santos smiled and then licked his lips.

"It's never come up," Knox said.

Her eyes went wide as she shook her head. "How? Have you seen him?" she asked, tipping her head in Santos's direction. "He's fine as hell."

"Don't inflate his ego," Knox joked. "His head's too big."

"Not right now," Santos mumbled.

Mary giggled and posed the same question to Santos. "Is he not your type?"

Santos laughed softly and looked from Mary to Knox. "He's very much my type," he said and threw his left arm over the back of the booth behind Mary's head.

Mary turned back to Knox, licking her lips. "Taste. So, do you not like pretty boys?" she asked. Santos groaned at his old nickname.

Knox rested his forearms on the table and leaned toward

her. "How'd you know we used to call him that in the Marines?"

"Makes sense," she said. "So...why'd you never hit that before?"

"Well?" Santos asked, waiting for an answer.

He shifted his gaze back to Mary, who was looking at him with the same eager expectation. She sucked her bottom lip into her mouth. When she released it, it was wet, and Knox couldn't look away.

"Never thought the pretty boy would be interested in me," he rasped.

"And now you know you were wrong," Santos said.

Mary and Santos moved at the same time, as if they were already completely in sync, pressing their legs against Knox's under the table, doing their damnedest to get him hard before they even had the chance to put their dinner orders in.

"Yeah," he moaned softly.

"I feel like I missed something," Mary whispered, her voice laced with lust.

Knox nodded once.

"Will you tell me about it?" she asked, unconsciously moving her hand to her chest to play with her right nipple through her shirt. Santos grunted and moved his foot between Knox's legs.

Knox licked his own lips, ready to tell her exactly how far he'd sucked Santos's shaft down his throat a few hours ago when Santos rained on their parade.

"After," Santos ground out.

Mary and Knox frowned at one another before turning to him in confusion.

"After we eat," Santos said. "We're going to need all the energy we can get." He turned toward the lunch counter. "Hey, Janine, we're ready to order."

"Who the hell is Janine?" Knox asked.

Santos rolled his eyes. "Our waitress. Obviously."

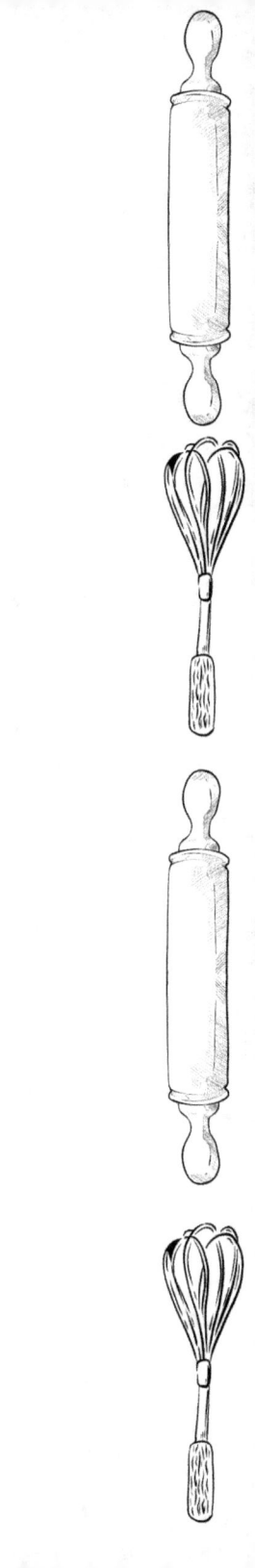

WELCOME TO SEA PORT

EIGHTEEN

Santos

S antos was worried dinner would be awkward or uncomfortable, especially once they had to do something as mundane as eating. It was hard to keep up a steady stream of flirting while shoveling Mr. Wright's food into his mouth, and if they couldn't flirt, Santos had to wonder if they had anything between them at all. He'd been waiting impatiently for this date all day and it was worth it because apparently, underneath the lust was a genuine interest in one another. Who knew?

Santos wasn't talkative, and when he and Knox normally ate together, Knox usually did at least sixty percent of the talking — and smiling — but Mary was giving as good as she got in both departments. Sometimes Santos worried Knox would get bored by his monosyllabic answers and incessant questions, but Mary and Knox were more than happy to talk each other's ears off, allowing Santos to contribute a little less frequently but just as enthusiastically.

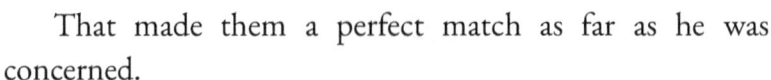

That made them a perfect match as far as he was concerned.

Mary added something to his and Knox's relationship that he couldn't put a name to just yet but liked. Immensely.

"So what'd you study?" Knox asked Mary, popping a fry into his mouth.

"Dead writers," she said nonchalantly.

"Dead poets?" Knox asked, laughing at his own joke. Santos chuckled and Mary rolled her eyes. Clearly, she'd heard that joke before.

"More like dead writers of political treatises," Mary said while she cut a piece of pork chop and popped it into her mouth.

"Oh," Knox and Santos said.

"Much less funny," Santos added.

She sighed sadly. "Yeah, that's how my students felt." But then she brightened. "The good thing is I never have to teach a class about women's memoirs ever again."

Knox smiled gently. "No, you don't."

Santos looked at Knox in his peripheral vision and studied his familiar face for a few seconds before Knox's eyes shifted and they made eye contact. They knew each other too well, especially after this morning, and that look made Santos squirm in his seat.

"What'd you get up to today?" Mary asked.

Knox eased back in the booth and smiled at her. "Same thing I do every other day."

"Which is?" she prodded in a soft, beseeching voice.

Knox's eyes shifted in Santos's direction with a nod. "Me and him met up for breakfast."

The shudder in his voice was subtle enough that Mary

probably thought it was his regular rasp, but Santos recognized it now. After this morning, Santos knew that deep wobble in Knox's voice got stronger when he was horny.

"Y'all do that a lot?" Mary asked.

Knox lifted his eyebrows and smirked. "First time, actually."

"Huh?" Mary hummed, shifting on the bench. "Was it good?"

It was the way she said it, the way Knox's eyebrows managed to lift a little closer to his hairline. But most of all, it was the way Mary was rocking lightly in her seat, her hip bumping against Santos's thigh rhythmically.

Santos's eyes shifted to the left and down, directly into Mary's lap. She'd moved her hand between her thighs and was rocking her pussy back and forth over her fingers. "Tell her," he said in a voice so thick and rough it hurt.

"You sure?" Knox asked, rationality sobering his words.

Mary was having none of that. "He is," she whispered. Moaned, really. "Tell me?"

Knox gave in just like Santos would've. And Santos wondered if his dick was half as hard as his at that moan.

"Santos stopped by my place with coffee today."

"Oh, you weren't at Sully's?"

Santos assumed Knox nodded his head in the silence, but he was too busy snaking his arm around Mary. She jumped lightly when his hand landed on her shoulder, right before she sank into his side with a soft smile on her face.

"Coffee was cold before we got to it, though," Knox said.

"Oh," Mary breathed. Santos's hand moved from her shoulder to her left breast, his fingers brushing her hard nipple. "Oh," she sighed with a soft smile.

"He got on his knees for me right there in my kitchen." She whimpered, nudging Knox to keep going. "He's got a serious tongue," Knox whispered.

Santos smiled at the compliment and because Mary shivered in his arms.

"That was one," Santos said.

Mary's body shuddered through another orgasm while Knox groaned and the bench squeaked while he shifted in his seat.

She turned and looked at him, her lips wet from her tongue. "It was your first time?"

"Yeah," Santos said.

"Was it as good as you dreamed it would be?" Mary asked because of course, she did.

"Better," he admitted, happy to finally have someone to share this with.

"Aw shucks," Knox teased.

There was a second of silence before they all burst into laughter. Knox covered his face in his hands, Santos had tears in his eyes, and Mary's hand was pressed to her chest as she leaned against the window and giggled.

Santos had often been on the fringes of a group with Knox plenty of times, and he normally hated sharing his attention for too long. Even worse, he'd discovered since moving to Sea Port, was pretending that he was hanging on Knox's every word just because they were friends. It wasn't, and he relished being free of that constraint he put on himself.

"Wanna hear about the goat?" Knox asked after they finally stopped laughing.

"What goat?" Mary asked, sitting up again and grabbing a fry from her plate and nibbling at it.

"Wait 'til you hear this mess," Santos breathed, nudging her plate as a reminder to eat. She looked from him to Knox, who sat in silence until she complied. It went unsaid, but Santos thought they'd all need the fuel tonight, so he set about finishing his own meal while Knox told his story.

Once Mary took a bite of her food, Knox pulled his mouth back to that easy smile. "So I got to my desk today after..." He stopped here and licked his lips before continuing. "Soon as I got to my desk, I get a call from one of the farms on the outskirts of town."

"So people really live on the farms? I thought most of them were abandoned." Mary asked.

"Some are. The Mayor's family has a few farms that no one lives on anymore. But some people do and some of 'em still work."

"Really? Why didn't anyone ever tell me?"

Knox smirked. "Probably 'cause a lot of the farmers are none too happy about us Transplants. They tolerate me and Santos, but that's about it."

"Oh," Mary breathed sadly, adorably hurt at the prospect that anyone wouldn't be chomping at the bit to get to know her, which was understandable since he was doing just that right now.

"You're probably better off staying out of their way for now," Santos beathed.

Knox nodded. "They'll come around soon, though. Especially once your bakery's open for real," he said with a wink that seemed to perk her up.

Santos could relate to that as well.

"So, anyway," Knox continued. "Me and Jones — one of my new volunteers — end up running around this field, trying to corral this damn goat onto a truck to take him back to where he was supposed to be," he said around his increasing laughter.

"So you got the goat home, right?" Mary asked.

"Now hold on, don't rush the story."

"He's dramatic," Santos said.

Knox didn't take his eyes off Mary. "Don't listen to his hatin' ass. I'm a natural storyteller," he said. Santos sighed aggressively. "And you don't mind, do you, sweetheart?" he asked in a deep, seductive voice.

Santos knew Knox used that tone of voice to get under his skin, and it worked, but not just on him.

"Yeah," Mary sighed and started bouncing softly in her seat, rubbing her thighs together. Her little movements made the hair on Santos's arms and the back of his neck stand up.

Santos glanced at Knox and found him watching Mary with a knowing smirk on his face.

"You look done," Mary whispered.

Knox's eyes shifted toward him and Santos blinked before realizing she was speaking to him. "Huh?"

Mary ignored his question. "I'm done," she said, dropping her fork. "What next?"

"What makes you think there's something after this?" Knox asked. He lifted his right arm over the back of the booth, mirroring Santos's body unconsciously.

"Dinner's a good date," Santos echoed.

Mary pushed her plate out of the way and leaned forward, smiling at Knox. "I think I deserve better than good, don't you?" she challenged. Knox opened his mouth to speak, but Mary cut him off, sitting back in her seat and slowly moving her hands out of view.

Santos's breath hitched when her hand landed on his thigh, caressing him under the table. He reached for his cup of water, mostly to hide the look on his face when her pinky nudged the head of his dick.

"It doesn't sound like Santos gave you a *good* blowjob this morning?"

"He didn't," Knox rasped.

"Did you return the favor?" she asked, her fingers ghosting the length of Santos's shaft.

Santos grunted.

Knox smiled smugly. "You heard the man."

"I did. So like I said, what's next?" Mary asked.

"When we leave here, we're gonna fuck," he whispered in an intimate and serious voice. They all shuddered at those words.

"We are," Santos groaned.

"I was hoping you'd say that. Why wait?" Mary said excitedly.

"She's got a point," Santos said, moving his hand from the back of the booth, brushing the side of her neck, and then snaking forward to her chest again.

Mary's pulse pounded against his forearm as she relaxed into his side.

But they were both watching Knox's face. His smile faded by degrees as Santos slipped his hand into the neck of Mary's shirt. Her skin was hot under his touch. Her breath was shallow, and when he lightly pinched her nipple through her bra, her hand was back on his dick.

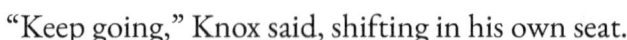

"Keep going," Knox said, shifting in his own seat.

Santos pushed his fingers into the cup of Mary's bra. Mary let out a soft, whimpering moan that made them all groan, although Santos was the only one of them with enough sense to pretend to cough as a cover. He didn't want to be impatient, but he couldn't stop himself from going straight for her nipple, rolling it between three fingers, enjoying how good it felt to be this free.

Mary started panting slightly as he played with her nipple. The rest of the diner was loud — bustling even, by Sea Port standards — but in their little booth, it was quiet, the only sound their rising, desperate breaths as they took their foreplay to the next level.

He didn't know how Knox was keeping himself together and his hands off his dick, but he was determined to break the man down.

Santos reluctantly pulled his hands from Mary's shirt, but only so he could pull the fabric up to her neck, exposing her body for Knox's pleasure.

Mary's shocked gasp mixed with a soft moan as she caressed Santos's dick with a little more pressure.

Knox's eyes widened, shifting to the diner behind Santos's head. Santos stopped, waited. "Keep going," Knox said after a while before moving his eyes back to Santos's hands on Mary's skin.

Santos pulled her bra cups down and lifted the fingers of his left hand to his mouth.

"Fuck," Knox hissed as Santos started twisting Mary's left nipple between his wet fingers.

Mary threw her right leg over Santos's left and moved her hands between her legs.

And finally, Knox broke. Both hands fell into his lap and he groaned.

"Keep going," she moaned, perfectly illustrating what Santos already knew — Mary was a perfect fit for them.

He covered her full breast with his right palm and squeezed until she let out a desperate whimper.

Both sides of the booth were creaking as they all squirmed in their seats. Mary reached for Santos's leg again and dug her fingers into his flesh. He hissed at the pain and Knox sat up in his seat, glancing behind them again. It was a good thing he had his wits about him, but Santos and Mary hardly cared.

"Does that feel good, sweetheart?" Knox rasped through a shaky smile as he turned his attention back to her face.

Mary nodded quickly, shivering through another little earthquake. Her eyes were closed and she was trying to take deep, even breaths. She was sexier every time he looked at her.

"You rubbing on your pussy for us, sweetheart?" Santos asked.

Knox groaned and Mary swallowed a high-pitched moan before nodding again.

That was all Santos needed to hear or see. He was done with dinner. Now, he was ready to fuck. "Time to go," Santos ground out. He started to pull his hands from her when Knox leaned forward.

"Don't," Knox said, and they locked eyes. "I'll get the check. Keep her pussy wet."

"Jesus," Mary sighed and then clamped her thighs shut.

"Yes, Sergeant," Santos ground out, his dick throbbing in his pants.

Knox grunted softly and then pulled his t-shirt from the waist of his pants. He stood, and Santos's gaze went immediately to the front of Knox's jeans. His erection wasn't completely hidden, but he did his best not to draw attention to it as he walked away. He placed a heavy hand on Santos's shoulder and squeezed.

Santos squeezed Mary's nipple in turn.

When he looked at her again, there were small beads of sweat at her hairline. "I'm going to come," she moaned.

"Shhh," he soothed her, still rolling her nipple between his fingers but softer. It was cruel, but he couldn't help but to bend forward and brush her ear with his mouth. "I don't want you to come until one of us is inside of you."

She couldn't bite back the cry, but thankfully, Mr. Wright's laughter drowned out Mary's moan.

"Maybe both of us," he added because he couldn't help himself thinking about what was coming.

He jumped when Knox returned and slapped his shoulder again. "Ease up on her, Marine. Let's get out of here."

Santos sighed and brushed a kiss against Mary's earlobe. He took specific care to tuck her breast back into her bra and right her shirt. They each offered Mary a hand and pulled her up, staying close until she was steady on her feet.

"God, I'm horny," she said under her breath.

"We all are," Knox said.

"Then let's get the fuck out of here and fuck," Santos grumbled.

And for once, they both did as he said.

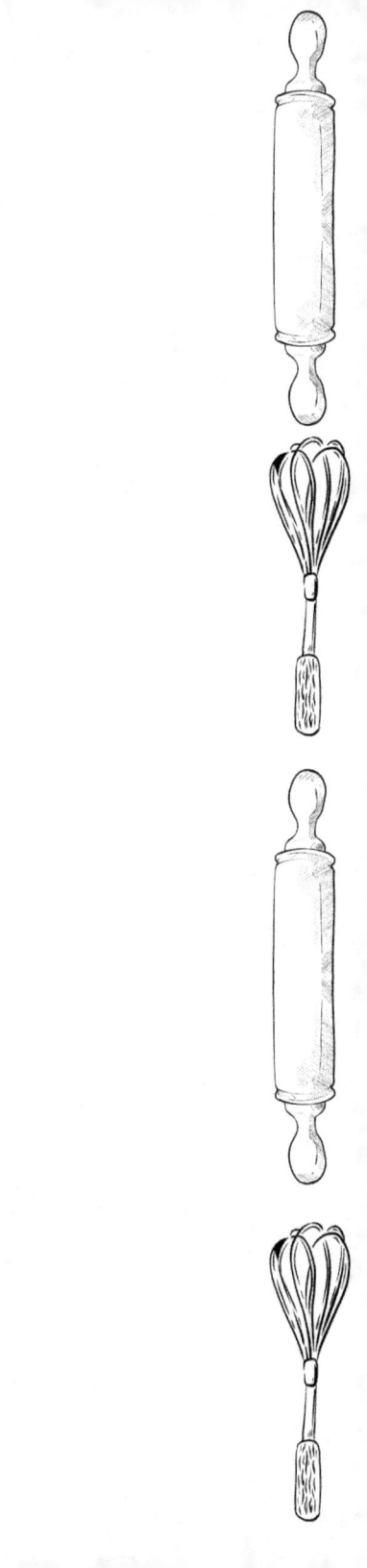

WELCOME TO SEA PORT

NINETEEN

Mary

S ea Port didn't have anything like a nightlife — no clubs, no bars open past nine, not even a movie theater. Most places closed around dinnertime, and the few places open through dinner were rushing their last customers out the door as soon as their plates were clean. The closest she'd got to experiencing Sea Port After Dark, such as it was, were the few nights when she'd stayed late at the bakery to work on some recipes. She'd walked home at dusk, enjoying the sound of cicadas in the trees or a bored dog barking at the stars. There was nothing much to see in Sea Port after dark besides the constellations and they were beautiful, but not enough to keep her out past sunset.

But the sun was completely gone when Mary stepped out of the Sunnyside with Santos and Knox hot on her heels, and the sky was a shade of dark blue; it looked almost black but for the tiny dots of stars in the sky. Sea Port hadn't invested in many streetlights and all of them were on Main, but Knox reached for her hand and led her down a darkened

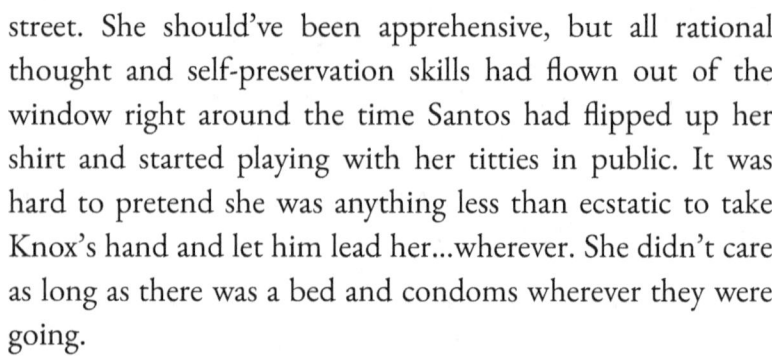

street. She should've been apprehensive, but all rational thought and self-preservation skills had flown out of the window right around the time Santos had flipped up her shirt and started playing with her titties in public. It was hard to pretend she was anything less than ecstatic to take Knox's hand and let him lead her...wherever. She didn't care as long as there was a bed and condoms wherever they were going.

Santos's touch was different — he didn't offer his hand but brushed the back of hers until their fingers entwined, holding onto her other hand with the same intensity as Knox. Sure, they were still complete strangers, but Mary had never felt as safe or secure with any of the other men she'd dated before.

"I'm so horny," she whispered excitedly.

"Where—" Santos started.

"My place," Knox cut in. "I live closest."

"How close?" she asked excitedly as their bodies bumped together with every step.

"Two blocks south."

"Thank fucking god," Mary said, walking faster, pulling them with her.

Mary didn't know where she was going, but she walked like there was fire licking at her heels. She couldn't even remember the last time she'd had sex, but it had been long enough that her vibrators had become her longest and most successful relationship. That might've been embarrassing, but maybe they'd been preparing her for tonight.

Just maybe.

What she did know was that her body had changed since she last hooked up with someone. Her thighs were thicker, her belly was softer, she felt more comfortable in her skin, and most importantly, when she looked in the mirror, she liked what she saw.

"Oh, you live here?" Mary cried as Knox led them to his building.

Sea Port had been an agricultural community since its founding, but Knox's condo building had once been the town's only factory. Mary didn't know what they'd made here — she'd honestly never bothered to ask — just that the building had been empty long before Sea Port's population started to decline until a few years ago when Mayor Waltham's father had started renovating it. But then he'd died, and the renovation projects had slowed was all Mary heard.

Nothing about the sexy firefighter who lived there.

"I do," Knox said, leading them inside.

"He's the only one who does," Santos breathed.

"Perfect," Mary said, stepping inside. "Then we can scream as loud as we want."

Knox choked on his laughter and Santos squeezed her hand reassuringly.

"You heard the lady, Sergeant."

"Shut up," Knox chuckled.

He gave Mary a cursory tour of the lobby, the elevator, and the hallways leading to his front door. She might've laughed it was so funny, but she too wanted to get to his apartment as soon as possible.

"And here's my place," he said, slipping his key into the lock.

"Finally," Santos grumbled.

Knox turned toward them, the glare already on his face,

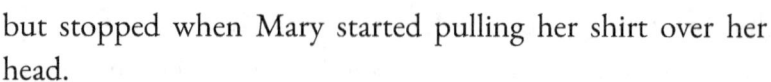

but stopped when Mary started pulling her shirt over her head.

"What's happening?" he asked, eyes moving from her cleavage to Santos and back again.

"Why wait?" she huffed, pulling her shirt off her right arm.

"I love a woman who gets straight to the point," Santos added seriously.

Mary turned to wink at him. "Thanks," she chirped.

"Don't you wanna slow down?" Knox asked, pushing his front door open. "What if we wanted to undress you?"

On cue, Santos unclipped her bra. Mary laughed, sauntering over the threshold and dropping her shirt, bra, and bag just inside the floor. She started kicking off her shoes and unbuttoning her pants. "Next time," she laughed. "Promise. How big is your shower? I've been in the bakery all day."

"What?" Knox whispered.

Santos had to push a shocked Knox into his own house and close the door. Knox was watching her with wide eyes and mouth agape. Santos stepped behind him and moved his mouth to the other man's ear. Mary started shimmying her panties over her thighs slowly as the quiet entryway filled with the sound of Knox and Santos's clothes rubbing together.

"She wants to know if your shower is big enough for all three of us," Santos said in that same serious, seductive tone he'd been using on them all night.

"Yeah," Knox whisper-groaned, and Mary pushed her panties to her ankles.

She cupped both breasts and played with her nipples as they watched each other in silent excitement. "Which way?"

Knox and Santos pointed to a door across the living room.

She held her heavy breasts in her hands, stepped out of her underwear, and turned toward it, knowing they would follow.

All day, Mary had soothed her frazzled nerves with a dream of stepping into the hottest shower she could stand, but when she walked into Knox's bathroom she wanted to cry. This shower was better than her dreams.

"Oh my god! It's beautiful," Mary gasped. "How much is your rent?" Mary loved her cottage, but it only had a tiny shower-tub combo in a cramped regular-sized bathroom. Meanwhile, Knox's bathroom was the same size as her bedroom *and* it had a walk-in tiled shower with a natural stone floor that was definitely big enough for three, maybe five in a pinch.

"Holy shit," she cried, spotting the freestanding tub on the other side of the room. It wasn't quite as big, but Mary could see two of them squeezing into it. Maybe the third could watch? "Do you need a roommate?" she asked.

"That's why you screamed?" Knox sighed, shaking his head.

"The bathroom in my house is half the size of this one. Less than half. Of course, I screamed. Must be nice to be blessed and highly favored," she said, rolling her eyes.

Santos chuckled, unbuckling his belt.

"This is what you get when you move here first and are willing to spend a little money on your own renovations," Knox said.

"Oh," she breathed. "I'm not doing that." She was about to say something flirty, but then Knox pulled his

shirt over his head and all the words on her tongue evaporated.

Vaguely, she heard Santos moving behind her and then felt his body heat kissing her naked back. She sighed when his mouth brushed the rim of her ear. "Do you like that?"

"Love it," she huffed. "How 'bout you?"

In lieu of a verbal answer, Santos pressed his groin against her back. She backed herself against the enticing pressure of his hard dick. "What do you think?" he whispered.

"What are you two talking about?" Knox asked, fingers prying his belt open.

"You," Santos said.

Mary smirked. "He said you should undress faster."

Santos's laughter was a soft breath against Mary's ear for a few seconds before his hands landed on both sides of her waist. "That's exactly what I said."

Knox swallowed hard at the sound of Santos's voice, but there was barely a moment of hesitation before he got back to opening his pants.

Mary licked her lips, watching him with a hunger their dinner hadn't touched.

Knox shoved his hands into his pants and waited. Santos's hands caressed her stomach and she held her breath as his fingers slid over her mound.

Knox's hand started moving inside his pants, tugging his shaft as he watched.

"Please," Mary whispered just as Santos's fingers brushed her clit.

They both grunted and Knox pushed his pants down his legs.

"You happy now?" Knox asked. His dick was dark

brown with a slightly darker mushroom head and it curved to the left, slapping against his thigh as he walked forward.

Mary shuddered in Santos's arms. "It's a start," she moaned.

Knox flattened his palm over the curve of her lower belly and moved his hand between her legs, his fingers slipping in her wetness and twisting with Santos's.

"Holy shit. I can't believe this is real," she said, closing her eyes and breathing through another mini orgasm with three of their hands on her.

"I know the feeling," Knox chuckled, kissing her cheek sweetly, as if his fingers weren't caressing her lips.

"It's real," Santos said, grounding them.

Mary laughed. "Apparently."

Knox kissed his way to the corner of her mouth. "You ready to scream for a better reason than a bathroom?" he asked.

Mary opened her eyes and leaned her head back onto Santos's chest. "Yes, please," she moaned.

Santos's rumble of laughter moved through her as he circled her clit.

"Yes, *sir*," Knox corrected, slipping a finger inside her.

"Fuck," Santos groaned, jutting his hips into Mary's soft ass.

"Tell me about it," Mary gasped.

WELCOME TO SEA PORT

TWENTY

Mary

I n her old life, Mary had been as close to touch starved as it was possible to get as her job became her entire life.

The semester before she graduated, Mary's mentor gave her a series of lectures on work-life balance and Mary had listened intently; she'd even taken notes. She thought she'd been prepared for what was to come, but that was just one more thing she'd been wrong about. Somewhere along the way, her job had pushed out everything else. All she had was work, no life, no friends, no hobbies. No one to come home to. No one to make quesadillas with her in the middle of the night. No one to go to the movies with or geek out with her about community theater.

No one to hug her when she cried.

It wasn't until Leah showed up to help her move to Sea Port and hugged her tight that Mary realized how much she'd missed being held. But sandwiched between Santos and Knox was a whole new level of intimacy she hadn't imagined possible.

Their breaths synced in slow, deep inhalations that seemed to bring them physically and emotionally closer all at the same time. Santos and Knox alternated between teasing her opening and massaging her clit in unhurried caresses. And because Mary was helpful, she was rolling her nipples between her fingers while the day's stress seeped from her pores.

"She's wet," Knox rasped, grinning while staring her deep in the eyes.

"Let me taste," Santos groaned into her ear.

Knox pulled his hand from her legs and lifted his wet fingers to Santos's mouth. Mary arched her back, craning her neck to watch as Knox slid his fingers wet from her pussy between Santos's lips. He grunted, sucking Knox's fingers deeper into his mouth.

Mary was so turned on she let go of her breasts and started caressing Knox's body, running her fingers through his coarse, curly chest hair, scraping over his smooth skin. Santos and Knox stared at one another with fire in their eyes while she squirmed between them and Santos's finger kept circling her clit. When Santos finally released Knox's fingers, Knox grabbed him behind the head and pulled him close. Their tongues slid together and they looked like they were trying to carefully devour one another with her pussy as the appetizer. Knox's tongue jutted into Santos's mouth and Santos sucked it between his lips with the same energy as he'd tasted the man's fingers. At some point, they became one writhing organism, both men humping into her as their kiss deepened. Mary had never been the creamy filling in a cookie sandwich, but she never wanted to be anything or anywhere else.

That thought and Santos's teeth sinking into Knox's thumb pushed her over the edge and she started shaking. Her fingers dug into Knox's chest and Santos slipped two fingers inside her.

He smiled against Knox's mouth as they pulled back from one another.

"Noooo," Mary moaned. Santos pulled his fingers from her sex. "No," she moaned again.

Knox stepped away, letting cool air replace his warm, hard body. Mary shivered at the loss.

Knox's smile had never been bigger. Almost as big as his dick, which was now hard and pointing right at them. "I thought we came in here for a shower," he laughed, walking backward.

"We were getting there," Mary sighed once her breath returned.

Knox trained his gaze directly on her. "Santos is looking a little overdressed, don't you think, sweetheart?" He stepped into the shower with a nod.

Santos kissed her cheek. "You heard the man," he whispered in a voice that was like molten lava.

Mary nodded, grinding back against Santos's dick before he spun her around to face him. A laugh fell from her lips.

"Undress me, sweetheart," he told her.

She nodded harder, laughing and moaning at the same time. Her hands were shaking as she pushed his shirt up and then explored his chest. "Damn," she muttered.

"I can't wait to get inside you two," Santos muttered

back. The word 'two' had never made her clit jump before, but there was a first time for everything.

He could've helped her, but he was rolling her nipples between his fingers instead. She finally had to push Santos's hands away so she could get back to the business of getting him naked. She refused to come on an empty pussy again just because she had sensitive nipples.

Mary felt wild and horny and Santos looked about the same. His light brown skin was flushed, his pupils were blown, and based on the bulge in his pants, he was ready to be naked.

"You enjoying yourself?" she asked, pushing his pants over his hips.

"Very. You?"

She smiled, kneeling at his feet and staring straight into his eyes as her face came level to his groin.

"Shit," Santos hissed, running his fingers through his hair as he looked down at her. He caressed her cheek with his free hand.

She lowered her gaze to his underwear. His dick was bulging through his briefs and Mary rubbed her thumb over the wet imprint of the mushroom head.

"Shh," he started again, but Knox whistled low, inter-rupting their moment.

Mary turned to look in his direction, caressing Santos's dick with her fingers because she could multitask. Knox was ripping open a condom wrapper, and she watched as he started rolling it down his length.

"Where'd those come from?" she asked.

"I believe in always being prepared," he replied.

"We've been waiting for this," Santos added. "For you,"

he groaned when she cupped his shaft through his underwear.

"Now come on, sweetheart," Knox said, tipping his head toward the shower. "Water's hot."

Santos grabbed her forearms and pulled her to her feet, spinning her around again. She could feel the goofy grin on her face.

"Someone likes getting manhandled," Knox said.

"We'll remember that," Santos promised.

"Shit, wait," Knox said quickly, and Mary stopped dead in her tracks. He darted from the room, dick bobbing up and down as he went, but he was back in a matter of seconds, fresh washcloths and a new bar of soap in hand.

"Well, aren't you a good host?" Santos teased.

Knox sucked his teeth. "Shut up."

"I think it's sweet," she whispered, making her way toward the shower.

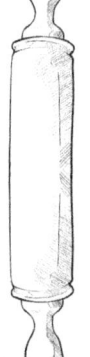

"And I think you've got the best damn ass I've ever seen," Santos groaned.

"At least we all agree on something," Knox laughed, following close behind her into the shower.

SANTOS

S antos had been unraveling slowly all day; he'd never
wanted anything or anyone as much as he wanted
Knox and Mary.

His heart was galloping inside his chest as he stepped
onto the cool tile.

Knox ducked his head under the shower spray. He'd seen
Knox do this before — hundreds of times, even — but never
like this. And never with Mary standing between them,
rubbing her pussy as she looked from one man to the other
and back again. Santos felt like every nerve ending in his
body wasn't just receptive but tender.

Steam tickled the hair on his legs, making his dick throb.
Santos had to reach down to grip the base of his dick so he
didn't spill too soon, remembering only when the packet got
in the way that he was supposed to be putting the
condom on.

Knox stepped from under the shower spray, smiling as
water cascaded down his head, face, and chest. He reached
for Mary.

"I can't get my hair wet," she giggled as Knox's hands
wrapped around her wrists.

"I'll be careful," Knox laughed, pulling her to him.

Santos used his teeth to rip the foil open like an
overeager but inexperienced teenager.

Mary and Knox started to kiss as one of her hands disappeared between their bodies. She swallowed Knox's happy
grunt while Santos pulled the condom down the length of
his shaft.

Knox opened his eyes and their gazes met. His hands
moved over her shoulders, down her arms, around her waist
and hips. He spread his fingers as his grip moved over her ass

and squeezed, and then he started walking her back, away from the shower spray.

Santos was trying to take it all in — the sound of water hitting tile, rivulets moving between all the gaps separating Knox's dark brown skin from Mary's slightly lighter brown. Santos wanted to bury himself in all those places, but there would be time for that later. For now, he grunted when Mary's soft ass bumped into his dick. And then he groaned when Knox's right hand wrapped around his shaft. It was looser than Santos's hold, but so goddamn good.

When Knox pulled away from their kiss, Santos's hand moved over Mary's throat and turned her head. She opened her lips and he sucked her tongue into his mouth. Meanwhile, Knox's hands were busy between their legs, jerking Santos with slow precision and, based on the sounds she was making in his mouth, rubbing Mary's clit.

Mary widened her stance and bent toward Knox's chest.

"Fuck," Santos breathed against Mary's mouth. "I need to be inside you," he groaned loudly.

"Me or him?" she asked in the sexiest voice.

Santos knew he wasn't going to last much longer and his brain was too clouded to answer. Thankfully, Knox was on top of it.

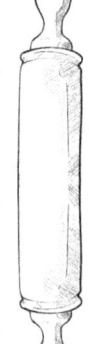

"You first," he smiled, kissing Mary's cheek. "You're so goddamn wet and he's hard as steel."

Santos grunted, but Mary spoke. "You're plenty hard too."

Santos's gaze dropped between their bodies and saw that both of Mary's hands were stroking Knox's dick in firm, tight pulls. That was all the encouragement he needed to get his shit together. In one smooth motion, Santos reluctantly

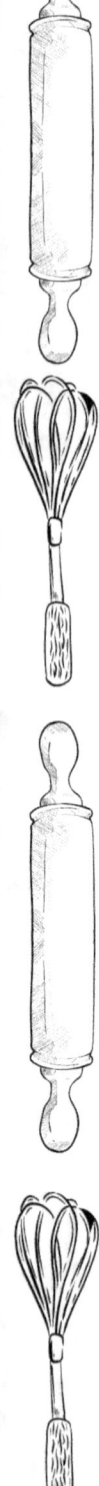

pushed Knox's hand from his shaft and nudged Mary's chest forward. She leaned against Knox as Santos bent his knees, grabbed his dick, and aimed the head toward her entrance.

Knox's fingers were in the way at first, but instead of sliding out of the way, Knox grabbed the head of Santos's dick and pulled him toward Mary's opening.

When Santos pushed inside Mary's hot pussy for the first time, it was with Knox's help, which felt fitting. And he definitely fit.

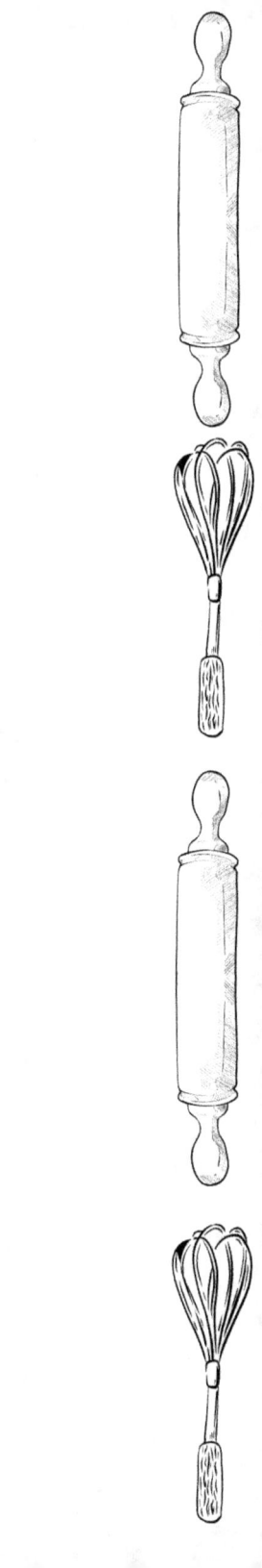

WELCOME TO SEA PORT

TWENTY-ONE

Knox

K nox had had a lot of sex in his life, but this was something else. The hot water beating at his back, Mary's hands caressing his dick, her big, soft breasts pressing into his chest to the rhythm of Santos's hips pushing against her ass. Santos wasn't fucking him, but Knox swore he could feel every inch of his length. He felt like one big nerve ending and the night had only just begun.

Mary shoved her face into the crook of his neck. Her soft, pitchy moans tickled Knox's beard. He happily held her up while she trembled in his arms. He was surprised at her steady hands on his shaft — surprised but very much appreciative. Santos's face was flushed and determined as he fucked Mary into Knox in long, deep strokes, his eyes focused on Knox the entire time.

Santos hit somewhere particularly deep and sensitive, making Mary moan loudly against Knox's skin. He responded with a full-body shudder that made his own toes curl.

"Harder," Mary moaned.

Knox ran his tongue over his lips. "She said 'go harder,'" he told Santos. "And deeper."

"Oh god," Mary groaned as Santos bent her forward and lowered his stance. Her face slipped down to Knox's chest. And on the next press of his hips, their skin slapped together, and a short grunt fell from Santos's throat.

Mary's hands tightened on Knox's shaft and he closed his eyes, breathing through his coming orgasm.

When Knox opened his eyes again, his gaze moved down the soft slope of Mary's spine, over the adorable little black butterfly tattoo at the small of her back, to the death grip Santos had on her waist. He couldn't see him pushing inside her, but just knowing it was happening was enough.

For now.

"What do you need?"

It took a few seconds for Knox to realize Santos was talking to him, but Mary was on it.

"My mouth?" she offered in a deep groan.

Both men's eyes went wide, but Santos's hips didn't stop.

"We're gonna run out of hot water," Knox said.

"Who cares?" Mary cried before lightly biting Knox's pec.

"Fuck, I'm gonna come," Knox said, shivering from head to toe again. He tried holding himself together, but Mary and Santos were making it really hard to do anything but fuck.

"That makes two of us," Santos ground out, the space between each word filled with the sound of their skin slapping together.

"Three," Mary groaned. "Fuck, three."

"Perfect," Santos moaned. He was holding onto her waist so tight, Knox worried she'd bruise and rubbed his palm down and up her spine soothingly.

Mary was unconcerned. "Keep fucking me. I'm so close," she gasped at the same time as she started using Knox's chest for leverage to throw her ass back into Santos.

"Shit," Santos hissed.

Knox scratched up her spine and grit his teeth as she started twisting her fists with each stroke.

"Make her come," Knox ground out. It went without saying that he and Santos would follow her lead.

Santos laughed drily and started moving his hips faster; he'd always been good at following orders. But in the end, it wasn't Mary that pushed them over the edge, it was Knox. Mary moved one hand between his thighs and started massaging his balls and it all suddenly just became too much for him to hold himself together. So, he let go.

Knox's head fell back and he started pumping his hips into Mary's hold as he filled the condom around his dick. Mary groaned loud while her shivering intensified.

Santos held out the longest, fucking Mary through her and Knox's orgasms before finally coming himself in a loud, pained shout.

Yeah, Knox had experienced a lot of sex before, but never anything like this.

Never anyone like them.

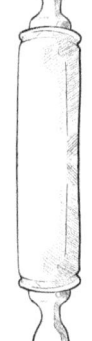

MARY

"It's a good thing you don't have any neighbors," Mary said with a soft smile on her face.

"This building is made of brick. They wouldn't have heard all that moaning you were doing," Knox said, tucking his own towel closed around his waist.

She laughed. "I don't care about that. But the water," she said, shaking her head. "If I came home from a long day of work and my neighbor had depleted the hot water having a threesome, I'd be pissed."

After that first shared orgasm, the hot water had turned lukewarm. They'd had to shut the shower off to actually clean themselves, rinsing in shifts, laughing as they maneuvered around one another in the surprisingly spacious shower. By the time they were done, the water had been ice-cold, but so damn worth it.

"How pissed? Would you go knock on their door to complain?" Knox asked.

"Maybe," Mary laughed.

Santos's body was still dripping wet, but he was patting his hair dry. "It'd be a foursome then."

Mary shook her head quickly. "That sounds a little too complicated for me. Too many legs. And arms."

Knox laughed. "And you don't think *this* is too many legs and arms?"

Knox's eyebrows were knit together in what looked like worry to Mary, but she was smiling excitedly. "Nope," she beamed, toying with the edge of the towel over her breasts. "We managed just fine on our first try. Don't you think?"

Knox ducked his head and smiled. "I mean, we..."

"We did more than fine," Santos interjected in his deep, serious voice. He didn't hide his smile.

"See?" Mary replied cheerily.

"Next time, we should use the tub," Santos said, tossing his own towel into the hamper by the shower before walking toward the door completely naked.

"See?" she smiled, looking between Santos's body and Knox, who rolled his eyes even as his own gaze jumped to Santos's hard back.

Santos stopped next to her. "You said something about your mouth."

Those words and the fire in his eyes made Mary's face light up. She turned to Knox, licking her lips. "I sure did."

Santos grabbed her hand and pulled her into the hallway. Knox grabbed the box of condoms and followed them toward his bedroom.

"So, did you decorate the space, or is there a Sea Port interior design company I don't know about?" she asked, marveling at the prints hung along the hallway.

Knox was clutching the opened box of condoms in both hands, a shy but eager smile on his face. "I did all this," he replied, his gaze trained on her ass.

The prints were all abstract florals in calming earth tones, which reminded her a lot of Knox. "You have good taste," she said.

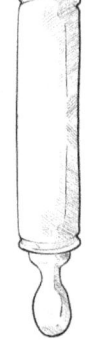

Knox's eyes lifted to her face. "You haven't had the opportunity yet."

Santos grunted out a laugh and pulled Mary into Knox's bedroom. "Let's fix that then."

"Oh, good, a king-sized bed," Mary cried out.

Santos stopped at the foot of the bed. It was a short walk, but his dick was already coming back to life. He plucked Mary's towel loose and then watched as it fell at their feet. Santos brushed his knuckles down her chest and circled her nipples, teasing them with his thumbs.

"Get on the bed," he rasped.

"Yes, sir," she moaned.

Santos and Knox groaned in return, the filthiest call and response of her life.

She climbed slowly onto the bed.

Mary gave herself a mental pat on the back that she'd left Cat-leen with a full water fountain and more food than she needed because Mary would not be home any time soon. Santos smacked her ass as she crawled up the bed, sending a shudder through her core as another moan fell from her lips. She was worried she'd be hoarse tomorrow with all this moaning and screaming, but it would be worth it.

Mary crawled to the head of the bed and leaned against the headboard. Santos and Knox waited at the foot of the bed and watched as she bent her knees, spreading her thighs for their viewing pleasure and her own delicious excitement. She moved her right hand between her legs, carefully massaging her clit while Knox stepped next to Santos and dropped his towel on top of hers.

They watched her for a few seconds before Santos turned in Knox's direction. Mary's eyes went wide. They were a study in contrasts, hard muscles but tender touches as their hands moved over soft skin. She dipped her fingers inside herself as they opened their mouths and their tongues slid together. They touched one another hungrily, hands gliding over each other's backs, hips, asses, anywhere they could touch, grunting softly into one another's mouths.

Mary had been getting along with her own fingers for years, but after Santos's dick, her two fingers weren't enough, so she added a third, twisting her left nipple as she tried to stay quiet.

Santos pulled back from their kiss and they stared at one another, having a silent, emotional conversation that made her worry this was all about to fall apart. She froze, fingers still stuffed inside herself, waiting, hoping, praying.

Finally, Santos spoke. "Get on the bed so we can suck your dick." But Knox didn't move. "Sergeant," Santos finally added in a voice so filthy, Mary's pussy clenched.

The bed gave way under Knox's weight. His head bumped against Mary's toes as he laid on his back and reached for her ankle while Santos rubbed his hands over his skin.

"Come here," Santos ground out, his lips kissing the side of Knox's shaft as he spoke.

Mary knew that command was for her and ecstatically complied, climbing to her knees. Knox touched her ankle lightly before he helped her shift until her knees bracketed his head, lovingly caressing the back of her thighs as she lowered her pussy onto his waiting mouth.

"Yes," she moaned as he teased her with one long, slow, deep swipe of his tongue from her clit to her opening and back again. Her eyes drifted closed in pleasure as Knox tasted

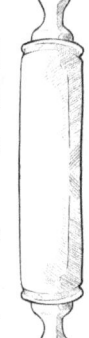

her, covering her clit with his soft lips, and dipped his tongue inside her. She could've stayed in this position forever and a few more days beyond that, but then he groaned against her sex.

She opened her eyes and got a front row seat of Santos's mouth filling with Knox's length. Mary involuntarily ground down onto Knox's lips before lowering herself atop him. She kissed the soft, curly hair below his belly button down toward his groin while Santos bobbed his head slowly, taking more and more of Knox into his mouth.

"Hi," she sighed happily.

Santos pulled back, stroking his hand over Knox's length. "You want to help?"

"Don't ask foolish questions," she said, licking the back of his fingers.

He angled the head of Knox's dick toward Mary's mouth and she sucked it between her lips. He watched her for a few seconds before pushing Knox's legs further apart and bending forward to suck one of his balls into his mouth. They shared a lovely purpose tasting Knox, smiling when he cried out, his ecstasy muffled by Mary's pussy. That sound, deep and desperate, solidified Mary and Santos's partnership; they didn't just want to make Knox come, they wanted him to come so hard and so often he wouldn't doubt how good the three of them fit together.

Santos moved his lips to the base of Knox's dick, licking and sucking on the sides of his shaft. Mary carefully lowered her mouth, taking as much of him as she could. When she needed a break, Santos happily took over, working more and more of Knox's length down his throat.

They had all night, and Mary was determined to make sure they used every minute.

Time was fake and Mary had lost track of it long ago. They'd been fucking for hours and they were exhausted, but they just couldn't stop. Not for long, at least. Sure, they took quick breaks to catch their breaths and reposition. At some point, while Knox had Mary face down, ass up, Santos left the room and came back with bottles of water. Mary downed half a bottle while Santos laid on the bed and she climbed onto his lap. Knox drank the other half of her water before crawling back onto the bed and slipping his dick into Santos's mouth; already moving like a well-oiled machine.

They had to take a little micro nap after that session, but when Mary blinked back into consciousness, Knox and Santos were already awake. She curled up next to them and watched Knox deepthroat Santos until she fell back asleep.

Mary had to be at the bakery no later than six if she wanted enough time to get her prep done before they opened. Sure, maybe she could count on Bria to start without her, but it was their first weekend as a real bakery, far too early to slack off. Knox had a training session with his volunteer firefighters that started at five, so he, too, needed to get some rest. But Santos had Saturdays off and that's probably why he had a battery in his back *all night long*.

And it was contagious.

"You tender?" Knox asked, caressing her hips.

She nodded, slow and tired, as her fingers nudged his head toward her opening so she could lower herself down his length. She let out a relieved sigh because every time was better than the last.

"We can stop," Knox groaned.

"Eventually," Mary gasped, lifting her hips halfway before she bore down again.

There was a small bruise on Knox's chest. Teeth marks. Mary didn't know if that was her bitemark or Santos's, and somehow, that gave her enough lust-filled adrenaline to move her hips faster.

Santos gripped her waist. "Slow down. Wait until I get inside you."

"Oh god," Mary moaned, falling forward.

Knox chuckled softly and wrapped his arms around her back. Santos rubbed lube around Mary's puckered asshole, easing one finger inside her to open her up slowly.

She gasped and let out the loudest moan of the night. "Holy fuck."

Knox kissed her shoulder, but his voice was as impatient as she felt when he spoke. "Quit teasing us," he said.

Santos laughed, not an ounce of exhaustion evident in his voice. "Us?"

"Us," Knox reiterated.

Mary wanted to agree, but she was too tired and too eager; too ready to finally do what they'd all been waiting for.

"You're gonna feel so full," Santos said just as he replaced his finger with the head of his dick.

"You're too big," Mary gasped, nerves catching up to her libido.

"I know, baby. I'll go slow," Santos said, holding still at her opening while Knox rubbed soothing circles across her back, breathing slow and deep with her.

"We won't hurt you," Knox whispered, moving his hand between their bodies to play with her clit until she relaxed.

Santos let Mary lead the way, only pushing further inside her when she circled her hips. They listened to her body, adding more lube the moment Mary seemed uncomfortable, massaging her clit and hips as she opened up. It burned, but it was a good burn she never wanted to stop.

She was too greedy to rob herself of this experience, so she pushed through until Santos's shallow thrusts deepened.

"Fuck. I can feel you," Knox groaned.

Mary shivered at how exposed she felt between them. How safe. "Fuck me," she whined against Knox's shoulder.

"Whatever you want, sweetheart," Santos ground out, pushing deeper on the next thrust.

What she wanted was every long, thick inch of them. What she wanted was the delicious tension in their bodies as Knox and Santos fucked into her carefully, rubbing against one another through the delicate membrane of her perineum. What she wanted was the moment when they found a rhythm and got bold, one pressing inside her as the other exited and then reversed. What she wanted was the moment they stopped being quite as gentle. What she wanted was their loud cries matching her own. What she wanted was one more shared orgasm as they came together before they passed out for good.

And unlike every man she'd ever dated before, Knox and Santos gave her everything and more.

WELCOME TO SEA PORT

TWENTY-TWO

Mary

Thank god downtown Sea Port was the size of a strip mall, or else Mary would've been egregiously late to work because she refused to skip a shower with Knox as they got ready for work while Santos slept.

They promised to keep their hands to themselves and they kept their promise. They didn't say anything about their mouths, so they got a little sidetracked, but early morning orgasms were better than coffee.

She rushed home from Knox's condo to change, pet Cat-leen, refill her food bowl, and give her a small pile of treats as an apology before power walking to Confections. She let herself into the back door exhausted, dehydrated, and sore all over, but it was five minutes after six in the morning, so Mary was counting that as a win.

"You're late!" Bria yelled as soon as Mary stepped into the kitchen. There was a streak of flour on her left cheek and a smug grin on her face.

"I'm the boss," Mary said in a hoarse voice.

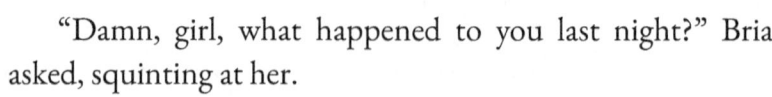

"Damn, girl, what happened to you last night?" Bria asked, squinting at her.

Mary's eyes widened and she turned toward the office. "Nothing," she squeaked out. Her face was hot from memories of everything they'd done last night and everything she wanted to do when she saw them next, but not an ounce of shame.

"I didn't sleep well," Mary said, which was true enough.

"Really? I was so damn tired, I passed out right after dinner. Yesterday was amazing!"

"It was," Mary said, dropping her purse in the office. Bria had turned back to the mixing bowl in front of her while Mary tied her apron behind her back. Mary watched Bria carefully fold chocolate into batter as she walked to the handwashing station. "It was better than I even expected. I guess the adrenaline threw me off and I was up all night." Again, not a complete lie, but definitely not the truth.

Bria nodded sagely. "That makes sense. Although... Never mind."

Mary's heart started racing. She wet her hands and started scrubbing them thoroughly. "What?" she asked, glancing briefly over her shoulder at Bria.

Bria didn't start speaking until Mary's hands were dry. "I was kinda hoping maybe you went out and did something fun to celebrate the opening." Mary was so happy Bria was focused on the batter because her skin was hot. She felt like she was standing in front of a fireplace as Bria inched close to the truth, but then Bria laughed sadly. "But it's Sea Port. There's nothing fun to do here after five."

Mary laughed softly as a bead of sweat fell down her spine.

"You would think with new people in town that y'all would make this place a little more interesting, but you haven't." Bria glared at Mary over her shoulder but then laughed. "I blame Willie. She promised us excitement when she was running for office. And for what? She ran unopposed."

"Maybe the next round of people will be more interesting," Mary said encouragingly.

"Maybe," Bria sighed.

"You wanna make some croissants?" Mary chirped, desperate to change the subject.

Bria groaned, sufficiently distracted. They'd been learning how to make croissants together for weeks. Every batch was better than the last, but the first batch had been atrocious, so their improvement was relative.

"If we must," Bria sighed again.

"We must," Mary said encouragingly. "But after that, we can work on a new icing."

Bria's eyes lit up. "Which one?"

"Ganache?"

"Yes!"

Mary did a little dance before she pulled the fridge open and started pulling sticks of butter out. Bria set the batter aside to rest and grabbed a square sheet pan. Mary dumped the butter on the worktable next to Bria and the brownies she was making.

Bria started preparing the pans but stopped to grin at Mary. "But if you hear anything about a secret underground dance party for Transplants, can you let me know? Just like, slide me an invitation."

Mary laughed. "Underground dance party?"

"Or casino," Bria offered. "I'd say sex club, but I doubt it."

Mary laughed drily, turning away to hide whatever strange look was on her face. "I don't know if Sea Port is the kind of place for a sex club."

"I know," Bria whined. "And the town ordinances won't let anyone open a casino."

"Ah," Mary said, "I see how you ended up at a dance party. What about an underground book club?"

"Have one of those already. They meet on the third Tuesday of every month in the library after they close, but they just read long ass fantasy series and talk about the likelihood of an alien invasion. They're always looking for new members, though."

Mary laughed. "I'll keep that in mind. What about a secret knitting circle?"

Bria cleaned the mixing bowl into the pan and started gently tapping it to get rid of air bubbles. "Got one of those too. Got started during the Korean War, I think. They like to make balaclavas for protestors to hide their identities."

"What?" Mary spun around to stare at Bria, certain she hadn't heard what she thought she had.

Bria, however, was unfazed. "Yeah, my grandma used to be a member. I only know because she babysat me until I was like five and took me to some of their meetings."

"But...how do they get in contact with protestors? 'Cause I know people aren't protesting in Sea Port."

Bria laughed. "Definitely not, and I have no idea." She turned to smile at Mary. "And even if I did, my Nana made me pinky promise not to tell anyone any more than that."

"Are you serious?"

"Very, and I don't cross old people in this town. Nowhere to hide from their wrath. Not even when they die."

Mary opened the oven for Bria to slide the pan inside. Bria grabbed the oven mitts and pulled out a full pan of chocolate muffins.

"So if I get you that invite to the underground dance club, will you invite me to the knitting circle?"

Bria stopped extricating the muffins from the pan to consider. "Depends. Can you knit?"

"A little, but I'm a fast learner."

Bria considered that while arranging the hot muffins on the cooling rack. "I can't say yes for sure, but I'd be willing to make some introductions."

"Deal," Mary cried.

"But if there's a sex club, I'll tell you outright, Nana be damned."

Mary gasped. "I'm gonna tell your mother you said that."

Bria laughed. "She'll understand. Anyway, if there's a sex club, I already know who I'll go to for details on that."

"Who?" Mary gasped.

Bria frowned at her. "Knox and Santos, obviously!"

Mary's mouth fell open. "Because Santos is a cop?" she asked.

"No! Because they're fine. Have you seen them?"

A pit formed in Mary's stomach. "I thought they weren't your type."

"Ew. They're not. But no one who looks as fine as them comes to a place like this and plans to stay single." She

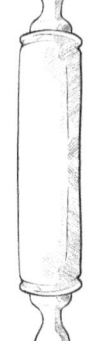

squinted her eyes conspiratorially. "They have to have a plan."

Mary started preparing her butter for lamination, mostly just to do something with her restless hands. "Um, being single is a far cry from starting a sex club," she laughed, sweat forming at the back of her neck.

Bria moved across the kitchen to the dish station with a laugh. "Sure, but Sea Port's in the middle of nowhere and most of the women here are married or over the age of sixty."

"They could be with each other," Mary interjected without thinking as an image of Knox's mouth wrapped around Santos's dick — and then the reverse — flooded her mind. She had to take a deep breath to center herself and get her pussy under control.

Bria sighed. "If that's true, then I feel bad for them. This is such a sad place to be gay." But then she perked up. "Even more reason to start an underground sex and dance club!"

Mary laughed. "So now it's both?"

Bria laughed right along with her. "In my mind, they're entrepreneurs. Also, it's fake and can be anything we want it to be."

"If that's the case, can we also make it a supper club?" Mary laughed and got back to work.

"That's a good idea," Bria cried. "And we can supply the desserts."

"You know, this little illicit business you've created isn't a half-bad idea. I'm glad I hired you."

Bria leaned against the counter and smiled triumphantly. "So can I get a raise?"

"Not that happy. Now, get started on your dough."

Bria wailed playfully but grabbed the canister of flour from the shelf above their workbench.

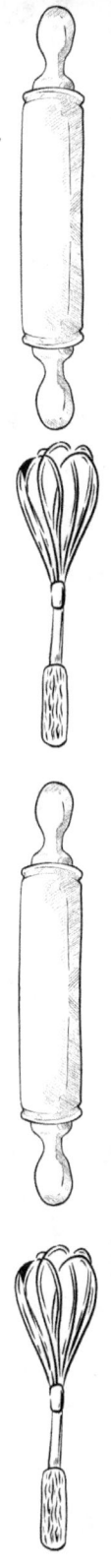

WELCOME TO SEA PORT

TWENTY-THREE

Santos

S antos preferred to plan how he spent his days off so he didn't waste a minute of civilian life.

The original plan for today had been a long run in the park, laundry, cleaning his bathroom, and grocery shopping — normal things. He'd left room for his regular coffee with Knox and maybe a pitstop by the Fullers to talk to them about their stud who kept breaking out of the stable. All normal errands he could run and still have enough time to relax — not that Santos really knew what that was.

But then he woke up mid-morning in Knox's bed, sore and sated and very fucking happy. All his plans went out the window.

He'd never been in Knox's apartment alone and didn't know what to make of the fact that Knox trusted him enough to leave him there without supervision. Or maybe, he worried as he walked naked from the bedroom to the bathroom, he'd thought so little of him. But as soon as he

stepped into the bathroom, those old anxieties melted away when he spotted the fresh toothbrush and towels Knox had left out for him. Santos wasn't sentimental normally, but that small gesture brought a smile to his face as he stepped into the shower.

After he was clean and refreshed, he walked naked around Knox's apartment. He stopped in the kitchen to make a fresh pot of coffee and then scrounged up a quick breakfast, surprisingly and completely at ease in Knox's home. Santos had perfected his one-night stand game while in the Marines, and his only rule was to never let himself get too comfortable. As soon as everyone came, Santos's brain turned to his departure, but he wasn't in any rush to leave Knox's place.

He took his coffee to Knox's bedroom and started stripping the bed. They'd done most of the work for him last night — the blankets were piled on the floor and the sheets were half off the bed — and Santos finished the job, dropping them in the small laundry room next to the kitchen. He had to carefully search Knox's closet for new sheets and blankets without infringing on his friend's privacy, even if he was desperate to be nosey. He remade the bed and straightened the bedroom and the kitchen before he threw on yesterday's clothes and left for home.

He had full plans to change his clothes and get back to his regularly scheduled chores, but as soon as he stepped outside, the air smelled like warm butter and sugar. His dick stirred in his pants and he adjusted his schedule for the day.

Santos stopped by his house just long enough to change into clean clothes and call his mom for their regular check-in before he grabbed his keys and left again. The slow walk downtown took about fifteen minutes and eased the sweet soreness in his muscles — a throbbing reminder of last night.

He walked past Sully's, which was at its mid-morning peak. Bria came barreling out of the front door as he passed.

"You here to arrest me?" She beamed at him.

Santos rolled his eyes. "It's my day off."

She lifted an eyebrow. "And?"

Santos sighed and the front door opened. "Hey, Bri— Oh, what's up, Santos? Missed you this morning."

"It's my day off."

Sully frowned. "When has that ever stopped you?"

He rolled his eyes again.

"Did you want me— something? I mean, did you want something?" Bria said, sounding flustered. Santos stared at the side of her face for a second, but she refused to look in his direction.

"Uh, yeah. Yes. Is there any chance you and Mary can make those almond croissants again?"

"Uh, the ones I dropped off this morning?"

"Yeah. I have one left, people loved them."

Bria bounced on her feet. "Ah, the boss is going to be so happy. I'll tell her and we'll talk, but I think we can make it work."

"Perfect," Sully replied.

And then they just...stared at one another until Santos cleared his throat.

Sully blinked a few times before she turned to him. "Coming in?"

"Not today."

"Oh. Okay. Cool. Um...bye." Sully aimed that last word at Bria before ducking back inside her café, red-faced.

"How's business today?" he asked, really just wanting to ask about Mary.

Bria was still staring at the front of the café, but she licked her lips and turned to him, her face shifting from a soft, happy grin to a sly smile. "Great, actually. No thanks to you."

"What's that supposed to mean?"

"It means you didn't stop by and support us yesterday. Mary is one of you, how could—"

"One of—"

"A Transplant," she said, exasperated. "Y'all need to stick together and support one another."

Santos had to bite back a grin at Bria's words. If she only knew. "I'll remember that."

"Good," she said, brushing past him.

He turned and called out. "Hey, tell Mary I'll be by later."

"We'll see," she said, waving a hand in the air without turning around.

Santos sighed and continued on his way down Main Street, around to the back of the town administrative building. The Sea Port fire department had one fire truck and it was always parked back here. Knox had an office on the third floor, but everyone who needed to know knew he spent most of his day down here in the small workshop full of tools to keep that ancient truck running.

And that's exactly where Santos found him, squinting at a computer, covering his mouth with his left hand to stifle a yawn.

"Either that report's boring," Santos said, leaning against the doorjamb, "or you're still tired from last night."

KNOX

K nox had been glaring at his laptop screen for what felt like hours when Santos interrupted him. He was trying to figure out next month's training schedule with his volunteers, but the problem with an almost all-volunteer force was that everyone had other things to do, and all those other things paid more than the meager monthly stipends a town like Sea Port could afford. Some months their schedules aligned perfectly, but apparently, next month wasn't going to be one of those times.

He was annoyed and exhausted, but Santos looked well-rested and happy. "It can be both," Knox said.

Santos shrugged. "One's definitely more fun than the other."

Knox turned his banker's chair toward the door. It squeaked loudly, like always.

"You gonna oil that?" Santos asked with a smirk.

"I keep forgetting."

"No shit. What are you up to?"

"Training schedule," Knox said, sitting back in his chair. "Same old bullshit."

Santos nodded and his gaze dipped to Knox's lap. Knox

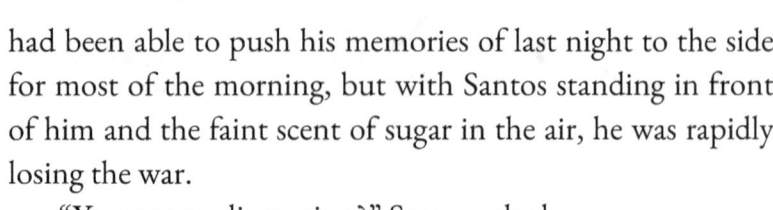

had been able to push his memories of last night to the side for most of the morning, but with Santos standing in front of him and the faint scent of sugar in the air, he was rapidly losing the war.

"You want a distraction?" Santos asked.

He posed that question to Knox at least once a week; usually, it was just an invitation to accompany Santos on his foot patrol. "That question would've been innocent a couple weeks ago," he teased.

Santos smirked, pushed off the wall, and stepped inside Knox's small workroom. "But it's not a few weeks ago," he said as the door slowly closed behind him. "And after last night, I think you know better."

The memories he'd kept to the margins of his brain started bleeding into the center — bright pink as Mary's pussy opened for Santos's dick, the taste of Mary's come when he licked it from the length of Santos's shaft before he plunged back inside her. He'd lived it, he knew every memory was real, but it was all so filthy, he could hardly believe it happened, let alone that it happened to him. All night.

"You sure about that?" Knox asked carefully.

Santos looked like he'd been about to perch on Knox's desk like he always did, but at Knox's question, he redirected his steps. "Pretty damn sure."

As Santos got closer, Knox shifted his feet wider apart. His heart started racing as he looked up at his friend.

"But if I'm wrong," Santos said carefully, "and there's still more for us to work out..." He let that sentence trail off and licked his lips.

"Shouldn't you be two loads of laundry into your day?"

Knox asked. He tried to ask that question in the same teasing tone he normally used, but this office was too small, Santos was too close, and it hadn't been that long since Knox was pumping inside Santos while he ate Mary out.

Sometimes, Santos looked at him like he knew what Knox was thinking, and this was one of those moments. He took a couple steps back and then bent forward, gripping the armrests so their faces were at eye level.

Eventually, Knox thought he might manage to remain calm when he was this close to Santos with years of sexual tension arcing between them, but that day wasn't today. Today he reached for Santos's face, the other man's skin hot under his fingers. He looked into Santos's eyes, surprised at how beautiful they were and how relaxed he was when they touched.

Knox pulled Santos forward, their lips spreading into matching smiles as they kissed. Each kiss was different, and this one was surprising in its tenderness, without any of the hesitation he felt just yesterday. Their mouths opened at the same time and their tongues searched for the other, like keys searching for a matching lock.

Knox was hard in an instant, groaning into Santos's mouth.

"I liked waking up in your bed," Santos mumbled against his lips.

"Fuck," Knox hissed, pushing up from his chair.

Santos grabbed Knox by the waist and pulled him close. They weren't careful with one another this time. Knox's teeth brushed Santos's tongue. Santos's fingers snaked underneath Knox's shirt so he could dig his fingers into his

flesh. They rubbed their bodies together, feeding one another with desperate grunts and eager moans.

Knox backed Santos against the door and moved his hand down Santos's chest to the front of his jeans. They stared at one another as Knox worked the button open and pulled the zipper down. Santos's dick was hard and practically spilled into Knox's palm as soon as he pushed the other man's underwear down.

"So you did want that distraction?" Santos joked.

Knox smiled and Santos licked the seam of his lips.

"Yeah. But not this," Knox whispered before crouching down. Santos groaned loud as fuck when Knox sucked the head of his dick into his mouth.

"Please," Santos begged, but Knox was already licking down his length. But then he stopped, his eyes shifting toward the doorknob. He thought he'd heard something, but—

"Okay, and when your damn barn burns down, don't say shit to me." Knox heard the voice through a vent that led to the corridor around the corner.

"Fuck," Knox hissed as they jumped away from one another. Santos turned away and stuffed his dick back into his jeans. Knox pulled his shirt from his pants to hide his erection before pulling his office door open. He stepped outside into the cool air and took a deep breath just as Old Mr. Brown and Mr. Tynesdale came around the corner.

Santos stepped from Knox's office just as Mr. Brown called out to him. "Billy, there you are. Will you tell this son of a bitch he can't burn his trash in his damn driveway?"

"It's gravel," Mr. Tynesdale said.

Mr. Brown rolled his eyes, but Knox held up his hands.

"I sincerely hope you two didn't stop by here just to pull me into your disagreement about nothing. Again."

Santos chuckled.

"Is arson nothing?" Mr. Brown spat back.

Mr. Tynesdale and Knox sighed.

"It's Saturday. Don't you two got nothing better to do?" Even as Knox asked the question, he realized it was a bad one. Of course, they didn't have anything else to do. This was Sea Port.

"You two been to Confections yet?" Santos asked.

It wasn't her name, but it was a close enough mention of Mary to make Knox's already excited dick throb.

"The hell is that?" Mr. Tynesdale asked.

"New bakery," Knox said.

"Oh yeah!" Mr. Brown cried.

"We're heading there after this," Mr. Tynesdale said.

"Heard she got teacakes."

"I ain't had teacakes since my Aunt Patty died."

"Mmhmm," Mr. Brown nodded.

"How 'bout..." Knox said, turning to his office door. He checked his pants pocket, making sure he had his keys on him, before leaning into his office and turning the lock on the doorknob. "How 'bout we all head on over there instead of talking about...whatever the hell you two are fighting about today?"

The two older men turned to one another in silent deliberation.

"Sounds good to me," Santos said, backing Knox up.

Knox pulled his door closed tight and the men finished their conference. "Alright," Mr. Tynesdale said. "We prob-

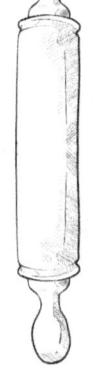

ably should get there before they sell out anyway. Heard the cases was barren yesterday."

"Mmhmm," Mr. Brown hummed.

"Heard that too," Knox said. "After y'all." He gestured for them to take the lead and set the pace, which he always did to the Porties over sixty. Which was most of them.

Santos shifted close and bent down to whisper in his ear. "Maybe Mary can help you finish what you started."

"Fuck," Knox hissed again.

Santos sucked the lobe of Knox's ear into his mouth before laughing and following the older men.

MARY

"Welcome to Confections, I'll be right with you!" Mary called over her shoulder as soon as the bell over the door rang out. The greeting had become a Pavlovian response over the last day and a half, a testament to just how busy they'd been since they opened, but Mary wanted to pound that damn bell into a flat disc.

Coffee and two donuts had gotten her through the morning, but now she was running on nothing but fumes. She couldn't wait to get the hell out of here.

"Take your time."

"We're not in a rush."

Mary's hands froze, her pulse started pounding, and her pussy shivered — a lot to happen to her tired body all at once. But both of those voices had moaned the filthiest things to her less than twelve hours ago.

She turned to look over her shoulder and found them sitting in two of the four chairs in her tiny seating area. The

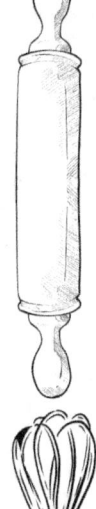

space seemed even smaller filled with their big bodies. She licked her lips, remembering how good it had felt being between them.

They were looking in her direction, but Knox tipped his head to her right. She jumped to find two other men standing in front of her display cases.

"Hey, Bria," Mary called.

The door to the kitchen swung open. "What's up?"

Mary nodded her head. "Can you—"

"Oh, for sure. Oh, Santos is here."

Mary nodded.

"I didn't think he'd show."

Mary nodded again, unable to trust herself enough to ask what she meant.

"Hey, Mr. Brown, Mr. Tynesdale. Y'all heard about our teacakes?" Bria called.

"Why else would we be here?" one of the men called back.

"Our cookies are damn good," Bria said.

"Watch your mouth," they scolded her.

"Sorry," Bria said, surprisingly contrite. But Mary couldn't focus on that transaction.

She finished boxing up the order in front of her and slid it into the fridge they reserved for phone orders once they understood that a number of older women had decided Confections took phone orders. All without consulting with Mary.

She wiped her already-clean hands on her apron as she walked toward the seating area. They stood as she neared, towering over her in a way that triggered a primal sexual response.

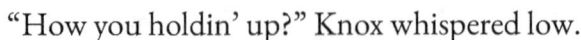

"How you holdin' up?" Knox whispered low.

Her mouth was dry, and when she made eye contact with him, all she could do was sigh.

Santos grunted out a soft laugh. "You eat lunch?" he asked.

Mary was similarly speechless when she looked in his direction. She shook her head.

"You need to eat," Knox said, a note of worry in his voice.

"And so do we," Santos said.

He could've meant a sandwich or something, but he said those four words in the same voice he'd used to talk her through an orgasm or two just last night. Mary knew deep down in her pussy that Santos wasn't talking about eating a bowl of soup.

"Hey, Bria?" Mary called.

"You should get six," Bria said to one of the men before turning to Mary. "What's up?"

"After these two, close up and take an hour for lunch."

Santos cleared his throat.

"Or two," Mary added. "Definitely two hours for lunch."

"You sure?" Bria asked with bunched eyebrows.

"Um, yeah. Yesterday, things slowed down around lunchtime anyway. We can open up for people who want a little snack between lunch and dinner."

"That's smart," one of the men said, nodding in Mary's direction.

"Thanks," Mary trilled.

"Alright." Bria shrugged. "So you still want four teacakes, Mr. Brown?" she asked with a smirk.

The man grumbled at Bria to just give him the half-dozen. Mary smiled, but then she saw Knox heading toward the door in her peripheral vision. Santos's hand nudged at her lower back.

"Let's go to my place this time," she whispered.

"Whatever you want, sweetheart."

And she was certain he meant *whatever*.

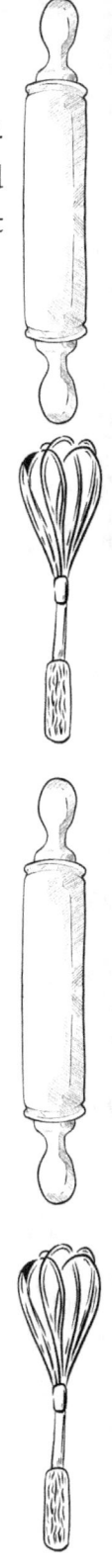

WELCOME TO SEA PORT

TWENTY-FOUR

Mary

By the time Mary led Knox and Santos onto her porch, she felt like she was floating through an alternate universe — you know, an alternate universe where she clocked out of work to get railed — and it was wonderful.

Somewhere in the back of her mind, she worried what her neighbors would think if they spotted her letting not one but two men into her house — and in the middle of the day, no less — but she didn't know any of them yet. She'd be ashamed later, if she had time.

Not now, though.

Her hands were shaking with excitement as she pulled her keys from her purse and unlocked her front door. "Get in. Hurry up," she whispered, trying to usher them inside.

They were crowded onto her small porch, laughing at her, but not moving toward her door either.

"After you, sweetheart," Knox said.

"Seriously?"

"You're in the South now," Santos added. "And he's a Southern gentleman."

Knox leaned against the side of her house with a gorgeous grin on his face.

"Didn't know Southern gentleman were into Eiffel Towers," Mary mumbled.

Knox tipped his head toward her door. "Well, now you do. After you," he said again.

Santos covered his soft laughter with his hand as Mary shivered and led them into her small cottage.

"Take your shoes off, please," she said, toeing off her own sneakers at the door.

While they were bent over their shoes, Cat-leen woke up from her nap on the couch, stretching her little front paws in the air.

"Oh, shit. Are either of you allergic to cats?" she asked quickly, already reaching for Cat-leen.

"No," Knox and Santos muttered at the same time.

Mary loved Cat-leen, but it was only upon adopting her that she discovered just how many people in her life were either allergic to cats or didn't like them. It broke her heart a little to realize she'd never be able to have big dinner parties with her friends, but she had so few friends in her last town that it hadn't mattered. Now, though, it mattered.

Cat-leen hopped on the back of the couch and stared at their guests with blank boredom. Mary moved forward and crouched down. "Cat-leen, these are my friends. They're nice, I promise."

"Well, hey there, Kathleen," Knox said, dropping his boots by the door.

Mary shook her head. "*Cat*-leen," she said.

Both men squinted at her in confusion.

"Cat-leen. I named her after Kathleen Cleaver. But you know, she's a cat."

They lifted their eyebrows and Knox sighed.

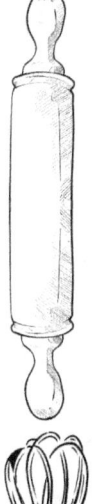

"The weird ones are always hot," Santos said with a slow shake of his head.

Mary stood and pressed a hand to her chest, unable to control the smile on her face. "You think I'm hot."

"And weird," Knox said.

"I'm not focusing on that right now." Mary turned back to her cat. "See?"

The only man in Mary's life — and, by extension, Cat-leen's — was her old vet. The vet in Sea Port was a man as well, but they hadn't met him yet. Either way, Mary wasn't sure how Cat-leen would adjust to strangers, and male ones at that, but she should've known her response would be indifference. Once Cat-leen realized their guests didn't seem to be a danger and Mary didn't have any new toys or treats for her, she stopped caring. She let Mary scratch her head for a few seconds and then crawled along the couch cushions until she jumped onto the window seat she'd claimed as her own.

"Okay," Mary said as Cat-leen settled back into her nap.

"That mean she doesn't approve?" Santos asked. There was a surprising note of worry in his voice.

Mary shrugged. "She doesn't approve of anything but crunchy tuna treats and ice cubes in her water sometimes. Anyway, I only have an hour for lunch."

"Or two," Knox corrected with a smile, offering his hand to her.

261

Their fingers twined together. "You're gonna have to make it worth my while to get that second hour."

Santos's hand nudged the small of her back again. "You know we will."

She believed them, but she kept her mouth shut, excited to make them work for every minute.

KNOX

A small part of Knox's brain had convinced himself that last night would be a one-off. It was his way of keeping his expectations in check; if they only had one night, it was amazing, no regrets.

But here they were in the cold light of midday, undressing for one another in Mary's bedroom with giddy smiles on their faces. Apparently last night wasn't a one-off and they had another hour or two.

Maybe more.

"Did you bring condoms?" Mary asked, pushing her leggings down her thighs. Knox heard her question but it took a second for the words to register because he was watching her breasts and stomach bounce as she got undressed, which was more than a little distracting.

"Huh?" Knox breathed.

"I brought some," Santos said, somehow already down to his underwear. He bent forward and pulled a sleeve of condoms from his pants pocket. "Someone's gotta be prepared."

"I used to be organized and super anal about it," she said and then giggled softly to herself as Santos's knees bumped into the side of her mattress.

"You seem pretty organized," Santos said, dropping the condoms on the bed and reaching for her.

Knox's dick was hard and in the way as he finished undressing as quickly as possible.

"I am," Mary conceded, lifting onto her knees. Her fingers brushed Santos's stomach and moved down to the waist of his underwear. "But it's not as bad as it was. I think Sea Port is teaching me how to loosen up."

Santos smiled against her mouth and kissed her lips softly before charting a path along her cheek. Mary's eyes shifted to Knox. She looked vulnerable and a little scared when their eyes met. "This isn't what I had in mind when I said I wanted better work-life balance, but I like it," she whispered.

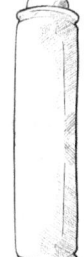

Knox pushed his underwear to the floor. "I like it as well," he sighed.

"Clearly," she gasped, her gaze trained on Knox's erection.

Santos grunted softly. Knox wasn't at all surprised to find that Mary had fished his dick from his underwear and was stroking it slowly. And considering how they spent last night and this morning, he wasn't surprised when she reached for him as well.

"Did you miss me?" she cooed as soon as her palm wrapped around the head of his dick.

"Is that question for me or my dick?" Knox groaned.

Mary smirked. "Are you and your dick in disagreement?" she asked with wide, innocent eyes even as she slid her hand down the underside of his shaft.

"No," Knox grunted.

"Didn't think so," Santos said, lifting his head from Mary's ear. He ripped a condom from the sleeve and passed it to Knox. "You two are lucky I even let you leave this morning."

"You were passed out when we left," Mary said.

Santos pushed her hand out of the way and started rolling the condom down his length. Mary scooted to the center of the bed and Knox got lost again watching their naked bodies twine together.

Santos climbed on the bed, bending over her body, kissing her shin up to her thigh. "Like I said, lucky," he mumbled against her soft stomach and the underside of her breasts before licking the circumference of her areola.

"Did you tell him how I said goodbye this morning?" Mary asked, sighing as Santos licked and kissed her breasts as if they'd been separated for days rather than a few hours.

Santos turned to Knox with lifted eyebrows, his mouth full of her nipple, while Mary started to writhe underneath him.

Knox ripped a condom packet from the others. "Our little baker said goodbye to my dick with her full throat this morning," he said, staring at Santos's tongue teasing Mary's nipple.

Santos's eyes went to Knox's dick and they both watched him roll it down his shaft. "You two could've woken me up for that," he mumbled against her skin.

Knox was worried jealousy might emerge between them,

but it didn't — not last night and not now, apparently, based on the way Santos was trying to inhale Mary's breasts and keep an eye on Knox's dick.

"Our little baker," Santos murmured.

Mary pushed his mouth back onto her nipple.

"Say it again," she moaned contentedly.

Knox climbed onto the bed. "Our little baker," he whispered, smoothing his hand up Santos's spine.

Mary let out another soft moan that Knox remembered from last night. Her legs wrapped around his waist, his hips shifted, and they both moaned as Santos sank inside Mary's pussy.

Her back arched from the bed. "Keep going," she sighed, reaching for Knox's dick. "Give him the dirty details."

Knox bent forward and kissed Mary softly. "Our little baker," he said and kissed her quickly, "pushed me up against the shower wall and got on her knees."

Santos shoved his hands under Mary's ass and pulled back slowly before slamming into her. The bed bumped into the wall with a loud creak.

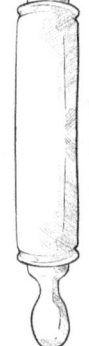

Knox started massaging Mary's right breast while Santos suckled the other, and he looked deep into Mary's eyes while he spoke. "She started sucking me off like we didn't have to get to work. Like she couldn't get enough."

"I couldn't," she groaned, reaching for him. Knox sat on his knees and let her pull the condom from his shaft. She sucked the head of Knox's dick into her mouth just like this morning, giving Santos the show and tell.

Knox moaned and closed his eyes while Mary's mouth explored his shaft and Santos fucked her with increasing speed.

"Just like that?" Santos asked, already panting.

"Yeah," Knox sighed.

Santos lifted to his knees so he could look Knox in the eyes. "Were you going to suck me like this earlier?" he asked, hips slapping against Mary's inner thighs.

"Tell me," she moaned against the head of Knox's dick.

"Fuck," Knox spat just before Santos's lips covered his.

Apparently, that story would have to wait for another day.

"I love the way you kiss," Mary moaned into Knox's mouth.

"Love it enough to give us that second hour?" he asked, licking the next moan from her tongue.

"Definitely."

His fingers were circling her clit while she stroked his length. He wished they didn't have to go back to work at all, but one more hour would hold them over for a little while.

Hopefully.

"I swear this wasn't part of my business plan."

"Sure, sure," Knox teased. "But before you got here, Mrs. Wright had the best dessert in town. I was just planning to seduce her. Ow," he laughed when Mary playfully bit his bottom lip and then kissed away the pain.

"Take it back," she said, moving her hand down his body to cup his balls.

"I'm just kidding," he said, just as she cried out.

"Oh fuck, right there, baby."

Knox smiled against her mouth and moved his fingers down her lips, the tips of his fingers brushing the wet space where Santos's dick pushed inside her. He moved his hand further and when Santos pulled back, Knox wrapped his fist around the base of the other man's dick, squeezing him tight.

Santos buried his face in the curve of Mary's neck while she cried into Knox's mouth. When Santos grunted again, Knox released him and he started fucking Mary harder than ever, gripping her behind her knee to hold her open.

"Fuck," she cried out again. Knox knew she was close. His fingers went back to her clit.

"I'm close," Santos said in a harsh whisper. He let go of Mary's leg and moved over her, shoving her face into the pillow. It muffled her cries but only so much.

Knox leaned back against the headboard and licked Mary's wetness from his fingers. Santos glared at him while his hips slammed into Mary's ass.

"You're next," he ground out.

"I ain't going anywhere," Knox replied, lazily wrapping his fists around Mary's hand so they could stroke his shaft together.

Surprisingly, those four words seemed to get Mary and Santos off at the same time.

They were definitely going to need that second hour.

MARY

Mary needed to get back to the bakery soon, but they all needed to eat. Her refrigerator was a wasteland, but they managed to find enough ingredients for some sandwiches they ate at her small dining room table. They were sated, showered, and smiling their asses off. A very good lunch hour. Or two.

Cat-leen decided to join them for her own midday meal, munching loudly in the corner.

"You really named your cat Cat-leen Cleaver?" Knox asked out of the blue.

"Sure as hell did," Mary chuckled, breaking off a piece of lunch meat and popping it into her mouth.

Santos had finished his sandwich in record time and was currently eating an apple Mary didn't even remember buying. He laughed softly and then leaned to the side to rub Cat-leen's head.

"It's not as strange as it sounds," she said. "I was teaching her memoir when I adopted her. It seemed fitting."

"Do you miss it?" Knox asked.

"Teaching?"

"All of it, I guess. I don't know anything about being a professor, but being a baker seems real different from that. I doubt you have to get up at six in the morning to go teach."

Mary shrugged again. "I'm in the shop by five under normal circumstances," she said with a smile, "but no, I didn't." She shifted her gaze to stare at a notch in the wood paneling around the fridge. "And the answer's no, I don't miss it. I hated it, actually. Every semester, every year. I was so fucking unhappy. And lonely. I don't care if I have to go into the bakery at midnight, it won't ever make me miss the life I left."

She forced a smile onto her face before she could manage to make eye contact with first Knox and then Santos.

Santos held her gaze. "Good," he said, bumping her knee under the table. "'Cause this feels right."

"A man of few words," Knox teased.

"And a big dick," Mary added.

"And don't you forget it," Santos added with a grin.

"You wouldn't let us," Knox sighed. Santos took another bite of the apple with a knowing smile.

Mary relaxed in her seat. "And I agree. This does feel right. What about you two? Do you miss your lives before this?"

"Not at all," Santos laughed. "I was living in my parents' basement, not sure what the fuck I was gonna do as a civilian."

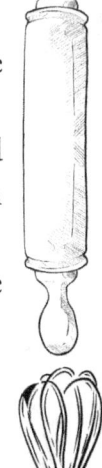

Cat-leen jumped into his lap. "Girl…" Mary warned.

"It's okay," Santos said.

"The fuck it is. She doesn't sit in my lap unless she wants something. I adopted you. I *feed* you." Mary slitted her eyes at her cat.

Cat-leen turned away to face Knox and he laughed before scratching at her head.

Mary sucked her teeth in disgust. "Who are you?"

"A lot like her mama, it seems to me," Knox said.

Santos chuckled softly, but Mary was too shocked and jealous to join him.

"What about you, Sergeant?" Santos asked.

"What about me?"

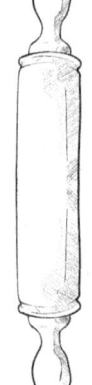

Santos sucked his teeth. "Do you miss your life before this?"

"I don't believe in regret or nostalgia," he said simply. "Never really had much to miss, honestly. And no one to miss me."

Mary tore her eyes from her traitorous cat to look at Knox. He was still focused on Cat-leen, but there was a sadness in his face that made Mary want to crawl into his lap and hug him. But they didn't have time for where that hug might lead, so she put her sandwich down, cleaned her hands on her napkin, and reached over to hold his hand.

When he looked at her, his face was soft, vulnerable, beautiful. "I know I don't know you that well yet."

"Coulda fooled me," Santos laughed softly.

Mary and Knox both smiled but kept eye contact.

"But I can already tell that however long we have together, I'd miss you if we drifted apart."

Knox started to smile, but Santos cut him off. "And it's bullshit if you think no one missed you. I missed you."

Knox's hand gripped hers, and his eyes were a little wet.

Mary lifted his hand to her mouth and kissed his skin. "And that was before he got all in your guts," she whispered.

This time, they all laughed.

Even Cat-leen meowed.

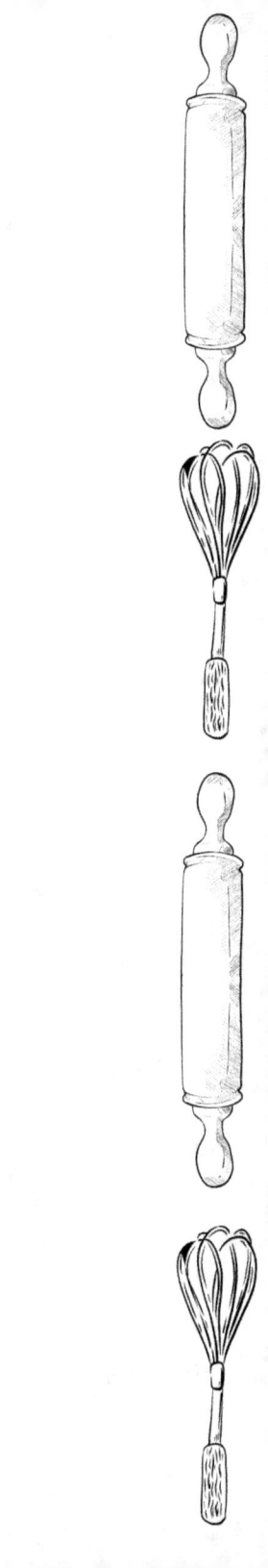

WELCOME TO SEA PORT

TWENTY-FIVE

Mary

Now that her bakery was open and she was getting regular dick, Mary was *really* living her best life. This morning, she woke up in Santos's cottage, sandwiched between his and Knox's bodies. They were all hungover once more from a night full of sex, and since they shared the belief that the best way to cure a hangover was to take one more shot, they snuck in a quickie, relatively speaking, before Santos dropped Mary off at home and went to Knox's — to get a little more sleep, allegedly — before they went to work. Mary, on the other hand, showered, got dressed, had a quick morning chat with Cat-leen about her nights away, and skipped to work.

All before she had a sip of coffee! If this was the kind of schedule her new life was offering, Mary was even more on board than she'd been before.

She let herself into the bakery kitchen and turned on the coffee pot before she did anything else.

Bria wasn't scheduled to arrive until after opening, so

Mary put on a little music and got to the business of making some dough. It was probably just a coincidence, but ever since she, Knox, and Santos got together, Mary felt like every part of her life was flourishing — her bakery seemed more popular every day, she laughed all the time, and even the onerous chore of doughmaking seemed to get easier and more instinctual with every batch. Okay, sure, the critical lack of sleep wasn't great, but besides that, she really couldn't complain.

She already felt comfortable in Sea Port, but over the last couple of weeks, Mary felt like she was well on her way to really making this place her home. She was even starting to learn more about Sea Port history through her chatty elderly customers, which was most of them.

Whoever originally inhabited the region had been terrorized out of the area soon after the American Revolution, like a number of their neighbors. No one Mary had asked yet seemed to know where they went or what happened to them, just that by the time someone sat down to record the town's history, all that early history had been forcefully forgotten. No one even knew the area's original name anymore.

At some point in the mid-seventeenth century, a group of people who were either delirious from hunger or high chose to settle here and try to farm — try being the operative word — as evidenced by the fact that they'd chosen to name it after a port on a sea that didn't exist then or now. The current town limits weren't decided by those first settlers but the ones who came later. Over the last few weeks, Mary had met more than a few elderly people who were the descendants of the first freedpeople to settle in the town after the

Civil War. Lots of Porties called that generation "The Firsts" and referred to it by the nickname those ancestors gave it, Free Port. The town's history started to pick up with the arrival of The Firsts. For a people recently denied every bit of humanity, The Firsts went about claiming their freedom in every way possible, creating a legacy that endured even today. The institutions of their freedom — the schools, churches, and newspaper — persisted even as the country turned back to shit after the brief, albeit bloody, reprieve of Reconstruction through the Second Reconstruction. Even as the rest of the region started to crumble because of economic changes, Sea Port had been built by people as distrustful of white men's institutions as they were invested in their communities. Sea Port wasn't immune to changes beyond its city limits, but The Firsts had trusted in their ability to survive above all else.

Unfortunately, they'd been so focused on building the town, they'd never planned for what would happen if people left — and in the last few decades, people left in droves. Still, the town survived through ingenuity and hard work because that was The Firsts' legacy. Or at least that was the legacy Mayor Waltham highlighted in the town's history on the relocation program's website. Mary already liked Sea Port, but now that her life was going so well, she could absolutely understand why Mayor Waltham was fighting so hard to keep this town alive.

She set her dough aside for the first rise and a quick knock on the back door startled her back into reality. Her heart started racing, thinking Knox or Santos had stopped by to surprise her. She rinsed her hands quickly and dried them on her apron as she walked to the door.

She pushed the heavy door open to the back alley with a big smile on her face. It wasn't Knox, Santos, or Bria, just a copy of the newest edition of the *Sea Port Sentinel* stuffed into the mailbox next to the door. Mary grabbed the paper, thin as ever, since not much happened in Sea Port, and walked back into the kitchen.

Over the years, the *Sentinel* had gradually transitioned to an online periodical, but they still published a monthly edition that mostly operated as the town's calendar. But even in its changing format, the *Sentinel* was still the best source for local news outside of sitting for a spell on old Mrs. Lincoln's front porch.

Everyone read the *Sentinel*, young or old, Black or white, politician, baker, fire chief, or policeman, which meant that by the end of the day, everyone would see the article on the front page. The headline would grab their attention, just like it grabbed hers.

Sordid Confections: Three's Company Downtown

"Holy shit," she breathed, staring at the paper in her hands.

If it had been a book, Mary would've bought it in a heartbeat, but it was her life on the front page of the small-town newspaper. The article was short and anything but sweet. It was, however, full of gossip about her relationship and unnamed testimonials from people who'd seen her around town with both men. Doing what? Mary was still unclear.

Well, she knew what they'd been discreetly doing around town, but the article didn't go into detail, thankfully. They'd held hands and hugged in public. And okay, one time Mary brought Knox donuts because he was still struggling with the volunteer schedule and that had led to sex in his office chair. And yeah, they'd forgotten to lock the door, but it was Santos who found them, and he wouldn't have told the newspaper *that*. Especially since he *had* locked the door before joining them. Mary thought they'd been very discreet! But apparently, a few anonymous Porties thought otherwise.

She read the article three times before a tear fell onto the paper. Her skin was hot with embarrassment and all the happiness she'd brought to work today seemed to seep out through her tear ducts. All the joy she'd been harvesting over the last few weeks was gone.

Mary turned off the ovens and tossed the dough she'd been working on in the fridge. Just before she left, she texted Bria that Confections was closed today, swallowing a fear that it might never open again.

She walked home quickly, glancing furtively around her, wondering which of her neighbors had talked to the newspaper and admonishing herself for being so reckless. She rushed inside her cottage, locked the door, and breathed through a wave of anxiety she hadn't felt in months.

Anxiety had run rampant through Mary's veins on campus. Every time one of her students asked a question she couldn't answer, or one of her colleagues interrupted the faculty meeting to exclaim at her lack of publications. Or when, for no discernible reason, she felt the prickle at the back of her neck as she walked across campus, feeling out of place and alone. Fear and insecurity never let Mary settle into her own skin there, but she had in Sea Port.

She thought she had before today.

Mary scooped Cat-leen into her arms on the way to the bedroom as she had thousands of times in their old life. She crawled into bed and held Cat-leen's warm, furry body against her chest as she fell asleep with tears streaming down her face.

Mary's life was decidedly not fan-fucking-tastic today.

KNOX

Knox had only one plan today and that was to barricade himself in his tiny office and finish off the stack of applications for every federal grant he could find. According to Mayor Waltham, most of Knox's job was to figure out how to fund his tiny little firehouse. Funding, Mayor Waltham said, was more important than putting out fires. Knox disagreed, but he had to work on these grant applications anyway.

His office door opened — no knock, no greeting — which meant it was Santos. "You need better manners," he said without looking up.

"Have you seen the front page of the *Sentinel*?"

Knox huffed out a dry laugh. "Not really a priority today. Or tomorrow. I'll check it out later."

He heard footsteps before the town's newspaper floated onto his desk. "Look now," Santos commanded in a voice he never used with Knox. Not outside of the bedroom, at least.

Knox only did as he said because he was busy. Grant deadlines were approaching and if Knox didn't get these applications finished, Mayor Waltham would be on his ass, and that's why one of the grants on his list was to fund another part-time staff member to help with the clerical load. If Knox never had to come up with another schedule, he'd die a happy man. But first, Knox gave Santos what he wanted and snatched the newspaper from his desk.

He started to lean back in his seat but stopped as his blood ran cold. "Fuck," he hissed.

"Yeah."

"Who the fuck..." Knox breathed, reading the short article a second time, refusing to believe what he was seeing was real.

Santos sat on his desk and shrugged, but his shoulders were tight. His mouth was set in a hard line.

"Where the fuck is this coming from? Had you heard anything?" Knox asked.

Santos shook his head.

"Is there something you're not telling me, Marine?"

Santos's back straightened but he didn't flinch. "I saw it and came straight up here. Calm down." Once he started speaking, Knox noticed the anger bubbling just under the surface, familiar to his own.

"What did you come here for? You should have gone to Mary," Knox said, tossing the newspaper back onto his desk.

"I knew you wouldn't see it. I came here to get you so *we* can go find her together," he said as if it was obvious. Because it was. Because of course, Santos would think of them both at the same time. Knox wasn't an afterthought to him.

He nodded and stood from his chair. "Alright, let's go find her."

"Find who?" Mayor Waltham called from the doorway. She crossed her arms over her chest and frowned at them like petulant schoolchildren.

Willie Waltham was...interesting. She couldn't have been older than thirty, but she had this way of talking to everyone as if she was ancient. When he first met her, Knox had assumed it was because most of the town had known her since she was a baby and watched her grow up. Her father was the previous mayor and had seemed to delight in taking his daughter to work anytime he could. It was hard to take over an authoritative role in that climate, but Willie had managed it deftly. She'd stepped into a role everyone agreed she'd been raised for, even if she took the position earlier than planned, all while grieving her father.

"Mary," Knox said.

"Does this mean you two saw the *Sentinel*?"

Santos sighed loudly.

"Yes," Knox echoed.

She frowned and stepped into the office. "Just so we're clear, I like you both. I like Mary. I like her double chocolate muffins better than any of you, but this town revitalization project is my baby. This town is my baby. Now you might not have realized it, but there are some people here who are less than happy about you Transplants."

"Can't help to keep calling us Transplants," Santos muttered.

Mayor Waltham shifted her eyes in his direction and held his gaze for a second before turning back to Knox. "I brought you three here to make this place better. I don't care what you do in your private life, but if you lose the support of the town, I don't have enough goodwill to save you."

"Is that a threat?" Knox asked in a voice teeming with rage.

Mayor Waltham laughed. Knox and Santos jumped at the loud bark. "Oh Lord, no. I'd never. It is a warning, though. Small town politics are a bitch. The City Council *will* call for a meeting about this. I can't stop them."

"You sure?" Santos asked.

"Very," she replied. "You'll have a chance to defend yourselves. Don't waste it. Good luck," she said, walking from the room.

Santos waited for her footsteps to fade. "What the fuck was that?"

Knox shook his head. "We'll figure it out later. Let's go."

WELCOME TO SEA PORT

TWENTY-SIX

Mary

"So what's the closest airport?" Keisha asked, the sound of her long acrylic nails tapping on her keyboard coming in loud and clear through Mary's cellphone speaker.

Mary was stirring cookie batter while Cat-leen cleaned herself on a dining room chair, watching over her after this morning's emotional naptime.

"Keisha, I don't need you to come down here and defend me," Mary said because it was what she knew she should say. But truth be told, having her best friend save her sounded amazing.

"Yes, you do. You should've gone to whoever's publishing that pamphlet of a newspaper and beat they ass," Keisha said.

"Alright, Killa," Leah whispered.

"Also, girl, if your shy, timid ass is out here getting it in with the cop and the firefighter, there must be something freaky in the water down there. And I am *parched*."

Leah laughed loudly.

Mary couldn't pluck up enough lightness in her chest to laugh, but she did smile.

Dominique exhaled in loud annoyance. "Can you take this seriously?" she scolded them.

"Oh, she's serious. Girl ain't had sex in like six months," Leah replied.

"Do you need to tell all my business?" Keisha said, loudly sucking her teeth.

"Let's stay on track and put together a plan for Mary's freaky ass," Leah said.

"Et tu, Leah?" Mary breathed.

"Et me," Leah replied around a laugh. "'Cause honestly, Keisha is right—"

"Thank you!" Keisha yelled.

"But we'll talk about you getting your groove... I can't even say *back* 'cause your sex life was worth less than Keisha's before this. But we'll talk about that later. For now, let's strategize."

"Right, thank you," Dom said. "We need to get you out of there as fast as we can. That's the most important thing."

"Is it?" Leah asked.

Mary had expected that response from Dom. Once she woke up from her nap and released Cat-leen from her death grip, she sent the SOS text message to the group chat and it made her feel better instantly.

"I'm staying right where I am," Mary said, feeling confident in that sentence now that she'd cried her eyes out and slept.

"You can't be serious," Dom said.

"I can. I am. I like it here. My bakery is doing so well.

Cat-leen has a great view of a bird's nest in a tree in our front yard. I've been getting my back blown out every night for a month."

"Goddamn," Keisha whispered.

"I'm happier here. Like I've never been happier than I have been here."

"Shit, I would be too," Leah breathed.

"But Mary—" Dom started.

"No, Dom," Mary said. "I love you so much, but I don't want to go back to academia. And I certainly don't want to leave Sea Port. Not even now. I needed to vent to my friends, not get a map to freedom." She felt sure when she started speaking, but every word made her feel stronger in her conviction. She'd freaked out this morning, but by the time she was done, Mary felt almost as light as she had when she woke up in Santos's bed.

There was a knock on her door, and Cat-leen interrupted her bath time to run toward the sound. Mary knew who was on the other side of the door by the giddy fluttering in her stomach.

"Hold on, y'all," she said.

"Ooh, now who is that?" Keisha asked.

Santos and Knox were crowded on her porch. Seeing them instantly brought a smile to her face.

"You okay?" Knox asked, his adorable face bunched in worry.

"I'm fine," she said, stepping back to let them inside.

"Fine?" Knox asked, toeing off his boots.

"Yeah, fine. I mean, I did cry this morning, but—" She couldn't finish that sentence because Knox pulled her into a hug.

Mary rubbed her cheek against his chest and wrapped her arms around his waist.

Santos massaged her shoulders and kissed along her hairline. She was considering slipping her hands underneath Knox's shirt when the sound of her friends' laughter interrupted their quiet.

"Oh shit, hold on." She had to squeeze her way out of the crush of their bodies to rush back to the kitchen.

"Who's that?" Knox called.

"Who's that?" Leah yelled back.

"I gotta go," Mary said.

"Is that them?" Keisha yelled just as Mary pressed the button to take her loud ass friends off speaker.

"Yes," she whispered. "And their names are Santos and Knox."

"Oh, yeah, I know they fine," Leah replied.

"Forget fine, let's talk about the sex," Keisha said.

"Let's not," Mary hissed.

"Who are you talking to?" Knox asked.

He and Santos stood shoulder-to-shoulder, filling the space between her fridge and the counter.

Mary tried to shove her lust back down, but it was very hard when they were so fine, so close, and before this shitty day had started, she'd sat on both of their faces.

"My best friends," she replied, licking her dry lips.

"Put them on the phone!" Dominique squealed.

"Nope. Definitely not. We're supposed to be strategizing," Mary replied.

"Strategizing about what?" Santos asked, grabbing her around the waist and pulling her between them again.

Mary exhaled softly without thinking.

"And that, ladies and ladies, is what a well-fucked woman sounds like," Leah said as Keisha howled from far away as if she'd dropped her phone.

Mary shook her head and gave up fighting the inevitable. She pressed the speaker button and leaned her cheek onto Santos's chest.

Her kitchen filled with the cacophony of Keisha's laughter, Leah's chuckles, and even Dom's frustrated sigh. Mary used her thumb to pull up her favorite picture of the four of them and started pointing each of them out so Santos and Knox could put faces and names to their voices.

"That's Leah, Keish—"

"Do either of you have brothers?" Keisha interrupted.

"Jesus," Mary sighed. "And that's Dom," she said, pointing to Dom's face.

"Wait," Keisha said, "are you showing them that picture of us at SeaWorld?"

"Yep."

Leah groaned. "I hate that picture."

"You look great in that picture," Keisha said. "Now, Dom..."

"Shut it, Keish," Dom said, speaking for the first time in a few minutes.

"That's not fair," Keisha whined. "They can see us, but we can't see them. Let's FaceTime y'all."

"No!" Leah and Dom yelled at the same time.

"Girl, I just woke up," Leah sighed.

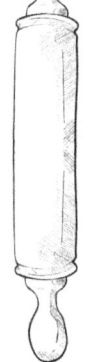

"Don't listen to them, Mary," Keisha said. "Do it."

Mary was about to respond when Knox pulled the phone from her hand and leaned into her back. He took a photo of them, and Mary smiled at their first picture

together. Knox handed the phone back and Mary lifted her chin for a kiss.

They moved into the living room and sat on the couch with Mary draped between them. She heard as soon as her friends got the picture.

"Oh my god, why are you three so cute?" Leah exclaimed.

"Are you shitting me?" Keisha yelled.

Dom had gone silent again. Mary started to worry until she heard her curse softly.

"Okay, the closest airport is...one I've never heard of," Dominique said.

"Oh, now you wanna get in on the girls trip?" Keisha cackled.

"I'm just looking. But whatever's in the water down there... I need it."

"Thank you!" Keisha yelled, vindicated.

Mary and all her friends laughed.

Santos and Knox gave her quizzical looks. Mary muted the call. "They think you're both fine as hell. We should tell the Mayor to put pictures of y'all on the website."

"You really are fine, aren't you?" Knox asked.

She snuggled against their bodies. "Now that you two are here, I'm great."

The sun set sometime after Mary's second orgasm and then she stopped keeping count. Her bedroom windows were fogged with steam, her bed was an absolute mess of sheets and their limbs, and there was a distinct ache building in her back, but she wasn't ready to stop yet.

Thankfully, Knox and Santos were on the same page.

She moaned.

Knox shifted next to her. He was rolling one nipple then the other between his thumb and forefinger. Sometimes he leaned forward to lick each one, but only for a second. For his part, Santos was slowly pumping one finger inside her while licking at her clit. None of it was enough to get her off because they didn't want Mary to come yet.

Not until they were good and ready. Never mind that *she* was well past good and ready and had been for a while.

Santos pushed a second finger inside her and Knox lowered his mouth to her breasts, but as soon as she started shivering, their mouths stilled, frustrating her again.

"Fuck you," she whined once the urge to come passed again.

"You're doin' that already." Knox breathed the words into the space between her breasts. He kissed his way up her chest, kissed her ear, and ran his tongue over her earlobe. "And you love it." That last word fell apart on a groan just as Santos's lips disappeared from her clit.

She looked down her body to find Santos sucking Knox's dick while his fingers started moving inside her again. "Oh my god," she groaned and fell back on the bed.

Once they'd gotten off the phone with her friends and she'd been filled in on Mayor Waltham's warning, sex had made the most sense as their next step. Their days had been

289

derailed already, what was the point of going back to work or stewing in their anxiety? Especially not when Santos really wanted to use his mouth to get them off before putting the head of Knox's dick at her opening, sucking at their joining while he pushed inside her.

Stress relief.

They started and couldn't find the will to stop. The only thing likely to get them out of bed was running out of condoms or whenever Cat-leen started whining for her pre-bedtime treats.

Until then, they planned to fuck and plot their defense between orgasms.

Knox started to slide inside her as Santos kissed his way up her lips to her clit, over her stomach, and up to her breasts. He stayed there, kissing and sucking at her nipples until Mary got impatient.

"Stop teasing me. You promised," she whined. Knox laughed into the crook of her neck as he moved slowly inside her from behind.

"We don't have anything to lose," Santos said, picking up the thread of their conversation from the last position.

Mary tried to roll her eyes, but she was quickly losing control of herself as yet another orgasm came rushing on.

"I have a lot to lose, actually. They could revoke my preferential loan," she said.

Knox's hips slowed. "How?"

"Morality clause," Mary panted. Those two words took a lot out of her.

Santos's dick bumped her clit, and she groaned. "Who still uses morality clauses?"

"A small Southern town in the middle of nowhere that

no one can find on a map," Mary replied automatically as the head of his dick moved through her folds.

Knox grunted, then the pressure in Mary's sex started to build as Knox pulled back and made room for Santos in her pussy.

"Oh god," she groaned as her eyelids fluttered closed.

"Tight," Santos grunted.

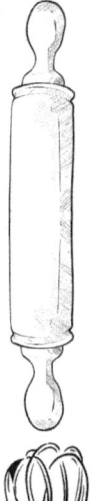

He pulled back and Knox pressed inside her, grinding against her before switching with Santos, back and forth, in and out. And then they pushed into her together. And deeper.

Mary felt like she was floating in the clouds.

"We could stop seeing each other," Knox said, and they all froze.

It was just a suggestion, but it made Mary feel like her heart was breaking. They were filling her pussy to the brink, but the thought of them breaking up made her want to cry.

"No fucking thank you," she moaned.

Santos laughed and started pumping again.

"Okay," Knox moaned, and that was the end of that.

In fact, that was the end of all their plotting for the moment. Whatever happened to one of them would just have to happen to all three.

WELCOME TO SEA PORT

TWENTY-SEVEN
Mary

Mary was trying to keep her hands and brain busy in the bakery, so she was making teacakes. She knew this recipe like the back of her hand; it was the first her grandfather ever taught her.

She'd gotten her love of baking from him. In the photo albums at her parents' house, there were dozens of pictures of her standing on a chair in the kitchen, helping him make these cookies. Whenever Mary was stressed or sad, her grandfather would show up at her parents' house, set her on a chair, and they'd make her favorite treats. Even when his arthritis made it difficult to hold his wooden spoon, making these cookies was how he showed his love. Now that he was gone, Mary made these cookies when she wanted to center herself in a happy memory.

She'd been making teacakes the day she was accepted into the Sea Port Relocation program.

Mary had been attached at either Santos or Knox's hips

— if not both — ever since the *Sentinel* had exposed their relationship. They'd been together when the City Council officially called a meeting to discuss the "unseemly" behavior of some in the Transplant community. Mary thought that was a bit judgmental, but she kept her mouth shut.

Even though most administrative things in Sea Port moved at the speed of cold molasses, the meeting was called for, scheduled, and here within days. Today, in fact, was the day.

"You're stressing," Bria said.

"Duh," Mary replied.

"Everything's going to be fine," Bria said, pulling two more trays of chocolate chip cookies from the oven.

"You don't know that."

Bria laughed. "Yeah, I do. This is the second batch of cookies I've made today. These aren't even for the cases."

"They're not?" Mary asked.

Bria shook her head. "These are for the elementary school. The kids have a spelling bee today and these are their treats."

"Aw, that's so cute," Mary said.

"No, it's a mercy. Before you got here, Mrs. Ball used to make the cookies. I think the kids used to bomb their words just to get out of eating them."

"Damn," Mary said, unable to stop the eruption of giggles.

"Exactly. They had to tell the kids we were making their cookies when they passed out the list of words to study."

Mary pressed her eyes against the sleeve of her shirt to blot the tears.

"Lord, not you crying!"

"I'm feeling emotional, okay?" Mary cried.

"Whatever. All I know is you better not be pregnant. I'm not ready to become assistant manager. You can't afford me yet."

Mary glared at her and Bria beamed back.

"Thanks for your support," Mary ground out.

"Oh, anytime! Besides, now that I know you're with Santos and Knox, I know my invitation to that underground dance club is a lock."

"Oh my god," Mary laughed.

Bria finished transferring one tray of cookies onto a cooling rack and started on the other. "Is it weird?"

"Is what weird?"

"Being with two people instead of one?"

Mary dumped the teacake batter onto plastic wrap and scraped the mixing bowl with her spatula. Bria wasn't the first person to ask her that question, but her answer was the same.

Mary had been single for so long that she couldn't remember what it was like to date anymore. What was weird when there was nothing of consequence to compare it to? Besides, no matter who she'd dated before, everyone came up lacking when compared to Santos and Knox.

There was so much to love about being with Knox *and* Santos. There was always someone around to taste her recipes. Knox had a readymade and eager audience for his endless stories. And because they liked him a lot, they made  sure to laugh at his jokes, even if they were terrible. In fact, Mary was starting to realize that they didn't just like each other, they loved each other, so laughing at Knox's jokes was becoming as easy as breathing. And once he'd told them about his traumatic childhood, Mary and Santos happily teamed up to make him smile and laugh and come. Even Santos, who seemed to need less reassurance in general, blossomed when they were alone together, smiling more, laughing more, even talking more.

Mary was happy with Knox and Santos; what could be weird about that? "Being with them is the happiest I've ever been," Mary said as she wrapped the thick batter into a roll, sealed the edges, and tossed it into the fridge.

The bell over the front door clanged, and Mary's heart started racing.

"I got it," Bria said.

"No, it's okay." Mary took a deep breath and walked into the storefront with Bria hot on her heels. "I said I got it."

"I know. I'm just here," Bria said. "Hey, Mrs. Gladstone," she called.

Mary's heart was pounding against her chest. She didn't know this woman by sight, but she recognized the name of the city clerk.

Mrs. Gladstone was a born and raised Portie, great granddaughter of two Firsts, and had held the same position for somewhere between forty and one hundred years — town gossip was inconclusive. She pursed her lips at Bria before turning her attention to Mary. "It's time," she said ominously.

Sweat collected at the small of Mary's back and above her upper lip. "Okay. Um... I'll be back," Mary said to Bria. "Soon? Sometime."

Bria nodded. "I'm gonna pack those cookies up when they're cooled, close down, and take them to the school."

"Okay. Yeah, that's good."

"And then I'll be by the courthouse."

"No, you don't—"

"Yeah, I do. I really want this job...and the underground dance club." She whispered the last half of that sentence.

"The what?" Mrs. Gladstone called.

"Nothing," Bria said, pushing Mary toward the door. Mary rolled her eyes and started to untie her apron, tossing it next to the cash register.

"Oh, wait," Bria called, heading back to the kitchen. She came rushing around the counter with a basket in her hands.

"I almost forgot," Mary laughed.

"What's that?" Mrs. Gladstone asked.

Mary flipped the tea towel to the side to show the assorted individually wrapped muffins. "Would you like one?"

Mrs. Gladstone shook her head, but her eyes were on the basket. She licked her lips, and Mary held her breath.

"Are you sure? Our dark chocolate muffins have a little sprinkle of flaky salt on top. They're to die for," Bria said, reaching into the basket to nudge one.

Mrs. Gladstone put up a serious internal battle, but in the end, no one could resist Mary's muffins. She snatched one from the basket as if they were dangerous and then turned and rushed outside.

Mary smiled at Bria, feeling for the first time in days as if maybe, just maybe, they had a chance.

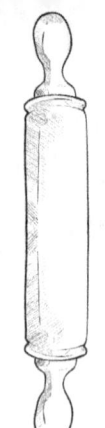

SANTOS

Santos was grumpy.

He had better things to do than sit in the City Council meeting. Mayor Waltham forced him to attend the meeting once a quarter, and it was always a waste of time. This one was even more of a waste of time than usual.

"Stop glaring," Knox said.

"I'm not glaring."

Knox turned to him, a wry grin on his face. "And my name's Boo Boo the Fool."

Santos laughed silently. "I'll try."

Knox laughed a little quieter than normal. "Guess that's better than nothing. Ooh, she's got that damn basket."

They both turned to look behind them at the front of the courtroom. The entire room turned toward her at the same time. Santos could read the nerves on her face, but she hid it well. And fuck if she wasn't beautiful. She was wearing a cute little lemon printed dress that showed off so much cleavage and thigh and most of her arms that Santos had to shift in his seat to relieve the pressure on his dick. Mary had an iron grip on her basket, and instead of walking quickly toward them, she snatched the towel off and started handing out muffins to anyone within arm's reach.

They'd decided on muffins together, a quick way to remind everyone that their relationship was sweet — techni-

cally. But each hand that reached into that basket made Santos frown harder.

"Damn, we shoulda met her at the door and grabbed our muffins first," Knox whispered.

Santos nodded quietly, glaring at Mr. Brown as he grabbed what looked like a blueberry muffin. Those were Santos's favorite.

Once Mary was close, Knox stood, tapping Santos's shoulder. He stood slowly and glared as Old Mrs. Lincoln's hands wrapped around an orange muffin.

"Hi," Mary said, joining them at the little table where the City Council president told them to sit. As if they were on trial.

"You alright?" Knox asked.

Her smile wobbled, but she nodded. "I think so." She reached into the towel and took out two muffins — dark chocolate for Knox, blueberry for Santos. "Here, I pulled these out for you two on the way over." She dropped the muffins into their palms.

He already loved Knox. Santos had loved him since he was eighteen. But this was the moment he realized that he loved Mary too. "I'm gonna make sure neither of you leaves the bed tomorrow," he whispered, rough and low.

Mary's face lit up. "Oh, so like every other Wednesday. Perfect."

Knox laughed, already ripping the plastic open. Santos pulled out her chair, and she sat next to them.

They jumped as the City Council President, Mr. James, dropped his briefcase onto the raised table at the head of the room.

He fixed his eyes on their table, glaring at them with an ornery scowl on his reddened face.

"Well, at least that mystery's been solved," she muttered. They'd been wondering who'd caused all this mess. He didn't know when they were going to vote on City Council positions, but Santos knew who wouldn't be getting his vote. He pulled open the plastic wrapping and took a vicious bite of his muffin.

Mr. James's eyes widened and he took his seat.

Technically, this was not a trial because they hadn't done anything wrong. But since Mary was the recipient of a preferential small business loan and reduced rent on her storefront for one year, with the option to extend her lowered interest rate for another year so long as her business was in good standing, the strings attached to Mary's fresh start were significant. Clearly, someone thought she was the weak link in their relationship and had made the decision to pick on her.

Santos was prepared to make them regret that decision.

Mayor Waltham strolled into the room with a bright smile on her face. She took the seat next to Mr. James and banged the gavel on the table three times — Mary jumped each time — officially starting the meeting.

"Well, well, well, this is the best attended Council meeting we've had in years." The crowd behind them laughed. "Everyone knows why we're here. A complaint has been lodged against Mary Woods for potentially violating the morality clause of her loan. Before we get started, I want to remind everyone that the Sea Port Revitalization Project aims to bring the best, brightest, and bubbliest to our town."

"How'd Santos get in, then?" Mary teased in a low whisper.

They laughed under their breaths until Mayor Waltham glanced in their direction.

"This meeting, however, is our chance to discuss that morality clause and Ms. Woods's alleged violation, to decide whether it serves the best interests of our town." She spoke in a grave tone but the smile never left her face. Santos generally like Mayor Waltham, but he gained a new respect for her in that moment.

"Now, let's get started. Mr. James, please, present your case."

KNOX

Knox and Santos didn't have to be here, they wanted to. Knox's job was to be quiet and smile unless asked a direct question, but this man was testing his fucking nerves.

"I mean, what kind of salacious element have we invited into our midst? Is this the kind of riffraff we want to repopulate Sea Port? The answer is no, good Porties," Mr. James said, turning to address the audience. Someone clapped once, but when they realized no one was eager to join them, they stopped. "No," Mr. James continued loudly, his forehead sweaty with exertion.

The man had been talking for nearly five minutes, and Knox was more irritated at every thirty-second interval. Santos spread his legs and pressed his left thigh into Knox's. His knee was jumping in barely suppressed anger. They looked at one another from the corner of their eyes.

"Who's glaring now?" Santos teased under his breath.

Knox smiled and rolled his eyes, but then Mr. James raised his voice again.

"Sea Port was a wonderful little town that my great-great-grandparents helped found after Emancipation. I have lived here all my life, and this place means something to me. It means everything to me, as I'm sure it means to y'all. So hear me when I say that I would rather see this town disappear into obscurity then hand it over to some Northern degenerates."

Santos had to grip Knox's thigh to keep him in his seat.

"Calm down," Mary whispered.

"I wanna calm my fist in that man's face."

Mary reached across Santos, offering Knox the bribe she'd set to the side. "Wanna try the new cranberry lemon muffin?"

Santos snatched the muffin from her hand. "He'll be alright," he said, tearing the wrapping open.

"You son of a bitch," Knox hissed.

Santos grinned around a bite of the muffin before offering the other half to Knox. He rolled his eyes but took it and popped it into his mouth.

"Thanks, sweetheart," he said.

"You're welcome," she beamed. "Nice to see you two eating my muffins with the same energy you eat my—"

Mayor Waltham banged the gavel again, and they all jumped this time.

Mr. James was back in his seat. His face was shiny with sweat accumulated over his impassioned speech. He dabbed at his brow with a cloth kerchief and nodded at the enthusiastic applause from a thankfully small portion of the audience.

Mayor Waltham cleared her throat and turned to Mary. "Your response, Ms. Woods."

Mary swallowed loudly, turning to them with a smile on her face before she stood. She cleared her throat before turning away from the Council toward the crowd. "Hi," she squeaked and then cleared her throat again. "Um, so... I know some of you, but I realize that most of you don't really have a clue about who I am. So, I'd like to tell you a bit about myself."

She took a breath here and licked her lips. Santos moved until his knee bumped into her leg, resting there for moral support.

"I moved to Sea Port because I needed a fresh start," Mary continued in a stronger voice. "I wanted to start over from scratch. I hadn't realized how sad and lonely and unfulfilled I was until I came here."

Knox saw Mayor Waltham move her hand to hide her smile and the stress he'd been feeling started to melt away. For the rest of Mary's speech, Knox watched her win the Council over, one sentence at a time.

"I realize that this is a small community, unused to change," Mary finished, "but you *have* changed." She turned her head to address Mr. James. "One of the things that made me happy about settling here was hearing how protective the

town had been of you and your husband, Mr. James. Any town, of whatever size and in whatever part of the country, that would fight *for* the rights of its gay citizens was a town where I knew I wanted to live. So, you might be able to imagine how much it pains me that you, of all people, would be leading the town mob against me and the men I love."

Mayor Waltham glanced at Knox and Santos, not bothering to hide her smile. It was clear by the look on her face that she guessed they'd prepared for this together.

"All I want is to live in Sea Port. I want to love in Sea Port. And I want to help this little town bloom," Mary said as the crowd erupted in applause.

She sat, wiping at her hairline and fanning her face. Knox threw his arm over Santos's shoulder and squeezed Mary's shoulder at the same time.

The Mayor let the applause continue for a few seconds before banging her gavel on the table to restore order.

It was standard for the City Council to retire for a few minutes to consider the testimony placed before them, but Mayor Waltham bucked that tradition like so many others since she took office. She stood from her seat and smiled at the room.

"I think everyone here joins our dear Mr. James in his love for Sea Port. From one descendant of a First to another," she added in a soft show of dominance, "I know that this town has a legacy we all cherish and want to protect."

She paused to let her words sink in before she continued. "But I don't want any of us to get into the habit of judging one another and calling it preservation. I'm ecstatic to hear that Ms. Woods loves Sea Port enough to learn our history. We can only hope that all our new neighbors feel the same.

This meeting reminds me of sitting in the audience just behind where Ms. Woods is standing, behind you at the time," she said to Mr. James, "as my father gave an impassioned speech in support of gay marriage. Of *your* marriage to Brian."

Knox didn't take any solace in Mr. James's chastened look, but he did decide to give him the tiniest bit of slack. He still wasn't going to vote for him in the next election, though.

"When the town elected me mayor, I promised you all that I would make Sea Port's rebirth my highest priority. And I am. That is why it's my pleasure to affirm that Ms. Woods has not violated the morality clause of her loan. And even if she has, it's written so poorly that it could open the town up to a lawsuit we can't afford. Tomorrow, I'll be contacting our lead counsel and the bank to remove this section from our preferential loan contracts. I also preemptively find, just in case someone is bored, that Officer Santos and Chief Knox are not in violation of the city's morality clause. We've seen far worse.

"And even though Mr. James has unfortunately shown his gender bias by *only* bringing Ms. Woods to the Council for complaint, as if men cannot violate the town's moral strictures, I acknowledge that this...unique relationship is not an aberration. But in our small Southern town founded on love, I decree that the love between the baker, the police officer, and the fire chief is not now, nor will it ever be deemed immoral so long as I am Mayor."

"Can she do that?" someone whispered.

"I can and I am. My mother has also asked that I make a formal request for cheesecake bites on the Confections

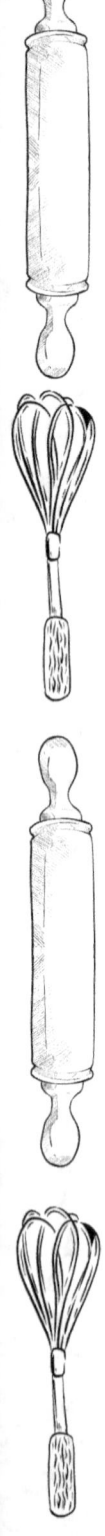

menu." She then banged her gavel, grabbed her notebook, and strutted from the room without another word.

And that was that, apparently.

Mary turned to them with a confused smile on her face. "Is that it?"

Knox sighed happily. "That's it."

The confusion shifted Mary's features for a while and then she shrugged. "This place is weird as hell. I think we're going to be very happy here."

For the first time ever, Santos's laugh was louder than all the others. And this was the moment Knox realized that this was his endgame. Santos and Mary were his home.

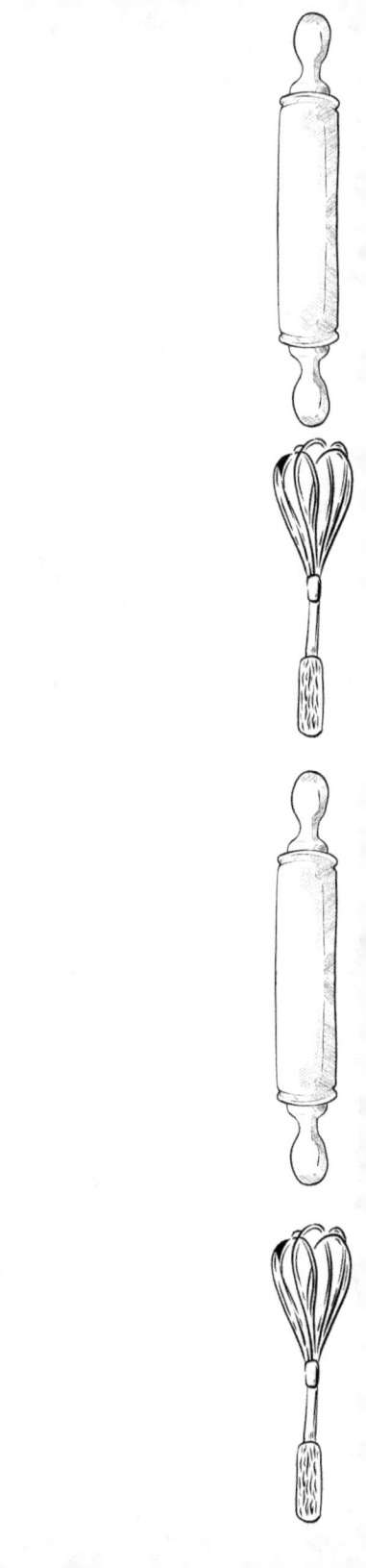

WELCOME TO SEA PORT

Epilogue

MARY

Three months later...

The best thing about living in a small town was that life just...moved on. One day Mary was sort of on trial for being in a polyamorous relationship and the next day, a couple of wild horses broke into the Waltham farm and half the town had bets on how many foals to expect.

Mary had been worried people in the town might see her differently, and they did, but their changed perceptions were more affected by her new donut flavors than the fact that she'd moved in with Santos and Knox.

In the past three months, Confections by Mary had gone from fledgling new bakery to small-town juggernaut. The second phase of Leah's business plan had set aside a bit of development money for Mary to experiment with new recipes, consider an online store for the masses outside of Sea Port, and explore a catering venture in a few years. But in just about four months, the catering business had developed

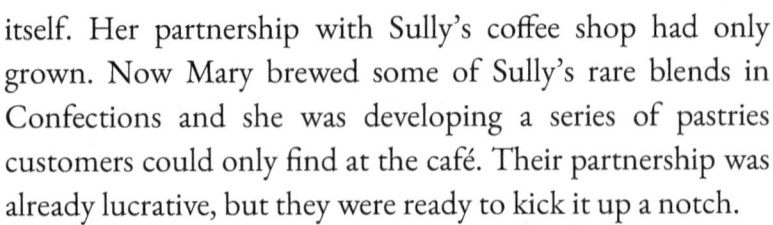

itself. Her partnership with Sully's coffee shop had only grown. Now Mary brewed some of Sully's rare blends in Confections and she was developing a series of pastries customers could only find at the café. Their partnership was already lucrative, but they were ready to kick it up a notch.

Confections had also taken over the Sunnyside's dessert menu. Mrs. Wright's arthritis was starting to worsen and she'd been relieved to hand over the responsibility of making the diner's pies to someone else. And based on Mr. Wright's new order for two more of each pie, she thought they were moving in the right direction. Bria was spearheading the development of Italian-inspired desserts for La Bella Rosa. In less than half a year, Confections had become the center of all Sea Port's baked goods, and Mary was ecstatic.

"If there's a Sea Port occasion, let Confections make your sweet crescendo," she whispered. "Sweet end. Sweet farewell?" She shook her head as she scribbled that tagline down. She could workshop the exact wording with Bria later.

Confections's unexpected windfall also meant that Mary could officially hire Bria full-time, plus a new part-time assistant.

Life was so good, even Mary's mother had stopped crying when they talked on the phone. She was still judging her, but she was doing so without the tears, and that was a marked improvement. Leaving academia hadn't just been a good decision, it had been the best decision of Mary's life. Professionally and certainly personally.

"Are the brownies done yet?" Knox asked, walking into the kitchen.

Their new house was just on the outskirts of town,

where they were surrounded by nothing but abandoned houses and empty fields. They'd wanted a place where they wouldn't disturb anyone with all their noise and they'd found it.

"Ten more minutes," she said. "But I saved the bowl if you want to eat some batter?"

Knox rolled his eyes. "Why even ask me that when you know the answer?"

Mary stood from the dining room table and pulled the mixing bowl from the fridge. She dipped her middle finger in the remnants along the edge and brought it to Knox's lips.

Her nipples hardened at his tongue gliding over her finger. When it was clean, she scooped a little more from the bowl and offered it to him again. Knox smiled and closed his lips around her finger, sucking again. They could do this all night.

Knox wrapped his arms around her waist and pulled her close. He was hard. He was always hard. And she was always wet. And Santos...

Santos called their names as he opened the front door. "I'm home!" he yelled. If she wasn't mistaken, Knox's dick jumped in his pants.

Mary set the mixing bowl aside. "We're in the kitchen!"

Knox started licking down the side of her hand while she rubbed herself against his bulge. They listened to Santos's regular routine, waiting patiently, hornily for him to join them. He took off his shoes, leafed through their mail, and cooed softly at Cat-leen Cleaver.

By the time he finally came into the kitchen, Mary was so wet her panties were clinging to her sex.

"Now this is what I like coming home to," Santos said,

fitting himself against Mary's back. His hands slid over Knox's at her waist and he pressed her closer into Knox's body.

She dipped her finger back into the batter and Santos took his turn licking the chocolate from her skin. Mary leaned back against Santos's chest. She angled her pussy even more firmly against Knox's dick and enjoyed watching these two men she loved with her entire heart kiss around her finger.

When Santos pulled back, he leaned down to say hello to Mary in the same way. She sighed into his mouth while Knox unbuttoned his jeans.

"You're just in time," Knox grunted, lifting the skirt of Mary's dress. He lifted one of her legs and slid into her as she sucked Santos's tongue into her mouth. Santos smiled against her lips as Knox pressed her against him and started fucking her right there in the middle of their kitchen. Santos moved his hands to her breasts, his body a firm wall of muscle for Knox to fuck her against until it was time to switch.

Coming to Sea Port had been a gamble, but not getting tenure had been a blessing in disguise. Mary started moaning into Santos's mouth, knowing that she wouldn't change a thing about her life in Sea Port because her new life was sweeter than ever.

Also by Katrina Jackson

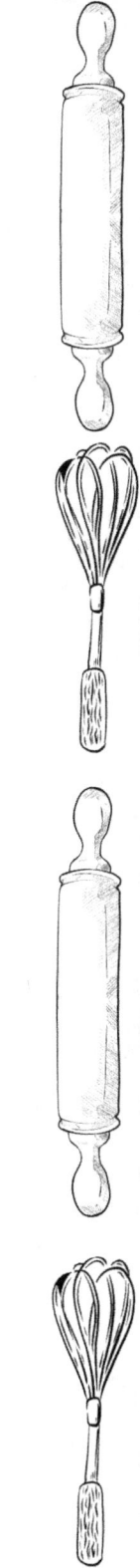

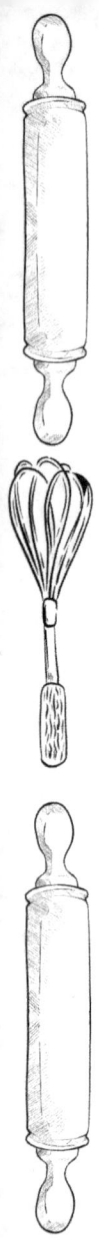

One More Valentine

Heist Holidays

Grand Theft N.Y.E.

The Family

Beautiful and Dirty

The Hitman

The Enforcer

Dolci

The Don

Dolore

-

Bay Area Blues

Layover

Back in the Day

Curriculum Vitae

Office Hours

Sabbatical

Mosley Coven

The Night Gate (website exclusive)

A Flicker to a Flame

Invocation

-

<u>Standalone stories</u>

Encore

The Tenant

Sex Toy Soldier

Looking

And When You Leave Me

Small Mercies

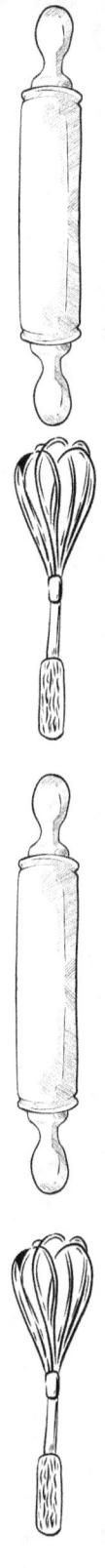